WARRIOR ROAD

WARRIOR ROAD

FRED GROVE

THORNDIKE
CHIVERS

This Large Print edition is published by Thorndike Press, Waterville, Maine, USA and by BBC Audiobooks Ltd, Bath, England.
Thorndike Press, a part of Gale, Cengage Learning.

The text of this Large Print edition is unabridged.
Other aspects of the book may vary from the original edition.
Set in 16 pt. Plantin.
Printed on permanent paper.

LIBRARY OF CONGRESS CATALOGING-IN-PUBLICATION DATA

Grove, Fred.
    Warrior road / by Fred Grove.
        p. cm. — (Thorndike Press large print western)
    ISBN-13: 978-1-4104-0916-4 (hardcover : alk. paper)
    ISBN-10: 1-4104-0916-3 (hardcover : alk. paper)
    1. Osage Indians—Fiction. 2. Racially mixed people—Fiction.
    3. Large type books. I. Title.
    PS3557.R7W37 2008
    813'.54—dc22   2008021515

BRITISH LIBRARY CATALOGUING-IN-PUBLICATION DATA AVAILABLE

Published in 2008 by arrangement with Golden West Literary Agency.
Published in 2009 in the U.K. by arrangement with Golden West Literary Agency.

U.K. Hardcover: 978 1 408 41299 2 (Chivers Large Print)
U.K. Softcover: 978 1 408 41300 5 (Camden Large Print)

Printed in the United States of America
1 2 3 4 5 6 7 12 11 10 09 08

WARRIOR ROAD

CHAPTER 1

Boone Terrell was late. He shifted into second gear as he took the dim road, angling like a badly healed old scar up the rounded hill to the cemetery and its ragged crown of blackjacks. Seeing the swarm of cars around the entrance, he pulled off and stopped, flushing a whir of grasshoppers from the dry bluestem grass, and turned off the motor, which died with a hushed cough.

As he softly closed the cutaway door of the flame-colored, two-seater roadster, he could hear the high wailing of the Osage women; and powerfully, as if beyond his will, he had the feeling of shedding the alien outer shell of himself and slipping backward into time, back to his beginning, back to where he belonged.

Striding along the road to the cemetery entrance and stepping over the cattle guard of oil-field pipe, he saw the mourners gathered at the north end for the interment, scores of Indians and whites. A big funeral, though for as long as he could remember all Osage funerals were big.

He hesitated, dreading to go on, dreading the sickening scent of banked funeral wreaths. Dreading the sight of the stiff-bodied mourners and of Lester Oliver, Paradise's lone undertaker since statehood, his unlined face as ruddy as a fall apple, ushering family and friends to chairs near the raw horror of the grave, signaling with nods and finger waggings and mouth grimaces, and despite his constant prowling, making no more noise than an apparition, never disturbing the solemnity of the ceremony. And the wailing, the primitive wailing. It was the wailing that tore at him deepest, because it came out of the past unchanged and, therefore, was true.

He moved on, wishing to reach the mourners before it was over, past the first uneven grouping of weathered headstones, like so many signposts, many remembered from his childhood; past where He-Lo-Ki-He (Bare Legs), aged one hundred and three, lay above the ground in his white man's red brick house of rest, facing east toward the rising sun. Here because the Osages had quit building cairns of stone around their dead after the country started

8

filling up with white people and the Osage graves were looted of the deceased's belongings.

Onward, walking faster, Boone met a richer field of stones, great shafts of marble — white, pink, black, beige — and gray stone angels poised here and there in hovering flight, soft smiles on their brooding faces. And again, as ever, he felt a dull resentment at the marbled extravagance encouraged by the monument vendors, who reaped so heavily when an Osage died.

A scene flashed before his mind, still vivid after these many years: Boone and his grieving fullblood mother and "Smiley" Kemp, his chicken-hawk features a mask of fixed condolence, murmuring: "Mrs. Terrell, I know you want something proper in memory of such a fine man." He appeared to consider at length. "That's a mighty fine stone over there — that black marble."

"Looks kinda expensive," Nellie Terrell said, her voice low and subdued. It was, Boone realized afterward, too soon following his father's death for her to make a sensible decision.

Kemp went on, his tone purring: "Don't you worry about that. Agency'll take care of everything, Mrs. Terrell."

"How much is it?" she asked wearily.

"Over in Tulsa they're gettin' twice what we do here in Paradise among home folks," he said, not without a trace of indignation.

"About how much, Mr. Kemp?"

He donned his most bountiful expression. "Four thousand, is all. An' I'll do a mighty proper inscription. No extra charge, you bet. Whatever you want on it." His face became mournful again. "Something like 'Until We Meet Again.' "

"I don't like that," Nellie Terrell said, shaking her head.

"How about 'The Memory of the Just Is Blessed'?"

She looked distressed. "I want something simple. Something short."

Kemp, in accord, pulled a worn little book from his hip pocket. "How's this strike you? 'Strong in Faith.' "

"He wasn't much of a church-going man, but he was a mighty good man."

"You bet — you bet he was," Kemp said, flipping a page, tracing with a grimy forefinger. "Here's a good 'un: 'He Lived and Died a Christian.' "

Nellie Terrell was near tears. "No," she said. Boone put his arm around her to steady her.

"I think I have it," Kemp said hastily. " 'His Memory Is Blessed.' "

"I like that. Use that and we'll take the black marble," she said, as if relieved to have made a choice, no matter the cost.

"That's right fine an' proper, Mrs. Terrell. Mighty proper. The highest respect we poor mortals can pay our loved ones is to make a shrine of their final restin' place. Now, would you like for me to carve a lamb or cherub or angel . . . to kinder set on top there? You know, like he's lookin' after things?" He paused expectantly, head cocked, breathing through a hissing gap in his stained teeth, mouth twitching anticipation.

"Guess not," said Nellie Terrell, and Boone led her away.

So black marble it was, at a price that would have caused Egan Terrell, who as a wandering, carefree cowboy had often ridden for twenty-five dollars a month, to turn over in his rocky grave had he known.

Boone came to the rear of the mourners and stood still, hat in hand, seeing the flag-draped coffin, listening to the final words of the old priest, delivered at a rapid, singsong rate, the meaning lost on the sobbing wind. Boone bowed his head.

When the droning voice ceased, he looked up and noticed seven uniformed men, three of them Indians, World War I veterans, their high-collared khaki blouses too tight for them by now, standing at round-bellied attention. A barked command. Up snapped the rifles. Another command. A volley crashed. The sliding clash of bolt actions. The acrid stink of gunpowder drifted to Boone. Again the command. Another volley. Then another, completing the twenty-one-gun salute for Acey Standing Elk, who had fought in France with the Rainbow Division and won a medal for killing eleven Germans and knocking out a machine gun nest. When he returned home, the Osages had honored him with a great feast and many fine presents. To Boone, too young then to go to war, Acey was a hero as well as his closest friend. At the moment that seemed a long time ago.

In the old days Acey would have been a leading warrior, bringing back Pawnee and Cherokee and Kiowa scalps and countless horses. Better, Boone reflected, had Acey lived then, before the Osages became oil-rich, when they had to hunt to live, when they lived in bands and the strength of the band was as a circle drawn around each person, before the whiskey that was now killing off a generation of young Osages — better had they all lived then.

As the shots died, an unseen bugler

12

sounded Taps to the muted roll of drums, the somber notes seeming to hang suspended above the blackjacks. Somewhere the keening started up again. Boone stiffened, shaken. Uniformed men, moving briskly, removed the flag from the casket, folded it expertly into a triangular shape, and then an officer presented it to a young white woman sitting beside a small Indian girl, who appeared to be with her, yet did not.

Boone had a sensation of great loss. Tears dimmed his eyes. Unashamed, he let them drop unchecked down his cheeks. Acey, his good and long friend, as close as a brother, perhaps closer, older by some three years, was gone, returned to Grandmother Earth.

Boone watched the young white woman. He didn't know her. However, the little girl, solemn and big-eyed and as motionless as one of the stone angels, had to be Acey's daughter, Mary Elizabeth. No more than four or five when Boone had seen her last, when Annie, Acey's Indian wife, was living. The white woman had to be Acey's second wife Boone had heard about.

An Indian man left a bowl of food at the head of the grave. The white woman rose and took the Indian child away. Slowly, the crowd began dissolving, receding in gradual ripples toward the cars, the Indians silent and undemonstrative, save for their grief-swollen faces. A hand-shaking white man moved among them, one by one calling their names . . . Charlie . . . Rose . . . Edgar . . . Grace . . .

Boone felt a stir of regret. Descendants of a powerful warrior race, the Osages were large people, notably Black Dog of the old ones long ago, who it was said stood seven feet tall and weighed two hundred and fifty pounds; now, through inactivity and the luxury of wealth, they had become too heavy and slow moving.

An ancient Indian woman caught his eye, blanketed, moccasined, her seamed face scarred as by fire, standing before a weathered angel. She reached veined hands toward the September sun boiling out of the blue sky. Her high-pitched wailing rose on a quavering note, beseeching. As suddenly, it ceased, and she scuffed off toward the cars, alone. She had, he knew, been praying.

He followed her with his eyes, understanding her, and proud of her because she cried openly in the old way, and he was left depressed because he could not convey his respect to her.

He became aware of movement near him, the tread of a heavy body upon the uncut

14

prairie grass. He turned, seeing a broad white hand outthrust before him. A diamond sparkled on the little finger. He looked up into the moon face and the blue-gray eyes he remembered so often on the streets of Paradise.

"Howdy, Boone," a resonant voice said. "Long time no see."

"Hello, Mr. Horn," Boone answered, taking the hand. Everybody in Paradise, Oklahoma knew Dane Horn. He was the town's most prominent citizen, if not of all Osage County, and in their local pride they said his influence stopped neither there nor the state capitol in Oklahoma City, but extended to Washington. You bet'cher boots. It was he who had greeted the Indians moments ago.

Just then a braided Indian man, whom Boone recognized as Louis Climbing Bear, plodded heavily up to Horn. "Thanks for bein' pallbearer, Dane," the fullblood said.

"Glad to," Horn replied courteously, shaking hands. "Acey was a good boy. We were good friends."

"Feast's at my place."

"I'll be there. Thanks, Louis."

"Boone," the Indian said, offering his slack hand, "you been gone long time. You and Acey went to school together. We want

15

you to come. You know where I live in the village." Louis Climbing Bear shook hands as the old ones did, ceremoniously, unhurriedly, his grip relaxed, not crushing your bones as some white men did. Boone thanked him.

"Where you been keeping yourself?" Horn asked curiously, turning to Boone as Climbing Bear plodded away.

"Here and there."

Although Horn was an aggressive man, he was also polite. He gave the impression of friendly interest alone, as if fearing he might be nosing into Boone's affairs, as he asked, "Hear you're racing cars?"

Boone nodded, not wishing to talk about it here.

"Hear you've won some good races?"

"Some," Boone said, smiling a little, "and I've lost some. I drive for a Fort Worth oil man."

"Making any money?"

"More than last year. I've still got a lot to learn."

"Well, you got your mother's headright and two from your grandparents and your own. You don't have to worry if you lose."

Boone kept his face impassive, while inside he felt a stinging heat of annoyance. Money talk struck him as out of place here.

16

It was an intrusion, wherever, when white people reminded you of how many head-rights you had, down to the exact number. It would be like telling a white man to his face that you knew how much money he had in the bank, or how many head of cattle or horses he owned, or how many acres of grassland. Except you didn't say that back, if you had manners. It seemed that head-rights were different, like public knowledge; everybody seemed to know how many you had, who had left you what and when. He let the feeling pass, and yet, when he spoke, his voice bore an edge that hadn't been in him when he left the Osage.

"Winning's important to me," he said. "I want to make it on my own, Mr. Horn."

"Mr. Horn!" Dane Horn exclaimed in surprise. "It's always *Dane.* Remember that. You've just been gone too long, Boone. Well, that's good. I say a man should do what's important to him. You young Osages need a goal in life. Do something! Don't end up like poor Acey — dead at twenty-seven." He slapped Boone lightly on the shoulder. "Come around if you need anything."

Boone nodded his thanks. You always nod-ded, he remembered, when Dane Horn invited you to come by, whether you were going or not. Many times Boone had heard

17

Dane Horn say that to Acey and the others and himself. For Dane Horn was a generous man. He never turned you down completely. He always let you have something when you asked for a loan. Yet Boone had never asked him for money; somehow he hadn't. He didn't know just why, because in those days he had drunk as much whiskey as the rest. Looking back now, he wondered whether it was pride or Egan Terrell's stern code taking effect: *Ask a man for favors and he'll come back on you someday; then he'll own you lock, stock, and barrel.* Come to think of it, Boone could not recall his father ever being obligated to Dane Horn or anyone.

Horn was making his way toward a red Buick touring, a heavy man picking up tallow around the middle, nevertheless moving lightly on booted feet, his genial voice rising and falling in greeting, mixing a little Osage with his talk, which always pleased the older Indians. To Boone he always looked the same, whether on the streets of Paradise, handing out silver to kids, or in the Cattlemen's Bank, which he owned, or in the Salt Creek Trading Company store, in which it was said he had considerable, if not controlling, interest. Always the white Stetson; thick white hair cut straight across

18

on the back of his stout neck; always the conservative business suit and bow tie and hand-made boots, always shined. Always smiling. A strong man with a strong smile, teeth as even as a horse's. It was also common knowledge that he owned or controlled fifty thousand acres of grassland and that, when he so wished, he ran the county's Democratic politics. There were no known Republicans in Paradise. You bet'cher boots there weren't.

Gradually, Boone realized that he was alone. Over there the grave diggers were shoveling in the last of the raw, dark sod. The mourners' voices faded, drowned in the roar of departing cars already raking up dust on the road to the Gray Horse Indian village.

One paying of respect remained. He walked through the thick grass to the black-jacks shading the Terrell family plot. Hands clasped behind him, he studied each stone for long and thoughtful moments. A kind of choking swelled his throat and a mist fell across his eyes, blurring the names and dates. But presently his eyes cleared and he felt an unaccountable ease, renewed, made stronger, sensing that through some mysterious source life continued on, indestructible.

Another lingering before the stones and he walked back toward the roadster, inhaling deeply of the sweet grass smell, face turned to the afternoon sun, relishing the rugged blackjacks and the hot, clear sky, like a blue Indian blanket overspreading the still earth. It was good to come back. The Osage hadn't changed, only its people. He was home.

He drove leisurely along the dusty, winding snake of the flinty road to Louis Climbing Bear's place, a simple frame house of canary yellow off the main road west of the little grocery store. The Indian village would have disappointed a visiting Easterner. Instead of hide lodges, it was an outscatter of white man's houses with wide porches. A long tent, spacious enough for a gospel meeting and open on all sides, sheltered tables laden with bowls and platters of food. He smelled the familiar aroma of dried corn, hominy, boiled beef and fried squaw bread and boiled coffee and fresh-baked pies. At the moment Louis Climbing Bear was giving bright new Indian blankets to the pallbearers.

Boone paused, rejecting the thought of food, but not to eat would be ill-mannered; and so he took a seat near the end of the first table and partook sparingly as the food was passed. Some of these fullbloods and mixed-bloods, like himself, he knew; they nodded and spoke with their eyes. Many of them he did not know, or he remembered their faces dimly but not their names. He could hear Dane Horn's voice now and then toward the end of the table, as distinct as a drumbeat, rising above the subdued hum of talk and the clatter and clink of dishes and cutlery. The old priest also sat near the head, eating his feast in silence.

Near the middle of Boone's table sat Mary Elizabeth and the white woman Boone assumed was Acey's widow. And again he sensed the apartness of the two. The woman looked about Acey's age: green-eyed, blond bobbed hair, a black silk dress severely encasing her slim figure. He felt a touch of sympathy for her. She's out of place among the Indians, he thought, and knows it. But it was the child who held Boone's interest, who deepened his sympathy. She seemed lost in a trance. A beautiful child. Skin the color of dusk. Eyes like smoke. As fragile-looking as a doll. And so still for one so young. Tomorrow he would go by the house; this evening was too early.

As these thoughts passed through his mind, the white woman rose; when the benumbed child made no effort to follow

21

her, as if unaware, the woman took her hand firmly, yet not ungently, brought her to her feet and turned her and drew her along to a yellow Packard sedan and drove away.

Four o'clock had come by the time the mourners got up to leave. Some lingered in the yard to visit quietly; some took food in cloths. Afterward, cars roared off onto the narrow, winding country roads, and the feast honoring the memory of Acey Standing Elk, a hero who had fought "across the waters," a feast given in the old and generous way, was over. It seemed all too brief, too transitory to Boone.

He was among the last to go. He headed west, trailing a wake of saffron dust, swung north at the first road leading to Paradise. Thinking, he puzzled again over the telephone call. He was gone when it came. A mechanic friend at the garage had answered the phone. "Just tell Boone Terrell that Acey Standing Elk's funeral will be at two o'clock tomorrow in Paradise." Click. A woman's voice, the mechanic said. No more. No name. Just like that. After being gone more than three years, from Indiana to California, he wondered how anyone other than Nate Robb would know where to locate him.

Perhaps it was the feeling of driving a familiar road. Suddenly he broke out of his musing. He rumbled over the wooden bridge spanning the railroad cut, gunned the roadster hard for half a mile, knowing in advance each twist and dip and rise; remembering the narrow concrete bridge over Salt Creek, he eased off the gas until he saw no one was approaching, then rushed across the bridge, the roar of the exhaust reboundings against his ears, and drove without letup over the flat to the Santa Fe tracks. Slowing down, he bounced over the crossing and continued west to the first principal street, where he turned north and entered the drowsy outskirts of Paradise.

The short, fast drive had relaxed him. An eagerness came, the desire to see familiar haunts again. Paradise, like everybody said, was an Indian town, and therefore an active trading center; and also a cow town and also a lawyers' hunting ground because of Indian clients. Four times a year, on the fifteenth of March, June, September, and December, Paradise throbbed to life when the Osages received and spent their quarterly payment checks from oil royalties, swollen by returns from the great Burbank field. In between checks the Indians charged their needs at the Salt Creek Trading Company and other firms, but the big store on Main Street received the bulk of their trade.

He was within a block of Main when, like a blow at the base of his skull, the thought exploded: How had Acey died? No one had said. There had been no opportunity for anyone to say, or for him to ask questions. He had supposed the usual cause: whiskey or a car wreck. Driving on slowly, he set the question aside for the moment to concentrate on the town.

It was ugly, really. Just a broad, bricked street flanked by commonplace buildings of red brick and sandstone. Nevertheless, Paradise was home and he liked it, and he smiled, remembering. No visible change met his eye. The Salt Creek Trading Company presented the same series of glassed faces, each opening on a different department — groceries and meat, furniture, hardware, clothing. In second gear, he idled past the Osage Nation Theater, where open-mouthed white and Indian boys alike had watched grim William S. Hart and resolute Harry Carey and showman Tom Mix and Tony the Wonder Horse. Past the Rexall Drug, and Haney's Hardware and Spitzer's Grocery, the bank corner and the office of the weekly *Headlight* and the Blue Bird Cafe.

As he loafed along, the same subtle oddness that he had experienced at the cemetery returned, an elusive sensation of differences. And at last he got it, at last he understood. Paradise was the same. It was Boone Terrell who was different, the Boone Terrell who had gone away and grown up and found himself, and in doing so had likely salvaged his life.

Impulsively, he turned in and parked at the curb before the Goodtime Billiards, got out and strolled inside, meeting the remembered staleness and the sour-sweet rankness of sweat and old clothes and plug tobacco and spittoons and roll-your-owns. The Goodtime was the main hangout for Indian and white youths and ranch hands and squawmen, the precise definition of the last being a ne'er-do-well or fortune-hunting white man who had wed a rich Osage girl for her money and, now at ease, slicked out in new boots and suit charged at the big store, spent most of his time in town, shooting pool or playing dominoes or drinking whiskey.

The domino tables were full, and the hunched players, all white men, could have occupied the same chairs when Boone had left the Osage. No one seemed to notice him. The click of balls drew him on. A game of snooker was in progress.

Boone stopped still, feeling a smile forming along his lips.

Fullblood Sammy Buffalo Killer, large and fat and jovial, blue shirttail out, leaned over the table and placed his left hand on the green cloth, tapering fingers just so, making a rest for the cue stick. He took two smooth preliminary strokes and drove the cue ball against a red ball, sending it flashing into a side pocket. The cue ball, with reverse English on it, backtracked and rolled dead, in prime position. Another tentative stroke and Sammy lined the cue ball against the number four ball, which darted into a corner pocket.

Absorbed as he studied the table with expert eye, he picked up a square of chalk and dusted the tip of his stick, drew bead on a red ball and drilled it home. Moving with deliberation, he ran out the table, while his opponent, a young white man, looked on morosely.

"Dang you, Sammy," he complained. "You're just too salty for me."

"Aw, I'se just lucky," Sammy said, sniffling. He dug into a trouser. "I'm payin' for the game."

As the white youth stacked his cue stick and went toward the front, the fullblood turned and discovered Boone.

"Hey!"

It made Boone feel good to see how glad

Sammy was to see him. Sammy gave him a limp handshake. "Hi, *Wah-Sha-She*," he said, smiling the old way as he spoke the old greeting. Boone wasn't certain what *Wah-Sha-She* meant, except that it went back to the early greatness of the Osages, and had a vague reference to The People, symbolizing power. Sammy used it half jestingly, half seriously, with an affection that warmed Boone.

Sammy's straight blue-black hair was slicked back and, as of old, he smelled pungently of brilliantine. Acey and Sammy and Boone had played football together one season, the year Acey was a senior, Sammy playing when the mood moved him. Despite bearing the name of a warrior family, he wouldn't hit people hard enough; for Sammy Buffalo Killer, a modern Osage, football was intended as a game of fun, not to be taken seriously. Seldom had Boone seen him out of sorts.

"A pool shark like you should be shooting a house stick," Boone kidded him.

"Nobody'll play me any more," Sammy said, his full, roundish face crinkling. "I have to pay for the games."

Boone sensed they were both avoiding talk about Acey. "I'll take you on," he said, simulating a brag. "Buck a game."

"I'll even let you break, *Wah-Sha-She.*"

Sammy called for a rack, and when the balls were lined up, Boone broke the triangle. One red ball dropped. He missed his next shot.

Sammy was drawing his first bead when the jest trailed off from his face. "You hear about Acey?"

"Yeah."

"Bad, ain't it?"

"I still can't believe it."

"Didn't see you at the funeral."

"Got in too late. But I made it to the cemetery and feast."

"Can't stand them feasts. Makes me sick." As Sammy sank a red ball and took aim again, two booted white men took the next table.

"What happened?" Boone asked softly.

Sammy looked at him sidelong, his hesitation brief but obvious. "Got drowned."

"Where?"

"Salt Creek."

"Drowned? Him — as good a swimmer as he was?"

Sammy nodded. He also missed his shot. "Hard to swim with boots on." He kept sniffling. His rich brown eyes were dull.

"When was this?"

Sammy glanced at the white men and

28

back, his reluctance growing. "Found him two days ago," he said briefly. "Creek was up. Just one of them things, ain't it?"

Boone let the subject drop. They finished the game in silence. Sammy played erratically, in contrast to his sure deftness the game before. Even so, Boone lost. He paid for the game and stuck a dollar in Sammy's shirt pocket and, as if of the same accord, they stacked cues and strolled out and stood on the sidewalk before the red roadster.

"Kinda lost your touch in there, didn't you?" Boone asked, amused.

"Aw, I'se just tryin' to even things up." Sammy's self-scoffing, however, didn't match his gloomy expression.

"Those two at the next table. Who are they?"

"Buck DeVore's hands."

"Buck DeVore? Never heard of him."

"You will, if you stick around. Heap big squawman, now heap big rancher." Sammy struck an exaggerated pose of self-importance, full lower lip hanging, arched belly protruding like a large melon, thumbs hooked at his belt. He rolled his eyes arrogantly.

Boone laughed. Sammy could always make you laugh. It was good.

"You settled down yet and got yourself a

good woman?" Boone teased him.

"Aw, them women, they keep chasin' me," Sammy retorted, putting on a bored expression, "an' I keep dodgin'. Have to move fast, this man."

"Where you live now?"

"Still in the old house."

That meant in town. Boone could understand Sammy's solitary life. Sammy's parents had passed on while he was in high school. An older brother had been a car wreck victim and he had no sisters, only a cousin or so, of whom Acey had been one.

Stepping to the roadster, Sammy reverently stroked the flame-colored fender on the driver's side. "Stutz Bearcat, ain't it? Straight eight? What'll he do?" (Sammy, like the old Indian men Boone had heard, always said "he" for "she.")

"Around a hundred," Boone said and recalled that the fun-loving, hard-drinking Sammy had owned two Cadillac tourings before he was eighteen. That he had wrecked them both, each time miraculously escaping injury when thrown out. Once on the road to Burbank, the other time west of Pawhuska, when he failed to round a curve, which he had explained he was trying "to straighten out." Afterward, the amused talk around town was that, being full of corn

30

whiskey, he had landed relaxed.

Sammy showed a lively interest. "Drive him in your races, this Bearcat?"

"No — a Miller Special."

"Them Tulsey papers play you up big." Sammy puffed out his chest, stuck out his lower lip, and spoke from deep within his chest: OSAGE INDIAN WINS HEAP BIG RACE, MAKES HEAP BIG DUST. (He pronounced it *Eendin,* the way fullbloods did.) At this moment he was the old Sammy, the clown, the comic, the genial spirit. They both laughed.

"What did they say when I went out after fifteen laps at Indianapolis this spring?" Boone came back. "You need some luck too. Well, there's always next year."

"Yeah. There's always next year." Surprisingly, Sammy's light mood was dulling again.

"Come out to the ranch with me," Boone suggested. "I'll bring you back after supper if you have to come in."

"No can do, *Wah-Sha-She.* Got to see Great White Medicine Man."

" 'Doc' Mears?"

"Yeah. I ain't feelin' so hot, this man." He sniffled again.

"I'll wait for you."

"You better go ahead. Thanks."

31

Boone, with regret, started to the car. He didn't know that he intended to ask the question until he swung around. It flipped off his tongue like a shot. "So Salt Creek was up when Acey tried to cross it horseback?"

"Yeah."

"Find his horse?"

"That horse came home. That was when Acey's wife, Donna, called in town for help. Bunch of us went out. Gettin' dark by then. Didn't find him till next day."

"Where?"

"Where the creek turns east in his pasture, caught in some brush." Pain crossed Sammy's face.

"Was there an autopsy?"

"Guess so. Doc Mears, he took a looksee at the funeral parlor. Judge Pyle was the — wha' d'you call it? — the coroner. He asked us boys some questions about this thing after we came in with the body. Then he called a jury. He said it was an accident."

"What do you think, Sammy?"

"Me?" Sammy looked confused, on the defensive. "Jesus, I guess it was. Why ask me?"

"Just wondered. If Doc Mears said bad whiskey killed Acey, I wouldn't think twice. But drowned? My God, Acey was like an otter in the water. Remember how long he could stay under?"

"Accidents can happen to anybody, they can."

Boone, nodding, had to agree. Why would it be otherwise? "See you around, Sammy. I'll be here a day or two." He opened the door and got in behind the wheel. The motor kicked off roaring. Sammy grinned his appreciation, and struck his heap-big-Indian pose. Boone slipped in the clutch and backed out, shifted gears, waved and took off north. A little way on he glanced back and waved again.

Sammy hadn't moved. He was still watching. He jaggled a hand back at Boone. At sight of the rumpled figure, aimless and pathetic and shiftless by white standards, and thus to be looked down upon, a wave of warm understanding swept over Boone. And there was no reason for it, because Sammy Buffalo Killer had never had an enemy during his carefree life, yet Boone would swear that his friend seemed afraid.

CHAPTER 2

He was truly going home now. Excitement pulsed in his throat. He rumbled across the Salt Creek bridge north of town and took the roadster around a curve. In the old days he would have picked up a pint of "Snipe" Murray's whiskey before heading home. He still drove fast, he always had. But he was cautious compared to then, when he and his friends raced each other on the narrow country roads, or staged races against time to Pawhuska, capital of the Osage Nation and the county seat. He wondered if Wild Boone Terrell still held the record: twenty-eight miles in twenty-five minutes to the bridge west of Pawhuska over Bird Creek, with Acey beside him as "official timer," an empty pint on the seat between them. They called it the Osage Speedway, and you followed the winding road Boone now traveled before coming out on the main highway west of Pawhuska. Other times they roared along the Arkansas River west of Paradise, or charged thirty miles southeast to Hominy.

He flinched at the remembered recklessness. Racing had taught him how to live within certain limitations. Even the best driver could die when a tire blew or a crankshaft broke; a driver overcome by heat exhaustion might dash straight into the wall. Only fools took unnecessary chances. You risked enough just competing, just getting out there on the track. Feeling the roadster swerve as the front wheels fought loose gravel, he slowed down until, pebbles raining against its underside, the salty Stutz straightened out.

Dusk was veiling the draws and purpling the eastern slopes of the shaggy hills. He reduced speed to indulge his eyes. It was not unlike turning the pages of a favorite book as first a knot of timber and next a particular rounded hill and then an outcropping of flame-colored rock passed before him. He tensed, waiting, knowing, and presently, sliding into view as the timbered hills parted as if painted on the landscape, caught in the last firebrand of the Osage sun — he saw the house where he was born. A distant bastion of red brick, two stories high, independent of its rough surroundings, and yet also harmonious because it had been there as far back as he could remember, its sturdy columns bracing the wide, cool porch.

By the time he had gone several more miles, early darkness was moving in. He switched on the headlights and drove faster, surrendering to his eagerness, his senses extraordinarily alive as he drew in the woody scent of blackjacks and the sweet intoxication of open-country grass. When he turned off the dusty road and rattled over the home cattle guard, at that moment seeing the old house up close, it appeared shockingly smaller, terribly shrunken and worn by time. He looked for light, saw none, and roared on to the rear. The kitchen was also dark. Flipping off headlights and ignition, he hurried out and was making for the back door when a figure bulged from behind the garage and growled, "Snub it right there, Buster — 'less you want some new buttonholes bored."

Boone jumped sideways, startled, scowling at the business end of a leveled shotgun, and then recognition came. "Nate," he said, not moving. "It's me — Boone."

Nate Robb stood very still, peering through the murk. Snorting self-disgust, he set the shotgun against the garage wall and, hand extended, his gruff voice apologetic, said, "Excuse the reception."

"What's up?"

After starting to explain, Nate reconsidered. "Come on in. Welcome home, stranger. Tell you later. It's nothin' much."

"Nothin' — when you greet a man with a shotgun?"

Nate's grunt was further dismissal. "I'll fix some supper. Had a decent meal since you left?"

"No sour dough biscuits, if that's what you mean?"

"That's what I mean."

Boone trailed him inside. Nate struck a match on his thumbnail and as lamplight spilled across the kitchen, Boone got the unforgettable redolence of baked bread and coffee and fried meat and kerosene.

Nate Robb appeared unchanged. Maybe more wizened and weathered. A drawn-up man in his sixties, bowlegged and spidery, and still as wiry and indestructible as ever. His eyes, as mere flint chips in a sharply chiseled face, bored into Boone.

"You've growed up, Boone," he said, approving. "With that Roman nose and them high cheekbones you could pass for a fullblood, which was what you said you wanted to be when you was little." His rubbery mouth formed a bantering smile. "Could except for one thing — you're too lean." At that, he stepped to the woodbox and picked up kindling and opened the grate and stoked the iron stove and lifted the stove lid with the iron handle and sprinkled kerosene from a can. Another match hissed. As flames leaped, he slammed the grate shut and plopped back the stove lid — never one, Boone recalled, to fiddle around when making a fire. Next, Nate Robb went to setting tin plates and cups and knives and forks on the oil cloth-covered table (you took spoons from an old mustard jar in the center of the table), and opening cans while muttering about the balky opener, and slicing bacon with his pocketknife. (He ran a house the same way he had a bachelor's cow camp in the olden days: strictly on a utility basis. Everything simple and usable. Nothing fancy.)

Affection was a rare admission for him, an outwardly gruff and unsentimental man, a product of that early era when Texas drovers began leasing the lush Osage ranges. He had never married. When his half-French, half-Irish friend, Egan Terrell, took an Osage wife, Nate became part of the little family, and there he had stuck, dour and reliable, a steadfast man who saw to things after Egan's death and, still, after Nellie Terrell's passing and Boone's long absence from the ranch.

On the back porch Boone dippered water into a basin, washed and dried on the roller towel. When he came back to the kitchen, Nate had tied a flour-sack apron around his skinny hips. Still wearing his battered hat, he took sour dough from a bowl on the stove and, turning to the flour bin — a ten-gallon lard can conveniently beside the stove — began shaping up supper biscuits.

Without glancing at Boone, he said: "So

that girl got in touch with you about Acey's funeral?"

"Girl?"

"That schoolmarm. Teresa Chapman. Right nice lookin' too."

"Teresa?" Boone felt a jolt of surprise. "How would she know where I was?"

"I told her. She came by here after they found Acey. Said she figured you ought to know."

"Glad you did."

"You ain't exactly easy to keep track of, you know. I was gonna call you, myself. Told her it was a gamble you might be in Fort Worth. Thereabouts or on the moon." The last was a deserved rebuke for Boone's inattention to running the ranch. Nate moved to the cabinet and pulled out a doughboard and finished working in the flour, cut out the biscuits with a baking powder can and laid them in a greased pan, shoved the pan into the oven, slammed the door, and, muttering, went to the back porch, where Boone heard him thumping through a sack of potatoes.

Teresa.

A warm feeling floated through him. So she had called him. He asked himself why she had bothered after three years. In thought, he entered the living room and

39

stood still, in the semi-darkness, smelling the mustiness of the years' disuse, his mind tracking back. Locating a kerosene lamp, he lit the wick, set the glass chimney back on the base, and carried it upstairs to his room.

Coming here evoked touching memories. A khaki-colored blanket covered his bed, and there was a bare pillow. Bit by bit he gazed about the room, seeing the Paradise High School pennant and the fearsome warrior crouching thereon, and the pieces of Indian handiwork, relics his mother had so prized: beaded elk-hide gloves, the buckskin vest of floral design — a handsome arrangement of red, blue, amber, and purple beads; moccasins bearing porcupine quills and the geometric designs of the Sioux, the distant linguistic kin of the Osages. The beaded horsehair bag and its red and yellow fringes of dyed quills. His father's twelve-gauge shotgun. Another pennant. The red and white of the Oklahoma Sooners, which inspired a pang of regret. He had made the University of Oklahoma's freshman football team as an end. It had happened then. For reasons he did not yet quite understand, he had quit school and come home to drink corn whiskey with his friends and race cars and waste himself in idleness and self-indulgence.

Why? Why? Who could say? All he knew was that a white man and an Indian had different motivations. He had taken the wild and destructive road until, for reasons likewise obscure, unless, dimly, he sensed some instinct of survival directed him, he had left the Osage and followed the breathtaking oil-slick tracks and disciplined living. If not, something reminded him, broodingly, he might lie on the wooded hilltop with Acey and the others.

Although racing was his need — not just the senseless charging back and forth on the dusty roads, or when you competed for money at the Speedway north of Hominy, or on tracks at Cushing and Tulsa — that was why he had received a local reputation for wild-Indian recklessness. Most of it deserved.

Step by step, thoughtfully, he circled the room, pausing to inspect each object. Everything was just as he had left it. There should be a pint of Snipe's foul whiskey in the bottom drawer of his dresser. Stirred by impulse, he opened the drawer and rummaged past folds of clothing and felt the rounded smoothness of the bottle. He held it against the light and shook. It was full and darkly swimming with murk.

At once, powerfully, he ached for a drink,

something he hadn't in a long time. His mouth juices ran. Now, just being back in the Osage, he craved whiskey. The realization shook him, because he thought he'd won his battle.

He stared at the churning stuff, hating it, damning it, wanting it. For an interval he considered pulling the cork and taking a shot, his mouth grimly set.

Suddenly, in self-disgust, he pushed the bottle back into the drawer, slammed it, and rushed from the room, conscious that he had been up here some time. Longer than he realized, because when he reached the kitchen, Old Nate had bacon, fried potatoes and eggs and canned tomatoes on the table, and was gingerly taking biscuits from the oven. He poured warmed-over coffee from a huge black pot and hooked his hat on a corner of the woodbox, the established signal to start eating.

They ate in hungry silence. (To Nate Robb you came to the table to eat. Talk came afterward.) When finished, he rolled a brown-paper cigarette.

Boone opened up: "When did you start welcoming folks with a shotgun?"

"Welcome, hell! Next time them hoot owls come around here somebody's gonna get his tail feathers dusted."

"Who's *them?*"

"If I knew, I'd swear out a complaint."

"What all's happened?"

"Started back in February. Little things. I'd find a pasture gate down, stock scattered to hell an' yonder. Made me think I was a little daffy, 'cause you know I never left a gate down in my life, by God!" Boone nodded affirmatively. "One morning I found a whiteface cow shot between the eyes. She was gonna have a calf in the spring. Another time I found the gate to the horse corral swung back — after I'd closed it."

"Why didn't you let me know?"

"Figured I could handle it myself."

"Doesn't make sense."

"Sure as hell makes sense to somebody." Nate's outraged eyes glittered. "That was just the start. Things got real spooky. One night — reckon it was after midnight — somebody ran up an' pounded on the side of the house. If I'd been a superstitious old fullblood, I'd a-run plumb to Pawhuska. Scared me, as it was. Time I got to the back door, they's gone. Little later I heard a car tearin' off toward Paradise . . . There'd be a lull. Maybe no trouble for two or three weeks. Then it'd start up again. One night I heard screams in the woods down the road. I just took my shotgun an' catfooted it right

43

down there." He built another smoke. A match hissed.

"Find anything?"

"Nobody there, course not. But when I got back to the house, the back door was standin' wide open — I'd closed it."

"What else?"

"Here lately they've changed their tune. Taken to roarin' up in the yard at night, then takin' off."

"Why, I wonder?"

Nate Robb's face was a study of concentration. "There's more to it than just tryin' to scare me. I'm too old for that."

"I don't get it. I don't get it at all."

The old man made a helpless gesture. "Ever stop to think what you got here? What's been left you? More than most folks can scrape together in a lifetime." He waved an encompassing hand. "A thousand acres of the best bluestem grass a cow ever got slick fat on."

Boone nodded soberly. "I don't understand it."

"You don't because you don't know what's goin' on in the Osage."

"Why would anybody do this?"

"You grew up in the Osage — yet you don't know?" Nate demanded, leveling Boone a scornful look. "It's greed — somebody wants this ranch."

"I won't sell it — never."

"If I scared out — moved to town — you'd be up the creek for somebody to look after a spooky ranch. Folks know you ain't interested in ranchin'. Know you're gone all the time."

Boone accepted the admonishment. Nate had long urged him to settle down. "I'm not about to sell this place, Nate. I want you to stay here as long as you like. It's your home."

"You forget I'm no young buck," Nate said, his seamy face softening slightly. "When the day comes I can't cut the mustard, which ain't too far off, you'll have to come back or hire somebody who'll likely let the place go to hell — do that or sell out."

"You can still cut it, Nate."

"The Osage has changed for the worse since you left. Ever' deadbeat in the country's swarmed in here. If they can't find some fool Osage girl to marry or some Osage family to hang around and potlick off of, they sell whiskey or steal cattle or take up hijackin' . . . Hell, other night three men robbed a rig crew up by Whizzbang. Came right on the rig floor — stuck 'em up." Nate's disgust flowed out through his intense eyes and his mobile mouth, which curled utter contempt. "Back in the early day we'd had a few necktie parties — got things regulated."

"I'll hire somebody to help you," Boone said.

Nate Robb drew back. His sharp-featured face became more edged. His mouth squinched defiance. "I ain't just about to nursemaid some drugstore cowboy that sleeps till five-thirty — wants his breakfast in bed. No — by God! When I can't cut it any more, I'll let you know."

Boone rubbed a hand over his mouth to mask his smile. Now he was hearing the real Nate, the old Nate. "All right. You let me know. Only I hope I never hear it." Boone reflected a moment. "Tell me about this Buck DeVore. Wasn't he the one you wrote me about who wanted to buy the place?"

"He's one of 'em. Squawman from the east side of the county. Well, he wasn't a squawman when he came here. But he changed that pretty quick. Caught him Acey's cousin, Rose Red Horse. Remember, her first husband got killed in a car wreck over by Ponca?"

"I remember."

"Buck started buyin' up land about the time you left."

"Maybe he's the one."

"Now don't get any sudden notions, Boone. Buck DeVore struts around Paradise like a big red rooster. Sure, he wants this place. So do three or four other outfits. They've all come by here an' asked if the place was for sale."

"What did you say?" Boone asked, smiling, knowing.

"I told 'em to keep right on down the road."

Boone rose and poured coffee and sat down. "What about Acey?"

"Drowned, they say."

"You believe that?"

Nate fixed him a sharp look, in his eyes some of the same surprise that Sammy Buffalo Killer had shown. "No reason not to. Why?"

"Dunno. A feeling, I guess. Think I knew Acey as well as anybody, better than most. He could swim like a big catfish, drunk or sober."

"Sure. An' Salt Creek was up. Maybe he hit his head on a rock or log, or got his spurs tangled."

"Could be." Boone was silent for a run of time. "I know this . . . Acey never hurt anybody in his life. Never intentionally. Just himself."

"You don't have to hurt anybody to get killed in the Osage. Just have something somebody wants."

"How's that, Nate?"

"Just sayin' how it is these days."

It had been a wearing day, Boone felt, the past catching up with the present, leaving him depressed and with the unreality of not actually having left the Osage. Yawning, he rose from the table. "Believe I'll turn in. Good supper, Nate."

Boone was at the doorway when Nate's voice, couched low, caught at him. "Don't go around sayin' in public you might be suspicious about what happened to Acey. Like I said, times have changed."

"What if I stumble onto something?"

"Keep it to yourself."

"God," Boone breathed, "times have changed when *you* talk like that, for me to say nothing."

"If you don't believe me, take a drive through the country some night. See the 'fraid lights."

" 'Fraid lights?"

"That's what they call 'em — 'fraid lights. Some Osages, mainly fullbloods, string up electric lights around their houses. They're afraid, Boone. Afraid."

Boone lit the lamp and ascended the stairs

and undressed for bed, considering what he had just heard. Lying in the warm darkness, he searched tiredly for meaning and order and found none, conscious somewhat of the returning inertia of his younger years. He thought of the bottle in the drawer, and he thought of Acey, as Acey used to be, and some lines from a poem whose author he could not recall rose to his mind:

Warm summer sun, shine friendly here;
Warm summer wind, blow kindly here;
Green sod above, rest light, rest light —

The last time he had seen Acey was in Paradise as they stood beside their cars in front of the Rexall Drug.

"Leavin'?" Acey asked.

"Yeah." It was bad Indian manners to pry, and when Boone saw that Acey wasn't going to ask more questions, Boone said, "I'm gonna drive racing cars."

"Hey, that's good, ain't it?"

Competition always appealed to Acey, any sort of game. He was drinking again — Boone could smell the sourness — as he had been, steadily, since his wife Annie's death; but save for a growing heaviness around the belt line and a certain puffiness in his face, you couldn't tell it much. He held his whiskey well, particularly well for an Indian, too well, which led him to drink even more. He was still straight and strong-looking and smooth-muscled and he hadn't lost his lithe grace. With his high-bridged Roman nose and the way he carried his head and the vigilant dark eyes, there was yet the look of eagles about him, this doomed friend. On weekends he played fullback for the Hominy Indians, the state's nationally known professional football team. The Sunday before last he had run back a punt for a touchdown against Memphis, and the car horns of the fans parked around the field sounded for minutes afterward. Sometimes he rode out to look at his cattle; other than that, he drank. He was like a bright but unsteady flame, likely to sputter out at any moment.

"Maybe you'll go Indianapolis, huh?"

"Maybe. I'd like that."

Acey smiled, the corners of his eyes like crow's-feet. The smile inspired a contagious confidence. "Ever'body's gonna be readin' about this Boone Terrell, this race car man. Ever'body's gonna hear about this Eat-My-Dust Terrell, this Osage man, this half-breed. You'll see." (The way Acey said it, the half-breed tag wasn't derogatory; it was more like a nickname.) He showed the amiable smile again and Boone grinned at the praise and was moved, because they were saying farewell.

"What about you, Acey?" Boone disliked asking.

One shoulder lifted and fell, a conflicting gesture which told Boone nothing and also much, which confirmed his fear that Acey would go on and on like the others and eventually drink himself to death, uncaring, or die in a smashed car, completing the unremitting cycle which so many young Osages followed, from primitive innocence to self-destroying dissipation, one from which Boone himself was about to flee. And then Acey smiled once more and it was time to go.

"Take care yourself," Boone said. What else could you say?

"You, too, ol' Half-Breed. Make 'em eat dust. I'll be readin' them papers."

Each extended his hand, lightly clasping for an instant. Each seemed self-conscious; slowly their hands dropped and each turned away and got in his car.

Boone left first. As he drove off, heading south, there was a thickness in his throat and he didn't look back.

Boone slept brokenly. Once he woke and was sitting on the edge of the bed, head bowed, hands pressed against his aching temples. His chest felt heavy, burdened. His mind seemed to glow and fade, glow and fade. He had been dreaming, though he could not recall his dream. He touched his face. His hand came away wet, and he knew then that he had been grieving while he slept and dreamed. Now, awake, his sense of loss did not lessen and his chest felt no lighter. On the grass-scented wind purring through the windows and billowing the curtains, the drawn-out singing of coyotes reached him. He listened, gladdened by the familiar foxlike sounds. For minutes he listened, as if the coyotes talked to him, to him alone. One voice seemed to rise off a ridge west of the house, which a higher voice answered now and then south of the house. They alone, he thought, haven't changed.

Lulled, he lay back and dropped into a deep sleep, hearing around him, last, the comfortable creaking of the old ranch house, and he was unafraid, because he had never feared darkness and night sounds.

Later, dreaming again, Boone heard drums. He knew not where he was in the dream or whence the drums came, which did not matter, for he heard them as distinctly were he attending the tribal dances at Gray Horse village. He was struggling to reach the crouching, weaving dancers, whose dim faces he could not recognize — save one, which was Acey's. Boone continued to struggle toward the circle of dancers and he was singing a warrior song, a Wolf Song. Just then an old fullblood rose and waved him back, shouting, "Go away — you're half white." Boone kept on. He seemed to be walking on a shifting mass that sucked at his feet and ankles, and now his knees. He sang louder, keeping his voice high and brave. No one turned to help; no one even noticed him. He forced his legs faster, and when he did they became heavier. He tried to shout, only to discover that he had lost his voice. Without warning he was floundering and finding no solidness under his feet. Just when he felt himself sinking to his armpits, the dancers vanished.

That broke his dream.

He sat upright in bed, a roaring in his ears like surf; and while he listened, all his senses rushing alert, the drums of his dream, diminishing, became the pulsating roar of a car traveling fast. He moved, trancelike, to the window, looking out at a sickle moon behind roving bands of clouds.

The roar came from the direction of Paradise. He spotted headlights bobbing like wolfish yellow eyes. As the driver approached the house, he eased off the gas. A moment more and the car was roaring again, past the house, racing on. The roar ceased suddenly, which Boone thought odd. He got the faint smell of drifting dust.

He went back and sat on the edge of the bed, thinking that if not for his nightmarish dream he wouldn't have waked to the car's racket. Some drunk, he thought, prowling the empty night roads as he used to.

He lay down and shut his eyes and was on the edge of sleep when he heard the cry. A cry that sounded vaguely north of the house, like the piercing yowl of a cat, yet not quite like a cat; too full and human-sounding, not high enough, not wild enough. Disturbed, he returned to the window and listened, hearing the wind's metallic rustling of the blackjacks on the west side of the house, but no cry. He turned and ran a hand through his hair, beginning to doubt his senses. No sooner his uncertainty than he heard it again, more distinct, more human, undeniable — real.

He went rigidly cold, shivering despite the warm night, head up, listening as the yowl climbed to a scream, then fell, then climbed again.

Just as he located it with some sureness

across the road, it ceased all at once. About half a minute passed before he heard the voice again. This time he moved with the cry, turning back into the room, slipping on trousers and shoes, and hurrying down the stairs to the kitchen and outside, drawn as much by curiosity as by angry determination to locate the source. And Nate. Where was he?

After several steps toward the cattle guard, he checked himself. The moon was sneaking out from behind the clouds, lighting up the road with silver. Turning back, he picked up a piece of firewood from the pile just beyond the kitchen and, circling west around the house, followed the fence line to the road.

Across the road it was blackjack black, and dead-still, and the awareness cut through him that he hadn't heard the awful wailing since leaving the house. Had he just imagined it after all? Was it part of his nightmare about Acey?

He waited, listening. When the scattering clouds darkened the moon again, he pulled up the top strand of the barbed-wire fence and eased through, and down the shallow barrow ditch, striding for the other side. His footsteps made no sound in the road's deep dust.

He wasn't ready when the screaming broke again, full-voice, not across the road where his senses told him it should be, but eastward, well past the house, moving away from him, it seemed.

He froze, his belly cold, his heart pumping against the wall of his chest. At once the cry shut off. Hard upon its fading, he hastened along the road, running lightly on his toes, keeping to the rim of the ditch. Up ahead he heard running.

As he spurted into a run, he was startled to hear a car start up and roar off. He could see nothing. He heard gears shift, rasping hard, and the roar of the motor deepening and tires slewing grit.

Not ten yards beyond Boone a shotgun bellowed. The car tore on, running without lights.

A moment later Boone heard the fury of a familiar voice cursing after the car.

"Nate," Boone called.

A figure stumbled out of the blackjack darkness beside the road. "Heard me and vamoosed," Nate Robb said, disgusted. "Damn a shotgun to hell, anyway. Not enough carry."

"Any idea who it was?"

"Naw. Just hope I dusted me some tail feathers."

The fugitive moon was free again, lavish with light. The narrow road was a trail of silver that disappeared into the mystery of the hills. They turned thoughtfully toward the house.

In the kitchen, Nate struck a match and lit the lamp. Standing over the glass chimney, the amber glow lighting the grizzled slopes of his weathered face, his old eyes flickering feeling, he said, "In the early day they used to say a panther's scream sounded like a woman, but tonight that was a man."

CHAPTER 3

When Boone came downstairs for breakfast, the events of last night seemed far removed from the greeting of this bright, clean morning, so cool for early September. A shower had caressed the hills while he slept. Mourning doves called. The sweetness of wet grass flowed off the prairie.

Nate Robb accorded him a nod and they sat down at the table.

"Guess you're heading back for Fort Worth?" Nate asked, after they had eaten.

"Not today. Going by Acey's. Then to town."

Nate put down his coffee cup. He looked questioningly at Boone. "Wouldn't aim to see Judge Pyle and maybe Doc Mears, would you?"

"I am."

"You figure something's wrong about Acey's death?"

"I don't know. It's just a feeling — that's all. I'd like to know more about how it happened. I won't feel right until I do know more."

"You won't find out much in Paradise."

"Maybe not. But I'm gonna ask. I want to know if they made a thorough investigation."

"Meaning if they didn't Boone Terrell will?"

"I'm no detective."

The old man bent forward, a movement of warning. "Let me tell you something, Boone. Acey never took a sober breath the last three years of his life. Whiskey'd got him if he hadn't drowned. Let it alone."

"If Acey's death was accidental, what's there to fear?"

"And if it wasn't accidental?"

"The more reason to look into it."

Nate Robb began clearing the table. He kept his head down, a sign of disapproval. Boone spoke from the doorway. "Is there anything you haven't told me that I need to know?"

"Come to think of it, there is," Nate snapped, pausing. "One of the best ways I know for a man to get his lamp blowed out is to nose in where he's got no business."

"But this is my business," Boone said. "Remember what happened at the Blue Hole?"

Nate seemed not to hear, and Boone went outside and stood under the blackjacks, his mind retreating. Seeing below him the mirror of the pool and the rimming rocks . . . the sheen of blue water as he dived headlong . . . as he heard Acey's shout of alarm and felt the first coolness of the water along his arms. Then the pain crashing through his head and the blinding, streaky darkness as he became strengthless, choking on water.

He remembered the extraordinary swiftness and strength of arms groping for his body and lofting him toward the dull light that appeared so far away, which was the last he knew until, in another world, he sensed, vaguely at first, that he lay with his head turned on a forearm and that someone was repeatedly jerking his belly against his backbone as the water ran out his mouth.

When he was pumped dry and he lay gasping on the bank, thunder rolling through his head, he saw Acey standing over him like a rebuking young god, his high-boned face a mixture of relief and anger.

"I told you to dive way out," Acey panted. "You fool half-breed, you tryin' to show me how brave you are, comin' close to them rocks?"

Boone was ten then, Acey thirteen, his sculptured bronze body beginning to fill out toward the promise of the natural athlete to be, deep-chested, smooth-muscled.

With an ache, Boone mentally rubbed out the picture. He idled out to the Stutz, his eyes straying to the road and down it, about where the night-owl driver had gunned his car. Brooding, Boone had almost forgotten. Walking through the cattle guard, he followed the fence line on the far side. In the grass alongside the bar ditch, he picked up Nate's empty shotgun shell. Some fifty yards on he saw a bent place in the grass where someone might have stood, and might have not. He crouched down. There were no heel marks, nothing. Maybe Nate was wrong. Maybe it was only some night-prowling drunk, which Boone realized was what he wanted to believe, and which, in all honesty, he knew he did not. He walked back to the car.

He was in no hurry as he drove. It was still a little early to call and pay his respects.

A schoolhouse, the Little Chief School,

shaped among the humping hills. It was high-peaked and white, quaint and sturdy, so small it appeared to be hiding in the grove of blackjacks. He repeated to himself: Little Chief School. There he had gone through the first eight grades; afterward to Paradise High School. South of the little school, in a tangle of shaggy hills, rose a special boyhood place with the special boyhood name of Medicine Hill.

A Hudson Super-Six touring was parked close to the schoolhouse. He reduced speed and turned in across the cattle guard, his anticipation rising, drawn by a sense of time passing, when the world was untroubled, gladdened to find the school there and in use. The place needed painting, but everything wasn't run-down. He could see two new outhouses, and there were more swings. A graveled road, no doubt laid through the courtesy of the district county commissioner looking ahead to the next election, led from the cattle guard to the doorway.

Now a woman came to the open doorway, sweeping vigorously, making the dust fly. He stopped with a jerking of the brakes. An electrifying feeling plunged through him. The woman was young, recognizable at twice this distance. He saw her head tilt up, saw her hands become motionless. An attractive frown of puzzlement puckered her brows, then disbelief.

He got out rather quickly, awkwardly, banging his foot on the running board, just now realizing that he had left the motor running. Reaching back, he snapped off the ignition. One step and he faltered still. He took off his hat.

"Hello, Teresa," he said.

Her lips moved soundlessly. She leaned the broom against the doorframe, her actions uncertain.

Coming forward at last, he stood at the foot of the wooden steps. "Pretty day," he said.

"Why, yes, Boone," she agreed, talking fast. "Yes, it is. School starts in a few days. I came out to clean up. There's so much to do." She gestured, making fluttery motions.

For lack of ease he looked around, seeing the tramped-down yard, bare of grass, and the building's peeled face, and inside, darkly, the rows of scarred desks. In a corner the American flag on a white oak stand. The teacher's desk and the world globe. And, coming to him pungently, the still-distinct musk of active young bodies, and the closeness of old books and pencil shavings. An eddy of nostalgia swirled over him. He looked at her. She seemed as mute as he, only her eloquent eyes speaking.

"I'm gonna do something," he said impulsively, taking the steps as he spoke. She stood back, surprised. Inside, he turned right. Just off the cloakroom he saw the bell rope neatly looped around a wooden peg. Uncoiling the rope and grasping with both hands, he gave a mighty yank and the bell clanged twice. He pulled again, harder, faster, and the metallic tones sounded again. He felt a delightful excitement.

He came out grinning. "That was one of my jobs," he said, strolling along the narrow aisle, touching the desk tops, past the iron, wood-burning stove and its black belly, on to the teacher's desk and back, in fancy seeing once more the young faces of white kids and Indian kids, penned inside like lively colts.

He hesitated as he stopped before her, for the first time looking straight into her face. She turned her eyes downward, then gazed straight into his.

His breathing shortened. He could find no words, for there were no words, seeing her not as he had left her, all long legs and arms and big eyes, seeing, instead, a full-bodied woman who had bloomed during his absence. Large hazel eyes set wide apart and rich chestnut hair drawn over her ears and pinned off her neck, the old-fashioned way he liked, rather than the bobbed hair that was the style of the day. She wore a blue gingham dress and her sleeves were rolled up to her elbows. He knew her birthday: May 18. That made her twenty-two past.

"You look fine," he said.

"Thank you. You look fine."

Words were becoming more difficult for him to find. He said, "I'm obliged to you for calling me."

"I looked for you at the church."

He winced. "Couldn't make it in time, though I did get out to the cemetery and the feast at Louis Climbing Bear's." An interval then, a further uncomfortable interval. By way of conversation, he said, "You're teaching school. How long?"

"I'm starting my second year here. Finished at A&M last summer. I always wanted to go to school here when I was little, rather than in town."

He was intent on her features. Her lips moved softly when she spoke, which brought out the fullness of her mouth and the sweetness he so remembered now. Awareness of his eyes pinked her neck and cheeks. She glanced away.

"Wish you had," he said. His mind swept

back to yesterday. "I saw Acey's little girl Mary Elizabeth. She go here?" He asked hopefully, not expecting that to be.

"Oh yes. You seem surprised."

"I'm glad. I was afraid she'd been shipped off somewhere. Some private school where she'd feel lost."

"She's very shy," Teresa said, manifestly welcoming the shift in their conversation. "Very quiet, very sensitive. I believe she likes it here. Likes the children. She's learning. She writes and draws beautifully. Most Indian children do."

"Good."

Again the stiff pause, as if each had run out of something to say, as if each avoided what yet had to be said.

"How long will you be home, Boone?"

"Day or two."

"Will you go back to Fort Worth?"

He nodded.

"Then?"

"California, I guess."

"You really like racing, don't you?"

"It's something to do."

"Not more than that?"

"It's my life." He smiled brokenly. "Keeps me out of trouble."

She began sweeping out the doorway again, short, aimless thrusts. She quit sud-

65

denly, moving back into the schoolroom, her knuckles white on the handle, and propped the broom against the wall. Her eyes deepened to pools, a reflection of bewilderment and hurt, deep hurt. "I waited a long time, Boone. But you never came back."

"I know."

"You didn't write. Not once."

He said nothing, his silence a confession.

"Not one word," she emphasized. "Why didn't you come back?"

"I couldn't."

"Was it . . . was it entirely the racing?" She was, he perceived, trying desperately to understand, and wanting to, and unable to because he couldn't help her understand.

He looked down at the worn planking smelling of floor sweep, incapable of telling her because he hardly understood himself at times. How could you explain when you were caught between two worlds, ashamed to admit that you had stayed away so you wouldn't turn into a drunk like Acey and others in the old bunch?

He heard her plaintive voice again: "Was it someone else, Boone? Did you find someone else?"

"No," he said, looking up, "and it wasn't all racing. I can't put it into words." His hands rose and fell, a gesture of futility. "Someday I'll know how to tell you."

"I'm afraid that will be too late, Boone. You see, I'm going to marry Andrew Horn next month. We've been engaged since May."

He took a backward step, as he might if recoiling from an unexpected and smashing blow, too shaken to speak. He opened his mouth and there were no words. Raising his eyes level with hers, he managed an uncertain control. "I hope you'll be happy," he said. "I mean that," aware that his shock betrayed itself in his eyes, in his voice.

"Thank you, Boone." She was being most proper, though he could scarcely hear her strained voice. Her eyes were enormous. She looked pale.

He could not help shaking his head. He kept doing that, over and over.

"I'm sorry," she said and put out her hand, but did not touch him.

"Don't be." There was a bitter edge to his voice. "You're right. Who wants to marry a drunk Indian?" And the moment he spoke he knew that he had been unkind, voicing a near self-pity, which he hadn't meant to convey, for he saw that he had hurt her; and having done so saw the flash of that deep hurt leaping out at him:

"I wanted to go away with you. Oh, how I wanted to! You'll never know how much. I wanted to run away with you, Boone. I'd have gone anywhere with you. *Anywhere.*" Her eyes were glistening wet. "Only you didn't ask me. You didn't even ask me."

"I couldn't."

She flung around, speaking faced away. "A woman can't wait forever, Boone. She just can't. Did you think I would? Did you?"

"I don't know what I thought, except one thing — I knew I had to get out of the Osage. I was drinking too much. Still, I never forgot you while I was away. I guess . . . I guess I thought it was better if you forgot me. That's the way it was."

"Oh, Boone," she said, turning back to him.

His throat filled. He felt stifled. And the distance between them appeared to widen, impossible to bridge, and the silence mounted and he couldn't break it. She looked into his eyes. Her mouth was trembling and she was very close to tears. That tore into him, that loosened him.

"Teresa."

He said her name and could say no more, and was reaching for her and expecting her to move away when, to his surprise, she came to him. He wrapped his arms around her and buried his face in her hair, the clean scent of her choking his senses, and became aware of her completely and warmly against him, each body niche of one seeming to fit the other.

He was still holding her when a steady roar invaded his consciousness. A car traveling at moderate speed. He tried to shut out the intrusion. And just when he thought it was passing, he heard it slow and clatter the cattle-guard pipes.

Boone released her. She stayed there another moment, looking up at him. "You were gone so long," she said. The car stopped with a crunch of gravel, and her face altered with the sound. Gathering herself, she brushed at her eyes, at her hair, pulled uncertainly at her dress. Taking the broom, she went to the door.

"It's Andrew," she said tonelessly. Facing the doorway, she seemed to force a wave.

Andrew, it sank through Boone. Why didn't she call him Andy? "I'll go," he said. "Maybe I can see you before I leave?"

"I don't think you'd better," she said, not looking at him. In one way her tone was final, in another it wasn't.

As Boone came outside, Andrew Horn was getting out of a brand-new blue Chrysler roadster with a distinctive winged goddess radiator ornament. He was a slim, blond young man, almost slight of build, wearing a neat dark blue business suit, white shirt and dark tie and western hat. Everything was right for him except the hat, Boone judged. Andy just wasn't made to wear a big western hat, no more than he was made to wear a football helmet. By the same token, however, few squawmen had the right to wear big hats, inasmuch as few of them worked cattle.

And as quickly, a still, small voice told Boone that he was prejudiced; that there was no such thing as the "right" to wear a big hat. Furthermore, Andy worked hard. He'd gone out for football four years in high school, finally lettering his senior year as a substitute end, where they put the lighter players. An example of dedication, the coach had pointed out to more talented players. Guts was a better definition, Boone knew, and he had admired Andy for sticking.

They said around Paradise that Andy was a bitter disappointment to Dane Horn because he cared nothing for the rough-and-tumble ranch life from which his father had evolved. By no physical feature did he resemble his father. Dane Horn weighed two hundred pounds or more, had thick hands and bull shoulders, and the big hat

70

he wore belonged. Whereas Dane Horn was dark and moon-faced, his son was fair and slim-faced, like his mother, a soft-spoken woman whose life was the Baptist Church; and whereas the elder Horn had penetrating eyes, the younger's gaze, though also blue-gray, was temperate.

Yet Andy had his father's sociability, a prerequisite for any successful business among the friendly, informal residents of the Osage, and he had his father's quick mind. As if recognizing the last two qualities, Dane Horn had sent his only son off to Yale and the Graduate School of Business Administration at Harvard, where he was graduated *magna cum laude* (which an impressed Paradise had paraphrased as "magnet come loud"), and put him to work not long afterward running the Cattlemen's Bank. Dane Horn preferred to keep his private office across the street, where he could see a stream of callers, ranchers and politicians and loan-seeking Indians, without disturbing the well-run operations of the bank.

Andrew Horn recognized Boone immediately and stuck out his hand. "Very pleased to see you, Boone." The slim face bore a look of sadness. "Back for Acey's funeral?"

Boone nodded. "At least I made it to the

71

cemetery."

"Sorry I missed you. Had to get back to the bank . . . Say, I'll never forget the time we played Pawhuska in the mud and Acey scored three touchdowns. Too bad he didn't go on to college somewhere."

"Yeah," Boone agreed, and sensed that he had no appetite today for rehashing the past, which was rubbed out, as the old Osages would say, and no keenness for discussing why Acey, who had had his pick of a dozen big schools, hadn't gone to college. He looked back at the old schoolhouse. "Was going by. Thought I'd stop." That, he would explain.

"Let's see. You went to school here, didn't you?"

Boone nodded, reminded that the Horns knew everything about you, which was one key to their success in business. "Teresa just told me the big news. You're a lucky man, Andy. Congratulations."

Young Horn's gaze flicked from Boone to Teresa, his eyes thoughtful for a moment, and back to Boone, smiling again. "I appreciate that, Boone. Come by the bank if you have time."

"Thanks."

Driving, Boone kept telling himself that he had no right to feel hurt. Everything she had said was true. Everything. But his shock of loss pained him terribly, and he knew it would for a long time. Conscious of the rushing wind, he glanced down at the speedometer. Christ, he was doing sixty-five on a road like this. Like a crazy drunk. He let up. Thereafter, he drove at a preoccupied forty-five, trailing a plume of yellow dust, unmindful of the passing hills and the massive swells of grass, his mind still back at the old schoolhouse, still seeing her engraved earnestness as she told him.

Acey Standing Elk's red brick house loomed broad and high among the blackjacks. The yellow Packard that Boone had seen at the feast was parked in the drive.

He saw no one. An acute dread overtook him as he left the car and, hesitating, went up the concrete steps to the front porch, nervous about coming here at such a time, concerned how Acey's widow, a white woman, would take his calling. The open door yawned on a dark, cool interior. He smelled heavy incense, exotic for the unworldly Osage. He rapped and stood back, holding his hat. No one appeared. He rapped again. After lengthy moments, he heard rustling movements and a woman emerged from the dimness and stood at the screen door. The same woman he had

73

observed at the funeral and feast with Mary Elizabeth.

He said, with a suggestion of apology, "I'm Boone Terrell — a friend of Acey's," and by her expressionless reaction he doubted that she was going to ask him in.

She drew back, well within the room's gloom, so that he could see no more than the indistinct oval of her face as she sized him up. He was prepared for her refusals, and hoping she would refuse so he could be on his way, when he heard her listless, "Come in. I've heard Acey speak of you a lot. I'm Donna Standing Elk."

She opened the screen door and held out her hand to him as he entered. At her gesture he sat in an armchair. Not until now did he notice that she wore a black slip which exposed the white, rounded points of her shoulders and her slim arms.

"Excuse my appearance," she said, though he had the impression that she was no way embarrassed by her state of undress. "I've been trying to rest."

"Sorry I got you up. I won't stay long. I'm leaving tomorrow or I'd come by later."

"Please stay. Excuse me a moment."

She disappeared up a long flight of carpeted stairs, stairs which had been bare the last time he sat in this room. He averted his

74

eyes from her shapely figure as she hurried away. Shortly he heard voices, briefly hers, raised a trifle, and a child's soft, blurred tones. Although he couldn't distinguish what was said, the voices brought upon him the uncomfortable feeling of eavesdropping, for he was privy to disagreement. Fixing his attention about him, he noted the dark furniture foresting the great room, the kind you bought at the Salt Creek Trading Company: heavy, ugly, overstuffed, overpriced. Incense stained the air.

When she came down the stairs, she was wearing a black dress, severely plain. Taking a cigarette from a silver box on the table near Boone, she lifted it to her lips and paused, a pause which he caught, and to which he responded by lighting her cigarette. She inhaled hungrily, letting the smoke curl from her mouth and nostrils as she said, "I see you're a gentleman, Boone. A rare discovery for a woman in the Osage."

He had to smile at her seriousness. She was not, he was beginning to see, of the openly brassy breed young Osages often married among the whites — on the make for easy living and Indian money, and when the inevitable breakup came, departing well-heeled, thanks to a clever lawyer. Not at all what he had expected: loud-talking, hard, unfriendly, coarse, arrogant, obscene. She possessed a remarkably good-looking, clean face. Bobbed yellow hair that showed care, striking green eyes and perfectly molded features — classic, he decided. A face you might expect to grace the pages of a New York magazine, and her cultivated voice was impressive to the ear. He wondered where Acey had found her. At the same time something about her bothered him, a discernment whose exactness eluded him.

"Acey was my best friend," Boone began. "We grew up together. Like brothers. Once he saved my life. We were swimming. I dived in and hit some rocks. He pulled me out." He had been speaking calmly. Of a sudden his voice faltered with feeling, and he asked her, "Is there anything I can do for you and Mary Elizabeth? Anything at all? If you're short of money . . . I know how an estate gets tied up."

Surprise was visible on her face. She said, "There's nothing. Thank you. I guess we'll go on living here, though I must say there's little I know about raising cattle. Not that Acey knew a lot either. He wasn't really interested in raising cattle. He was more interested in . . . well, having a good time. However" — she corrected herself, showing him a wan understanding — "I guess we're

76

all like that. Guess we'd all rather have a good time first."

"I wish I could do something."

"I'm grateful for your kindness, Boone. Friends — old friends — mean so much at a time like this. Time heals all wounds, I've been told; but I wonder if it isn't the very old who say that. I believe it was Mark Twain who said [she gazed thoughtfully toward the ceiling, a searching upon her well-made face], speaking of expressions of sympathy when his daughter Jean died, 'They cannot heal the hurt, but they take away some of the pain.' "

He nodded in return, impressed, while still puzzled, still disturbed, why he knew not. A silence swelled between them. So it was time to go. When he stood, she held out her hand. "How nice of you to come, Boone. How very nice."

Looking at her once more, he experienced the sharp discovery of what bothered him about her. It beat through him even as he resisted it. Donna Standing Elk showed no outward marks of grief — that was it. Just a little weariness — that was all. Her green eyes were perfectly clear, her face smooth and unshadowed.

He dismissed the observation as soon as it stabbed him. Was he fair to compare her grief, that of a white woman, to the anguish of wailing Osage women, whose contorted faces became as ashes? Some people controlled their sorrow, others did not. And she was a white woman. How could he tell how she felt?

He turned away to cover his shame.

He was at the door when a subtle whisper of sound pricked at his ears from behind. He turned. A small figure, clad in a plain brown dress, her grave eyes and braided hair suggesting a solemn Indian doll, stood at the foot of the carpeted stairs, one hand resting lightly on the banister. She was staring at him. A faint bafflement kindled the smoky eyes.

Donna Standing Elk's scolding voice came sharply. "Mary Elizabeth, you should be upstairs resting."

"I broke my doll."

"How?"

"It fell off the bed."

"I'll get you another next time we're in town. Go on, now, dear."

He continued to watch the child, held by the unnatural pallor of her face, its daubed-on pasty whiteness, and felt himself drawn toward her, speaking as he did so. "Mary Elizabeth, do you remember me? My name's Boone — Boone Terrell. I used to come to your house. I remember you when you were little."

Before he could reach her, she whirled and fled up the stairs. During that one moment, however, when she faced him before retreating, had he imagined a gleam of recognition? Or was it merely the nameless appeal of a lonely child, frightened and confused, too young to understand what had happened to make her house so still? Why strangers came, why stiff-bodied adults spoke in hushed voices?

He went back to the door, where the Standing Elk woman, in apology, said, "That strange child. She keeps putting flour on her face, the poor little thing. I was just talking to her upstairs about taking it off if she came down."

"Flour?" He was aghast. "Why?"

"I'll tell you." The classic face was calm no longer. "She's ashamed of her Indian blood — ashamed of her father, who was a drunk. That's the whole story, Boone. You might as well know it. There's no use pretending any more. It's been hell for both of us."

She spoke the truth. He couldn't deny that. But somehow he resented the way she said it, the flatness of her voice, the hidden harshness pealing out at him, as if her previous barriers of restraint were down and she was somebody she had pretended not to be earlier.

"I understand," he said earnestly. "I'm sorry."

Going down the porch steps, he had again the choking sensation that was becoming familiar, which persisted as he started the Stutz and drove out on the road. There, by habit, as he took a backward glance at the house, he spied the pallor of a small face at a second-story window over the porch. A small hand fluttered up and vanished with the ghastly face before he could wave back.

CHAPTER 4

As Boone continued toward Paradise, he sank into a troubled musing, thinking of the haunted child back there, conscious of a damning accusation, dark and heavy and true: that the Osages of his generation were not only destroying themselves, but likewise were crippling their children, scarring them for the rest of their lives.

Better if oil had not been discovered in the county, if, instead, the Osages were as poor as the Pawnees and the Otoes, as poor as the white men had intended them to be after moving them off fertile Kansas lands to these blackjack hills and prairies and rocks, not knowing oil existed here in quantities that would make the Osages the richest Indian tribe in the United States, and as he had heard white businessmen proudly proclaim, "the richest people in the world per capita." And wasn't Osage County the biggest in the whole state? It was, which implied that it also was the best.

He remembered his parents reminiscing of an evening about when the tribal roll was closed in 1907, and the Allotment Act, which broke up the reservation and each Osage or part Osage on the roll got a homestead and other shares of land. How the mixed-bloods wanted allotment in the name of Progress, and the fullbloods, holding to the old ways, didn't. And a smart young Sioux, married to an Osage woman, had inserted in the allotment bill the shrewd provision that all mineral rights on the reservation should be held as community property and divided quarterly on a per capita basis among the two-thousand-odd allottees on the roll. And eventually how the tribe received one-eighth royalty on each barrel of oil. As events turned out, other Oklahoma tribes without the community provision experienced the extremes of affluence and poverty. The Creeks, for instance.

One man with oil on his land would be rich, another without oil would be poor.

Long ago Boone had learned a truth about himself. Reared as a white boy because of a white father and because his mother wanted him to be educated in the white man's schools, he was more white in his ways than Indian. Yet, at heart, emotionally, he was an Indian. It pleased him further that, save for the lightness of his skin, he looked like a fullblood. And so he had grown up much like a spectator viewing both sides from the vantage point of the middle, while simultaneously aware that he belonged fully to neither.

Now, he knew, the old fullbloods were right. The reservation should not have been allotted, because allotment had attracted the quick-witted lawyers and bankers and merchants, and soon land was passing from Indian hands. Among the waves of people that followed allotment like flies were types who had been failures elsewhere, Egan Terrell used to say.

Although what had happened was not to the advantage of the Osages, Boone understood the impelling force behind the newcomers. It was a continuation of the American dream of "westward expansion," a second chance to start over again. And as oil production increased, more white people came. He liked best the idealistic school teachers and the grim coaches, and old-time cowmen like Nate Robb, both a father and an uncle to him after Egan Terrell's sudden passing, because the old-timers also appreciated the wind-singing prairies. In that link of nature they were akin to the tribesmen. The teachers were forever appealing to you to "hitch your wagon to a star," which meant going on to college and later "carving a niche" in the business world and "amounting to something." The coaches, deferring to natural athletes, were continually reminding you to "train hard — stay outa the Goodtime and get in early. Let the girls alone."

Boone drove on. Seeing Andy Horn's car parked at the schoolhouse, he drove faster and began to assess the time left him. Some good state fair races were coming up late September and early October. He should go back to Fort Worth and get things ready. Leave tomorrow. Somehow or other, thinking of cars and tracks failed to interest him today. He felt purposeless and ineffective.

He turned in at the Terrell ranch and decided to talk to Nate again. In the kitchen he called for Nate without answer. Standing there, delaying what his conscience told him he must do as a friend, go into town and ask questions, he could feel anew the creeping apathy that he thought he had overcome forever. He seemed about to slip back into the skin of that old Boone Terrell as the eye of his mind took the steps one by one, to his room, to his dresser, to the drawer and the bottle.

No — no.

Groaning, he lurched outside and down to the barn. The horse corral was empty. Nate was out riding. Restless and indecisive, Boone spent an hour or more walking around the old place. The idling didn't help. A familiar inner voice whispered that he tarried because it was futile for an Indian to raise questions of the Paradise town officials, and if he did he'd get no straight answers. But a new and stronger voice said he had to ask the questions, anyway, whatever the pre-established answers.

By now the sun was midway across the sky. He ate a cold lunch and still lingered, no more at peace with himself than when he had returned from Donna Standing Elk's. His thoughts kept shifting back to the child and the shock of seeing her flour-whitened face. He had to do this thing.

It was past two-thirty when Boone started for town.

Paradise stirred sluggishly as he drove down Main. As usual, the Goodtime was busy. Through its murky windows he saw figures hunched at the domino tables, and taller shapes at the pool tables. The Blue Bird Cafe looked empty. Several heavy-bodied Osage women waddled into the big store.

He made a U-turn at the far end of the street and retracked. Driving past the Cattlemen's Bank on the corner, he saw flaked gold lettering on the dirty window of a small office: CHAUNCEY PYLE, JUSTICE OF THE PEACE.

As Boone parked in front, town marshal Sid Criner left the office. He nodded and passed on toward the bank, taking the mincing, pigeon-toed steps Boone remembered. Criner had a noncommittal face the color of a faded gray shirt, an aloof, inconspicuous man, lean, close-mouthed. Townsmen and Indians gave him a wide berth. For there were ugly whispers about Sid Criner, among them that Criner wasn't his real name in Texas. That he had used his gun overzealously keeping "the lid on" in such Oklahoma oil boom towns as Healdton and Cushing and Shamrock, to the extent that as the towns settled into respectability the local fathers had told him to move on. At

Shamrock, in Creek County, the story went, irate citizens had further hastened his departure after the controversial wounding of a driller.

Criner's main duty in Paradise was jailing drunk Indians, which usually he accomplished without show of force, thanks to his reputation, generally just a "come along" sufficing; then, following an overnight stay in what local wits referred to as the city's "Crossbar Hotel," bringing the hapless victims before Judge Pyle. However, Sid Criner's tenure spoke for itself. There were few violations of the public peace in Paradise. No burglaries that Boone recalled, no bank robberies. Such envious tranquillity was in sharp contrast to the violence at Shidler and Whizzbang, the oil-field camps some miles to the north.

Flies buzzed around the screen door of Judge Pyle's office. Boone rattled the door a couple of times to shoo the pests and entered.

The cadaverous, dark-suited figure behind the desk continued to read his newspaper moments more before he laid it reluctantly on the desk, the paper shaking in his palsied hands, and lowered his pale gaze, squinting over steel-rimmed glasses resting far out on the long jetty of his nose.

Boone didn't know where to begin. Chauncey Pyle's title of "Judge" was strictly honorary. For a lawyer who had served in Oklahoma's first legislature, and helped write the Oklahoma constitution, it was said, he had fallen on less dignified times. Enfeebled now, he held on to his modest post by levying fines neither too high nor too low, and because other Paradise lawyers, riding the affluent pastime of representing Osage clients in estate and divorce cases and drawing comfortable fees as Osage guardians, didn't covet it. His jurisdiction was limited to hearing minor offenses, mostly public drunkenness, which led to a wide acquaintance among the younger Indians, and presiding at infrequent preliminary hearings involving felony cases, which less frequently he committed to a higher court for trial; at which times the dingy confines of his office, which originally had housed a saddle shop, took on a certain faded official decorum. On those noteworthy occasions Chauncey Pyle lined up the chairs, got out his gavel, and attired in white shirt and black bow tie, called the court to order. Once, Boone remembered, "Judge" Pyle had addressed his high school civics class on the formidable subject of "The Formation of the State of Oklahoma." He had seemed quite old, even then. An austere figure nodding owlishly to the teacher's courteous remarks.

When Boone introduced himself, Pyle nodded. "I knew your father. Onetime he brought charges in connection with the disappearance of two prime whiteface cows. Held the preliminary right here in my court. Yes, sir. Your father never did recover his cows. I think the defendant had eaten them." He chuckled. And as Boone smiled, Pyle asked tolerantly, "One of your friends in jail and you want to bail him out?"

"Not this time," said Boone. Then courteously: "Judge, I understand you're the coroner in the Acey Standing Elk case. We were close friends. I've been gone. I'd like to know what you've found out."

The geniality of old times gradually ebbed from the lined face, leaving a guarded officiousness. "He drowned in Salt Creek," Chauncey Pyle said.

"Did you examine the body personally?" Boone asked, projecting the question with distaste.

"I did, with the coroner's jury."

"Any marks?" Boone felt cruel. Judge Pyle was so old.

"Now see here, young man." Suddenly and surprisingly active, Pyle scraped back in his chair. "You'll have to ask Doc Mears about the medical side."

"Isn't that part of the coroner's report?" Boone went on, a doggedness coming through his voice.

The judge, his official dignity ruffled, rose stiffly and, holding himself straight, strode to the door and closed it and faced about. "Are you questioning the jury's findings? The case is closed. Acey Standing Elk drowned — that's the evidence in the case. It was clear-cut."

"Judge, I'm inquiring as a friend of Acey's, in case you found anything unusual about the circumstances? Even the faintest evidence of any foul play?"

"If there was, I wouldn't have closed the case."

The pale old eyes met his straight on, causing Boone to doubt his purpose here, and yet, a moment after, he heard himself persisting, "I'd like to see the report."

Pyle, as if foreseeing that turn, took dignified steps back to the desk. His air was patronizing as he opened the middle drawer, shuffled papers, and made a show of presenting an official-looking sheet to Boone, who began reading the old-fashioned scrawl:

It is the finding of the jury that the

deceased, Acey Standing Elk, an Osage Indian, died by drowning in Salt Creek, Osage County, Okla., between September 4 and 5, 1924.

Below, he read the signed names:

Dane Horn, foreman
Dr. H. B. Mears
L. S. Kemp
Bart Murray
Newton R. Chapman
Herb Staley

Boone knew them all except Staley. L. S. Kemp was Smiley Kemp, Bart Murray was bootlegger Snipe Murray, and Newton R. Chapman was Teresa's father, general manager of the Salt Creek Trading Company.

"That satisfy you, young man?"

"What did the Osage agency say?"

Judge Pyle looked further imposed upon, near the limit of judicial tolerance. "In response to my call, the agency sent Tan Labeau over. He was at the funeral parlor when the jury investigated. He read the report. He raised no objection to our ruling."

Boone sat back and crossed his legs. "Was anyone with Acey when he drowned?"

"What kind of fool question is that?" Pyle exploded, as if in the role of attacking prosecutor, lips bared on pipe-worn yellow teeth. He spluttered indignation: "Acey Standing Elk left the house on horseback. He did not return. He was found drowned. How would the jury know whether anyone was with him?"

"That's what a jury's supposed to do, isn't it, find out such things?" Boone asked, feeling a new tenacity.

Pyle retreated into miffed silence, and Boone rose and walked to the door and opened it and turned his head. "I believe the main question still hasn't been answered, Judge," Boone said, knowing that he was pushing hard on an old man accustomed to riding the fence these many years. "I mean if there were any marks on the body." He waited.

Chauncey Pyle was busy stuffing tobacco into a pipe bowl, spilling as much as he kept. His vein-swollen hands closed over the bowl. His voice was steady again. "Had there been any that would have been noted in the jury's findings."

Boone hung on. "Just one more question, Mr. Pyle. If the case is so clear-cut, why close the door?" He went out.

A crowd had gathered on the sidewalk

near the Rexall Drug. A man in jeans and blue cotton shirt and straw hat was waving his arms as he talked. Boone recognized Bert Woods, a small rancher on Lucy Creek, and strolled closer to hear. Bert Woods was saying:

"They lost everything. Only clothes they got left is what's on their backs. Fire started while ever'body was asleep."

There was a ripple of movement as the crowd opened a path for Dane Horn, who nodded here and there, not missing a face. "Who is it, Bert?" he asked courteously. As he spoke, the perception sank into Boone that Dane Horn never failed to address a man by his first name, which made the other, particularly a poor man, feel more equal, and Bert Woods was dirt poor.

"Al Sanders an' his family," Woods said, not unimportantly. "Been farmin' on shares. Lost everything. Al's got four kids, an' his wife's sickly."

The scene, Boone sensed, belonged to Bert Woods, a man seldom the center of any gathering. And Boone saw that Horn was fully cognizant of that as he raised his hand for attention, his manner of one hesitating to intrude when another man had the floor. He said, "We could take up a collection. I mean something besides clothing and bedding and groceries. What do you think, Bert?"

Dane Horn was asking his opinion — him, Bert Woods! A stooped man bearing the print of hard times across his crimped mouth, Woods appeared to grow a little taller. His voice came stronger when he said, "You bet, Mr. Horn. Anything we can do."

"Where's Al's family?" Horn inquired politely.

"At my place."

"Good. That's mighty neighborly, Bert. I've always said you can't beat Osage County folks," Horn said, nodding left to right, and everyone nodded in concert. "Here . . . maybe this will help," he continued, and opened his wallet and removed a bill and handed it to Woods.

The Lucy Creek cowman's eyes bugged. "They'll sure appreciate *that,* Mr. Horn. You bet! I'll tell 'em who gave it."

"Never mind," Horn said. "Just say it's from the folks in Paradise."

"You bet — sure."

Dane Horn turned and the crowd parted for him, his departure much the same as a notable actor exiting from the stage after a memorable performance. Boone erased the judgment as it formed. Horn was a friendly, generous man; nobody could deny that. No man in town was as generous. More than once Boone had seen him surrounded by kids on Main Street, handing out nickels and dimes, excluding no one.

Off to one side of the crowd Sammy Buffalo Killer was waiting for Horn. He shuffled his feet and looked down at the sidewalk. Horn, as if anticipating what that apologetic gesture portended, greeted him with a resigned, "Hello, Sammy."

"Dane . . . I mean, Mr. Horn."

"What is it, Sammy?" Horn asked, lowering his voice.

"Need a little loan till payment."

Horn pressed a hand across his paunch. "How much you need, Sammy?"

"Twenty bucks — that's all." Sammy's voice had a pleading quality.

"That's all?" Horn echoed, yet understanding tempered his amusement. "You'll just buy whiskey with it."

"I'm hungry."

"You with three and two-thirds headrights and you're hungry?" Horn expelled a hearty laugh and shook his head. The watching faces were grinning. "Well, all right. But I want you to walk straight down to the bank and tell Andrew you want to sign a note for it, payable the fifteenth. I'm not like you Osage boys. I have to work for my money."

The watchers silently applauded, nodding.

"Sure, Dane," agreed Sammy, brightening as Horn took a bill from his wallet. Then, again shaking his head at such spendthrift ways, he crossed the street to the big store.

Boone compressed his lips, pained by what he had seen. His face burned. Ashamed for his friend, he turned away before Sammy could see him. A few years ago Sammy wouldn't have begged in public, which was what it was, begging. And the *three and two-thirds headrights.* That burned, too. Dane Horn knew exactly. Everybody knew.

Reminded that Horn was on the jury, Boone started to follow him, then changed his mind. The store was no place to talk. He'd catch Horn a little later. Maybe in a few minutes, if he went to his office over the drug store. Waiting by the steps leading to Horn's office, Boone leaned a shoulder against the wall and watched the crowd.

Bert Woods was still talking and waving his arms as he retold his story, adding extra flourishes, sweeping his hands upward to indicate the sudden onset of the flames while the family slept, gesturing dramatically as he described Al Sanders snatching up his children and rushing from the house. Whites and Indians handed him money and lingered as Woods continued to throw in more details of the burnout. By this time he was repeating himself third telling around. Boone smiled as the audience edged away. Woods stood alone. He looked around. But there was a snap to his walk as he took his departure.

At times Boone nodded or spoke a greeting, and his reflection grew that he knew fewer people than he used to. He had the detachment of a distant observer, of returning home a near stranger. There was a fairly steady current of expensive cars passing on the broad street as drivers made U-turns at both ends of Main and circled back. Occasionally one parked in front of a store and went in, or the occupants sat in the cars to watch the people on the street. A taxi driver with two large Osage women as passengers cruised past; the carefree laughter of the women reached Boone. The taxi sagged to its haunches.

A big-hatted squawman and his Indian wife wheeled a purple Cadillac to the curb beyond Boone. She got out, a heaviness to her movements, and without word to the white man climbed the high curb and went into the drug store. Boone recognized her. Rose Red Horse. Acey's other cousin. Now Rose DeVore, according to Nate. She wore mourning black and the wake of her grief was visible in her swollen face. She seemed to see no one. Boone remembered her as an extremely good-looking woman, four or five years older than Acey. Although she was getting too heavy, she retained her straight, well-formed stature and carried herself proudly.

Her husband, who looked younger than she, continued to sit behind the wheel of the Cadillac, a bored expression on his restless face. When minutes passed and she did not come out, he suddenly got out and slammed the car door and posted himself on the curb and looked up and down the street. He set his dove-gray Stetson at a slanting angle. He was red-faced and chunkily built and the candy-striped silk shirt made him appear broader. His hand-tooled boots shone like glass. He swaggered as he shifted about. A diamond glittered on his left hand as he brought out a pocketknife and began paring his nails while he chewed on a match, assuming the importance of a recently rich man. Boone thought of what an old fullblood might say: "He's big man, ain't it?"

Two cowboys loafed on the other side of the drug store entrance. One, a rake-thin man whose brown face wore the haggardness of lean times, scrubbed a hand across his chin and came out to the curb where the squawman stood. Boone heard the cowboy say, "Howdy, Buck. Remember me?" He held out his hand, smiling.

Buck DeVore regarded him blankly, distantly. He took the hand briefly.

"Remember? We used to work together around Avant for Old Man McKay. I'm Billy Cochran."

"Can't say I do."

The other's smile faded. "Wondered if you could use a good hand?"

"Don't need anybody."

"I'd be willin' to take just a day or two's work. Chop wood. Build fence. Anything." There was urgency in his voice, a quiet desperation of need without pleading.

"Can't use you," Buck DeVore said and went back to paring his nails.

"Know anybody that needs a hand?"

"Sure don't."

"Well, see you around, Buck."

Angry hurt marked the gaunt face as the puncher rejoined his companion. He was muttering under his breath. "That uppity son of a bitch. Acted like he didn't even know me, now he's married him a rich Osage. I can remember when he drifted into the Osage from Texas, when he was damned glad to sweat for a plate of beans, biscuits, and sowbelly with the rest of us."

The two moved off.

Old Hunky, a braided fullblood, shuffled up and stood in front of the Rexall. He wore a blousy Indian shirt of many colors, rusty brown trousers tied at the waist with a piece of cotton rope. He could have been in another world as he stared at the passing traffic without expression. A blocky, once-powerful man, Old Hunky had played first team guard at Carlisle Indian School years ago, and when he got drunk those glory days possessed his mind.

Sometimes late at night Boone and his high school friends used to see Hunky on the street, generally around the Blue Bird Cafe, and invariably drunk. He would weave out of the semi-darkness and try to throw his arms around the neck of the nearest Indian youth, and his breath of Snipe Murray's corn whiskey tainting the air, he would ask over and over, "All time frien', huh?"

"Sure, we're your frien', Hunky," the amorous-designate would say, knowing the one sure way to sidetrack his tribesman. "How about showin' us how you played at Carlisle?"

"Carlisle?" The slurred voice quickened. "I was star there long time ago. Big star.

99

First team guard." And Old Hunky would crouch and assume a blocking stance, and "dig in" and, snorting, charge imaginary linemen, bowling them this way and that, on and on, as if he must drive them to the end of the playing field. By the time he had turned around, triumphant, the amused boys were gone.

Now, Boone spoke to him, and remembering that Hunky raised a few cattle, he inquired, "How's ranching?"

Hunky glanced up and down the street before he answered, and then warily, swiveling his head from side to side. "Son o' bitch," he said, "I don' like that white man."

"What's wrong?" Surely Boone thought, judging from Hunky's troubled face, something very bad had happened.

"Three times him steal my cow," Hunky said. "Three times me buy cow back."

Boone's smile was incredulous. "You bought the cow back three times?"

Hunky nodded solemnly, as if there had been no other alternative. "Son o' bitch," he said, "I don' like that white man."

"Who is he?"

Again, Hunky's wary eyes scouted the street both ways. He seemed about to reply when across the street Dane Horn left the

Salt Creek Trading Company and paused in front.

Hunky looked at Dane Horn. Hunky's mouth stirred, then settled, still. He did not move. When Dane Horn turned up-street toward the Packard agency, Old Hunky shuffled suddenly off in the opposite direction.

Boone watched the fullblood go on. Had he meant Dane Horn? Had he? That was hard to believe. And yet Hunky would tell Boone, an Indian, what he would not a white man.

All at once the street, the cars, the people, their voices, everything, wearied Boone, and a restlessness fell upon him. He turned away.

The office of Doc Mears was on a side street, a block off Main. There a puffy-fleshed woman, looming large and formidable, her starched white uniform appearing to add to her dimensions, nodded vaguely to Boone as she penned entries in a ledger.

"Doctor's busy right now," she said, glancing up.

"I'll wait."

"May I have your name?"

"Boone Terrell. I want to talk to him in private."

Her somewhat knowing expression said that was not an unusual request for a young man.

"Don't believe you've been in before."

"No, I haven't." He seated himself and waited.

A sudden outbreak of voices at the door of the doctor's treatment room commanded Boone's attention, and Sammy Buffalo Killer came out talking. "See you Friday, huh, Doc?" Sammy looked happy with the world, an aboutface from the subdued full-blood Boone had seen begging on the street for a loan until payment. Sammy's dark brown eyes sparkled. His voice was rich and lively, the fun-loving Sammy of old. He shook Boone's hand, joking, "Hey, there, *Wah-Sha-She.* You don' look sick."

Boone smiled evasively. He couldn't get over Sammy's abrupt transformation.

"Want to see me, son?"

The doctor was calling Boone, who saw him slap Sammy's shoulder and go back into the treatment room.

Dr. H. B. Mears hadn't "doctored" Boone's people. Boone knew him only by sight and word of mouth. The doctor, a general practitioner, had turned up in Paradise soon after World War I, when the Burbank field was swelling the quarterly

Osage payments, arriving with the locust swarm of lawyers and merchants and car dealers. Boone knew that Mears had soon established a profitable practice, and that he was well-liked and considered competent. It was said that he had an unusually heavy practice among the young Osage men.

Stout and quick of movement, his iron-gray hair cut short, Army style, Mears briskly motioned Boone to sit down. "Haven't been careless, have you, son, banging around up at Whizzbang?"

Boone shook his head, half smiling.

"Don't. Place is lousy with the clap. It's those worn-out Kansas City floozies they're bringing in. Every young buck in town seems to think the grass is greener up that way. Hometown pussy is harder to get, but it's a damned sight safer, believe me." He smiled his broad understanding of life, revealing white, even teeth. "I've raised hell galore with the county officials to clean up the joints there, but they say there's nothing they can do." He tapped a Camel on an evenly trimmed thumbnail and lit up, a frank interest moving into his scrubbed face. "What brings you here?"

Boone told him in few words, while braced for the doctor's affront at invasion of his official domain.

"Don't blame you a bit," Mears said agreeably. "I'd ask questions too. An old friend, you say. An excellent swimmer also. However, my examination revealed no indication of foul play. None whatever."

"Was he drunk?"

"Wasn't he always?"

Boone felt a blast of irritation. "Were you his doctor?"

"I was not. Don't know that he even had one locally. I was referring to his reputation as a heavy drinker. That's all, son."

"He was that, all right," Boone agreed, "and I guess he took the Keeley Cure at Kansas City more than once. But there had to be times when he ran out of whiskey, when he wasn't drinking hard. So I wonder if you can tell me . . . was he drunk when he drowned?"

The doctor had an air of straightforwardness, of looking you in the eye when he spoke. He said, "To tell you the truth, son, I didn't check the alcoholic content of his blood. Didn't think it necessary, since there was no evidence of foul play. Not sure the test'd be accurate by then, anyway, him in the water about two days." From the reception room a young Indian's voice, heavy and slow, cut across the tail end of the doctor's remarks. Mears glanced at his gold pocket watch, his first indication of impatience. "Anything else on your mind?"

Boone, not yet rising, flung up a hand and let it drop carelessly. "Any lumps or marks on the body?"

Now the doctor did look impatient.

"I keep thinking he hit his head on a rock or log, maybe. Was knocked unconscious."

"Could be. However, there was nothing to indicate that."

Boone rose. "Thanks, Doc."

"Come back, anytime. I have a good many friends among the Osages. God knows they need somebody to take their side, somebody who understands them." Mears went briskly to the door and opened it for Boone.

A young fullblood Boone didn't know was waiting in the reception room. One of the young ones, he guessed, who had grown up during his absence.

Downstairs, Boone checked his step, rehearsing what the doctor had said, which totaled zero. Not that Boone was surprised. Nobody was going to tell him anything, if there was anything; and maybe there wasn't. He sensed that he was merely making motions, knowing each outcome in advance. And the truth angered him.

He foraged for alternatives. Exhume the body? Permission would have to come from

Donna. And discovery of a bruise wouldn't be conclusive proof of foul play, for Acey could have struck an object in the water, or a floating log could have struck him.

Coming to Main, he could tell by the thinned-out traffic that the afternoon had wasted away. He climbed the noisy wooden stairs to Dane Horn's office. The frost-paned door was closed. He grasped the knob. Locked.

On the street once more, walking north to his car, he noticed movement behind the glassed front of the weekly *Headlight,* which reminded him that he had overlooked what the paper had to say. A woman sold him a copy. There it was on the front page. His eyes raced over the column:

OSAGE INDIAN'S BODY
FOUND IN SALT CREEK

Acey Standing Elk, Well-known
Rancher, Athlete, Drowns;
Burial at Gray Horse

Acey Standing Elk, well-known member of the Osage tribe, was found drowned Tuesday in Salt Creek north of town.

He had left his ranch early Monday on

horseback. When he did not return that evening, his wife, Donna, called officers in Paradise. A searching party was organized immediately. Recent flood conditions made searching difficult, authorities said.

Justice of Peace Chauncey Pyle was notified and a coroner's jury, consisting of Dane Horn, foreman, Dr. H. B. Mears, L. S. Kemp, Bart Murray, Newton R. Chapman, and Herb Staley, rushed to the scene late Tuesday.

After the jury viewed the body, it was removed to Oliver's Undertaking Parlor. There an autopsy was performed under the direction of Dr. Mears and Judge Pyle, who issued a unanimous verdict of accidental drowning.

Besides his widow, Mr. Standing Elk is survived by one daughter, Mary Elizabeth. Services were conducted at St. Joseph's Church, with burial in the Indian cemetery at Gray Horse. Bearers were Dane Horn, Jimmy Whitehorn, Kip Jackson, Bill Drake, Harp Carter, and Pat Harlow.

Mr. Standing Elk, a graduate of Paradise High School, is remembered as an all-state fullback for two years. He played with the famous Hominy Indians' professional football team several seasons. In recent years he had operated a successful cattle ranch.

In World War I, he was decorated by the French government for bravery. The deceased leaves a host of friends.

The deceased leaves a host of friends.

Nothing more, Boone thought. Nothing. At the same time he could hardly expect the *Headlight* to abandon its bland ways after years of sidestepping controversy and devoting its columns to eulogistic obituaries and reports of civic meetings, local items, and routine school events . . . Miss Twila Brown played two numbers on the piano which were well received. The meeting was well attended . . . There will be a pie supper at the Blackjack School, starting at 6:00 p.m. Saturday. Everybody is invited . . . Mr. Lester Oliver attended a morticians' meeting in Tulsa last week. He reported a good turnout . . . The New Idea Club will hold its monthly meeting at 2:30 p.m. Monday in the home of Mrs. Daisy Drake, who urges all members to attend . . . The Chamber of Commerce had launched its annual membership drive. Let's all put our shoulders to the wheel and boost Paradise . . . Mr. Dane Horn reports range conditions extra good

108

in the Osage for this time of year . . .

He knew that he was being unfair. The *Headlight* wasn't about to rock the boat and dig deeper than the bare facts of the inquest, any more than the jurymen would talk about it. He faced around to stare out the window, watching little whirlpools of dust spinning along Main.

Across the street Andrew Horn left the bank and cut across toward the newspaper office. He had a rolled-up sheet of paper which he carefully protected against the gusty wind. Hurrying inside, he hailed Boone and went to the counter. The woman beamed.

"Just a rough layout, Mrs. Early," young Andrew said. "I've finally convinced Dad we should advertise more. We're going to run a two-column ad each week." He unrolled the paper. "Think we'll make this our theme: 'A Friendly Bank in a Friendly Town.' "

"Sounds good to me, Andrew."

"Perhaps you have some suggestions?"

"I might suggest a light border, and we'll find some art in our mat service to illustrate it. Should have a proof for you by early tomorrow afternoon."

"Fine, Mrs. Early. Thank you."

He came to the window. "Glad you're still

with us, Boone. Wish you'd make it permanent."

"May do that one of these days. Got a minute, Andy? I'd like to talk to you."

"You bet. Come over to the counting house. I'm still winding things up."

They crossed the street and Andrew unlocked the door, smiling as he said, "Don't ever believe that fable about banker's hours. Everybody's gone but me."

As Andrew went from window to window, drawing the green blinds, Boone's thoughts turned inward. He looked deeply within himself. Boone had never felt close to him, and he wondered why. Andy was always friendly and unselfish. Reviewing those years, Boone could see himself exhibiting the superiority of the natural athlete toward the less gifted, the struggler, while Andy, without complaint, carried water and wrapped bandages and taped and rubbed down the stalwart young gods of the gridiron. Yet Andy had scored in more important and long-lasting ways, as a scholar and first-team debater and class leader. Had Boone wished him well? Boone's self-reproaching honesty said he had not enough. And now, when Boone needed help, would Andy confide in him if he knew anything about Acey? Or would he show the usual vague indifference?

Boone asked him point-blank, as young Andrew came behind the teller's cage, "Do you think Acey's death was accidental?"

Andrew closed a drawer and locked it before he answered. "Guess I'm like the town gossip, Boone. All I know is what I hear."

"What have you heard?"

"Just that he drowned."

"You accept that?"

"Frankly, I haven't questioned it because there's been so much tragedy. So many young Osages dying. Do you realize, Boone, that of all the fullblood boys we went to school with, only two or three are living? I've thought a great deal about that. It saddens me."

"What if somebody came up with a different set of facts about Acey?"

"Like what?"

"That somebody was with him."

Andrew's brows flew up. "Then I'd say that possibly it wasn't accidental." He laid a sharpening glance on Boone. "Have you found out something contrary to the story?"

"Nope. I'm just asking questions. I want your opinion."

Young Horn left the cage and came around, a frown on his slim, intelligent face.

"You asked me, now I'll ask you. What do you think?"

"It's more feeling than fact. I knew Acey pretty well."

"You and Acey were close friends, I remember. I'm sorry to say that I seldom saw him these past few years. Maybe when he cashed a check, which wasn't often. He borrowed from Dad."

"I can't see anybody fool enough to cross Salt Creek, drunk or sober, when it's flooding."

"Guess Acey figured he could make it. Danger never slowed him. He liked to take chances."

There was much truth in that, Boone conceded, nodding.

"He was daring in everything he did," Andrew went on, his tone reminiscent. "Thing was he had the ability and the confidence to carry through. He made great plays look almost routine. I saw a lot of big games when I was back East in school . . . Army, Navy, Yale. I never saw a single player who was Acey's equal at throwing or kicking or running with the football. He was another Jim Thorpe. Remember the time he kicked a muddy ball eighty yards on the fly, and raced down the field, made the tackle, recovered the fumble behind the goal line, and we won the game?"

"That was against Ponca," Boone said, breaking out into a broad smile, warmed that Andy remembered.

"The year he led the state in scoring."

"Yeah," Boone said.

"Remember when Pawhuska kept kicking the ball away from him, and he took the punt five yards behind the goal line and scored? I remember I got so excited I fell over the water bucket, and two guys landed on top of me . . . One of 'em was Sammy Buffalo Killer . . . Boy, did the Indians parked around the field honk their horns!"

Andrew Horn's eyes were moist. So were Boone's.

For the next several minutes they rehashed other Acey Standing Elk feats, dwelling on crucial games, recalling as well the fights that broke out as the crowds tramped the sidelines following each play, the rough oil-field workers openly betting, and how sometimes the officials ran for their lives the moment the game ended.

"You know," Andrew concluded, excitement flushing his face, "if Acey had wanted to cross Salt Creek, he'd have made it." Of a sudden he started and became still, an awareness surfacing up through his eyes as he looked at Boone. "What am I saying,

Boone?"

"That he didn't try to cross."

As they stood there, locked in thought, Boone felt a wordless understanding pass between them, a bond he was reluctant to break with words. For another moment they regarded each other, then Boone said, "Maybe I'll see you before I leave," and turned to the door. He looked back.

Andrew Horn was silent, upon him a studied thoughtfulness. "OK, Boone," he said quietly. "Good luck."

Boone walked slowly to his car and sat behind the wheel, conscious of a new strength. On toward the south end of Main rose the stone-studded yard of Smiley Kemp. Boone couldn't read the sign against the coming dusk, but he knew what it said: Monuments of Lasting Remembrance.

Tomorrow, he thought.

Chapter 5

Around nine o'clock the following morning Boone parked the Stutz in front of Kemp's monument works, wincing at the memories the sign evoked.

As he passed through the screenless doorway of the place, which was more shed than building, he heard the chink of hammer on chisel and the bite of chisel on stone. A dusty figure crouched before the half-finished face of a graystone angel. Nodding absently to Boone, Kemp straightened and stood back to admire his handiwork.

"Right nice and proper," he approved. "For Charlie Runs-Deer, a Hominy full-blood. Buried two months ago at Gray Horse. OK just came through from the agency this morning. 'Bout time. Family's gettin' upset. Nothin' worse, I say, than an unmarked place of rest." Had Boone desired to comment there was no opportunity as Kemp, his mournful, chicken-hawk face bearing a patina of gray dust, waggled a bony hand at a nearby shaft of pink marble. "Old inscriptions are always best, I say. Put one of my favorites [which he pronounced *favor-ites*] on there. Lookee."

Boone's eyes followed the spectral hand, his mouth firming, his revulsion climbing, and read: GONE BUT NOT FORGOTTEN.

"I'd like to talk to you, Mr. Kemp," he said, and it occurred to him that Osages were always too nice, too meek, never aggressive like whites when they had to know something. "You may not remember me. I'm Boone Terrell."

Kemp studied him a moment. "I never forget anbyody whose departed ones I

115

helped lay to rest." His nose was leaking. He swiped a forefinger across and sniffed. His tongue moistened the dusty trap of his mouth. "I recollect you now. Don't believe you got your mother's stone from me, though."

"No," Boone said, almost with relish, "I got it at Pawnee. You were too high. Neither was it black marble like my father's, which came from here."

Kemp's shoulders upped and fell, as if to say Boone's past decision mattered not. Still, he asked, "What'd you get?"

"Granite."

"Hmmmnn. Not as purty, an' don't match."

"Nor as expensive," Boone said and curbed himself at that point. The conversation, fueled by old feelings, was nearing self-defeat. A little more and it would get out of hand. "I'd like to talk to you, Mr. Kemp," he said again.

"You're doin' most of it, boy, a-comin' in here — same as accusin' me. What else is stuck in your craw?"

"You were on the coroner's jury that examined Acey Standing Elk's body."

"Who told you that?"

"Nobody. I read the coroner's report in Judge Pyle's office, and it's in the *Headlight*."

"And a sad duty it was, boy," said Kemp, calming down. "Only a little whipstitch ago it came to me that his widow would like to look at some right nice stones . . . maybe an angel or cherub or lamb —"

"— to kind of set on top, like it's looking after things?" Boone provided, unable to resist the opening.

"That's it exactly," Kemp followed, not a whit disconcerted. "Acey, him bein' a big war hero an' all. I tell you things need to be done proper at a time like this." He regarded Boone at length, expectantly. "Maybe you're here as a friend of the bereaved, come to pick out a proper headstone?"

"I didn't come for that, although I am a friend of the family."

Kemp's look of anticipation collapsed.

Boone thought, Is he mocking me? He said, "Some things don't quite stack up, Mr. Kemp. Acey was a crack swimmer — drunk or sober." The voice Boone was hearing didn't sound like his own. "I want to know if you saw any bruises or marks on the body when the jury examined it at the funeral parlor?"

Turning, Kemp put down the hammer with care, then the chisel, eyes fixed on the dusty floor, his attitude that of obliging recall. Suddenly he cut his glance at Boone,

117

a close scrutiny. "You talk to Judge Pyle?"

"To him and Doc Mears."

"What did they have to say?"

Boone had the impulse to flare out at him. Christ, did Kemp think he didn't know where the question led?

"I want to hear what you saw."

"Now," said Kemp, his easy manner returning, "I guess they said no, else you wouldn't be here."

"And maybe they said they did see something."

"In which case I figure you wouldn't come around here, interruptin' an old man at his God-given work. Wouldn't be necessary. That's what I mean, boy."

"I'm not a boy any more, Mr. Kemp. I just want the truth. Maybe you saw something they didn't?"

"No offense — no offense," amended the hasty voice on a purring note. "Look at it this way. A big man like Acey was, with a big shock of black hair, could get a lick on the head from the saddle horn or a rock or a log floatin' by when he went down, an' you'd never see it. . . . He was all swole up, too, him bein' in the water that long. Besides, folks don't like to tarry around a funeral parlor." Finished, Kemp retrieved his tools. "That's how it was, boy," he said.

Turning his back on Boone, he set to work on the angel's incomplete face. *Chink. Chink.* He was tapping on the angel's nose.

Unforeseen, the smell of raw dust and the cold-looking stones and the sight of Kemp bending over the imperfect face, as yet ungentle, which instead appeared deformed under his dusty hands and dirt-encrusted fingernails, affected Boone as a desecration.

He said, "I knew you wouldn't tell me anything, Mr. Kemp. I think you're afraid. This whole town's afraid of something. I can smell it."

Chink. Chink.

Boone turned on his heel.

He had driven two blocks on Main before he realized fully where he was, so deep in thought. At this moment he was passing the second glassy-eyed entrance of the Salt Creek Trading Company. He parked and turned off the motor, eyes unseeing on the store window. After a while he noticed certain bright, miniature figures. Dolls. He returned to his ponderings. Other than to help satisfy his conscience, he had managed to acquire only a feeling of futility as he asked questions. The dolls invaded his attention again, and in that frowning moment the small, haunting, flour-daubed face materialized before him. Leaving the car, he

strode to the window and was at once disappointed. These were dolls from foreign
lands. All but one, on the end there. Navajo-
looking.

He turned in quickly, acting on an impulse
that raised him up and dispelled some of
the morning's frustrations. This one thing
he could accomplish before he climbed the
stairs to Newt Chapman's office and
launched more unproductive questions.

An Indian doll? The woman clerk, flus-
tered momentarily, said, "There is one — a
display model in the window."

"That's the one I want."

Something in his eyes moved her. She had
the doll when she came back. No Indian
had made the imitation buckskin dress and
the beaded necklace and felt moccasins, but
the eyes were a deep brown and the black
hair was braided and the painted face was
copper-colored.

"It's ten dollars," she said, hesitating a
little over the price.

Boone smiled and paid. He had expected
more. "Wrap it up for me, please. I'll be
back in a few minutes."

Upon entering the vast store he never
failed to feel the immensity of its beguiling
wares. He felt so again as he took in the
smell of fabrics and leather, as he trailed his

eyes over the stacked shelves and counters and tables and racks of quality clothing, and the piles of colorful Indian blankets. To his left, centering the massive north wall, a boxcar-size sliding door, halfway open, seemed to wink customers into the grocery department, complete with meat market; beyond, unseen from here, he remembered that another giant door opened into the hardware department, then into furniture. Voices hummed, the busy undertone of trade. Two prices, he thought. One for whites, another for the gullible Indian trade, charging from a habit established in the early days of paternalism and seldom asking an item's price. The store was what Nate Robb called "a bird's nest on the ground." At the same time, the big store's critics agreed that it carried the most up-to-date, quality goods in town, and that the friendly, efficient clerks had nothing to do with the prices.

Moving on, Boone passed to the rear of the store, his even steps producing responsive squeaks from the polished wooden floor, and climbed the long stairway to the business office.

Newton R. Chapman, peering through thick glasses, was as intent on his ledgers as a circling hawk and did not look up until

Boone coughed. There was a blinked surprise, then an amiable nod. As Dane Horn was generally good for a small loan, or even a big one, so Newt Chapman was good if you needed credit until next payment. A pale-skinned man of medium build and mild of manner, he rose and shook hands.

"Glad to see you, Boone. It's been some time. Too bad about Acey Standing Elk. Sit down."

Boone sat, debating where to start. By now his questioning had the mechanical routine of rote, and so he held off, replying to Chapman's queries with generalities. Did he like racing? Yes, very much. Wasn't it dangerous? Yes. But you soon learned not to take unnecessary chances. How long was he going to be around? A few days. Paradise was on the boom. Had he noticed? Yes, he could tell it was lively. Had he heard the good news about September payment? No. Well, it was going hit close to three thousand dollars per headright.

Ceremony taken care of, Boone began. He was asking as an old friend of Acey's. In fact, Acey was his best friend. He just wondered if Mr. Chapman had knowledge or suspicion of foul play?

"If there was anything wrong, it didn't come to my attention," Chapman said, perceptibly surprised at the question. "Certainly nothing I saw at the inquest. I knew Acey well. He traded here." A small crease ran across the pale forehead. "In fact, there's a sizable unpaid balance on the books right now."

"Was Acey having trouble with anyone? Did he ever say he'd been threatened?"

"Not to my knowledge." As Chapman went on, Boone sensed the caution of a man avoiding involvement, the guardedness of a Judge Pyle or a Smiley Kemp. "What makes you think something's wrong, Boone?"

"I don't say there is. It's just that in the first place I can't see him trying to cross Salt Creek in a flood. In the second place, I can't see him not reaching safety. He was a great swimmer."

"Unless he struck his head on something."

"Or was knocked in the head."

Chapman sat upright. "You think maybe . . . ?"

"Just a possibility. By the way, Mr. Chapman, was any money found on Acey?"

"Come to think of it there was. Lester Oliver told us there was fifty dollars in bills and a pocket watch. Which would scout the robbery motive. Too bad, too bad. A fine athlete at one time. Too bad he never went on to college. Just got to drinking too much." Newt Chapman lifted one corner of a ledger page and let it drop like a back-to-work signal. The interview was over.

But as Boone stood, something in Chapman's actions detained him. The man's sudden nervousness, his uncertainty. A sort of determination pushing through his customary affability. "Have you," he asked, "seen Teresa?"

"Saw her at the schoolhouse."

"Did she . . . ?"

"Yes, she told me the news. Andy's a fine fellow. Well-educated. Up and coming. I wish them well."

"I'm glad you understand, Boone," Chapman sighed, getting up, relief gushing redly across his paleness. "I appreciate your manly attitude . . ." His speech was stumbling. "Yes, indeed . . . You can understand my position, Boone . . . and Mrs. Chapman's . . . Teresa's our only child."

Boone replied before the full impact of what he was saying occurred to him. "I understand, Mr. Chapman. You want her to marry a white man instead of a wild Indian." And having said it, he wished he hadn't, for Mr. Chapman's pale, bookish face was flaming and he was saying, "I didn't mean to imply that . . . if I did, Boone."

They stared at each other, Boone seeing

the naked truth. Down below on the main floor a voice, resonant and genial, was calling out greetings and booted steps were ascending the stairs, the solid tread of a heavy man, and advancing to the doorway behind Boone, who turned and saw Dane Horn.

Horn's face lit up. He waved an expansive hand. "Don't tell me you're here to hit Newt up for credit till payment?"

"Me, with four headrights?" Boone answered, grinning back. He had countered without thinking. "Not today, anyhow. I've been inquiring around about Acey. If he'd had any trouble with anybody."

"The jury's verdict was accidental drowning."

"Yeah. I read it."

"That's the way it looked to all of us, didn't it, Newt?" Chapman nodded. Dane Horn went on: "Accidental drowning. God knows what might happen to a man when he's drunk. Tell you what I think. Acey fell outa the saddle — that's what I think happened to him, Boone. Fell and swallowed a lot of water, and that was it. Yet, who knows? Who can say exactly?" He swept a deploring hand about. "Whiskey — it's the bane of the Osage nation. For a lot of white men, too . . . Well, go on with your visit. Come by the office before you leave for Fort Worth, Boone — even if you don't need a loan to get you by till payment." He winked broadly. Boone found himself smiling back, affected by Dane Horn's unquestioned friendliness, which was one root of his power.

"Need something, Dane?" Chapman asked as Horn started to leave.

"It can keep," Horn said.

Boone watched him go down the stairs. Soon Horn's full voice sounded again in greeting. An Indian woman laughed, her voice heavy and rich. When Horn spoke a few Osage words, the woman laughed again, pleased. The voices fell to a murmur.

Horn's voice was still in Boone's consciousness as he nodded to Chapman and took his leave.

"Wait."

Boone turned curiously, drawn by the way Chapman had spoken. His voice was quite low.

"You might see Tan Labeau at the agency."

"He knows something?" Boone came in a step.

"I believe it's customary to check with the agency officer when an Osage dies under other than normal circumstances." Chapman's face was noncommittal, smooth of any opinion. He sat back down at the desk and resumed his entry-making.

If Newt Chapman was afraid, he didn't show it; and if he was being helpful, he scarcely showed that either. As the agency officer, Tan Labeau was a logical person to check with and one Boone already had on his mental list after seeing the jurymen, so Chapman's suggestion hardly could be classified as a tip. Viewed in another light, it was one way to be rid of a nosy Indian.

Downstairs, Boone picked up the doll, boxed and wrapped, and walked outside and left it on the car seat. His attention lifted across the street, where in black-lettered propriety against a white background hung a sign over two second-story windows: OLIVER'S UNDERTAKING PARLOR. And below that smaller lettering which read: INTEGRITY, DIGNITY, BEAUTY.

Boone had decided earlier to see Lester Oliver, after the jurymen, and now was the time. Then Tan Labeau, before he saw Herb Staley and Snipe Murray.

He could sense the dregs of an old depression as he took the wooden stairs, and he jerked as a bell chimed when he opened the door. He froze in dread, feeling the thick, dark red carpeting underfoot and smelling the sickening leftover of flowers past and the heaviness of embalming fluid fouling the stifling air. Somewhere an electric fan droned. A small chapel opened ahead, as grim and cheerless as a jail cell; and directly off it, door open, yawned the embalming room and the long table and the clutter of dark bottles. Why'd they have to leave the gruesome place open? He had asked that long ago and been told that it was to help the air circulate.

"Yes?"

Boone turned toward a soundless figure gliding out from a curtained-off office, meeting the eternal face of Lester Oliver, lineless against the dim light. A white carnation like the eye of a headlight in the buttonhole of his blue serge suit. Oliver spoke — the hushed voice that was stamped in Boone's memory: "Is there something I can do for you?" His smile, which Nate Robb used to describe as "goin' up and down like a window shade," came on, an immediate salutation that bared dull gray teeth.

"I remember you," he said as Boone gave his name, and he pointed toward the office, bowing a little as he did. When Boone was seated, Oliver handed him a cardboard fan, commenting, "Worst time of the year in the Osage. Summer hanging on. I'll go get a fan and plug it in here." He glided away, his steps noiseless.

Boone, glancing at the cardboard fan, noted the quotation thereon in gold italics:

Life is but a day at most,
Sprung from night — in darkness lost.
— Robert Burns

The heavy-scented horror of the place bore down upon him. Twice he had come here, the first time with his broken mother to arrange for his father's funeral . . . His fullblood mother, whose parents had walked the trail southwest from the Kansas lands to the new reservation of rolling blackjack hills and bluestem prairie. His fullblood mother. Inscrutable yet emotional. Primitive yet complex. Modern, wanting to prepare her only son for new ways, yet bound in spirit to the old. His fullblood mother, who keened like an ancient one at funerals while dressed in the Salt Creek Trading Company's finest black dresses. His fullblood mother, who taught him never to stare at people, to be brave, to be unselfish; who loved Egan Terrell, this ready-smiling man of French and Irish blood whose neck was broken when his sorrel roping horse stepped in a prairie dog hole and fell with him.

Mr. Carlson, a local minister, his craggy face an etching of absolute hell and damnation, came to Lester Oliver's Undertaking Parlor to pay his respects, for Egan Terrell had been a generous and well-known cowman.

"Reverend Carlson," said Nellie Terrell, overcome again, dabbing a silk handkerchief to her swollen dark eyes, her voice a wail, "I want to join your church."

Carlson, a tall, dignified man, looked down at her in surprise, then understanding. "Whatever I can do for you, Mrs. Terrell."

Although he drove out to the ranch several times and sat in the high-ceilinged living room of dark, heavy furniture from the Salt Creek Trading Company, his funereal bass filling the sad house, she never joined Mr. Carlson's church. He could promise her only suffering. Perhaps that was why she did not.

It was said in Paradise that Nellie Terrell grieved herself to death. His childlike, full-blood mother . . .

The last time steadfast old Nate was beside Boone. Nate in the straight jacket of his stiff-collared white shirt and outmoded blue suit, when Boone was too broken up to make the necessary arrangements alone. With Nate, he entered the storeroom where Oliver kept the caskets on display. When

Oliver snapped on the one dim ceiling light, Boone got an instant garish effect of ornate horror: the lids open, the bulk of the coffins revealing the red satin lining which the full-bloods favored. Boone's insides kicked and his breath shortened. A close terror seized him, a clutch of panic.

"Now you'll want something with dignity and beauty," Oliver assured him, hushed. As he talked, his face smoothing, his blood-less lips pursing, Oliver steepled his white, plump hands, forming an attitude of prayer.

Boone knew only that wildly he longed to flee this dark and horrible cavern of semi-darkness with its smell of death. He nodded numbly. Tears blinded him suddenly.

The hushed voice whispered again: "This one is very nice. Very fitting for a mother."

Bronze, barbaric, hideous, it glistened under the half light, awakening Boone's rooted distress of before, springing afresh upon him with a sense of suffocation. His impulse was to take it and be gone, but an unexpected and helpful logic came to him, and he asked, "About how much is it, Mr. Oliver?"

"Let's see now." And then so hushed Boone just caught it: "Three thousand."

Nate Robb glanced warningly at Boone, whereupon Oliver amended, "I can come down to twenty-eight hundred, Boone. That's a very fair price."

And as Boone considered, his mind bending before the gray-toothed smile, the long-ago black marble monument raked across his consciousness, giving him strength, and he said, "Show us something more conservative, Mr. Oliver. Nice but conservative in price."

Now the image slipped away, thankfully gone, as Lester Oliver brought in a revolving electric fan. He plugged it in. When it was rotating, he seated himself, hands steepled, his timeless face inquiring. "What's on your mind, Boone?"

"It's about Acey Standing Elk," Boone said, hastening to the point.

"Poor boy," Oliver said. "In the prime of life. Heavy drinker. I guess you've been gone. Did you view the remains?"

"No." Boone felt like shuddering, glad he had not. He wanted to remember Acey at his best.

"A beautiful corpse, if I may say so. A rather difficult job it was, too, considering the circumstances of his passing. The Osages said we did a good job too. They painted his face." Oliver smiled faintly.

"They did that so he'd be recognized in heaven."

"I'm for preserving all the old customs," Oliver said, acquiescing, "as primitive as they seem to some. Such as burying a cedar pole at the foot of the casket, and leaving food at the grave."

"Cedar symbolizes eternity," Boone said earnestly. "Cedar smoke also purifies. The food left at the grave is for the journey to heaven. Indians believed in the Great Spirit before the white man came."

"Say, you kinda go for that stuff, don't you?" Oliver said, and Boone saw the faint amusement light up his face again.

"As symbols, yes. The cross is also a symbol, you know."

"I've handled a good many Osage funerals over the years," Oliver said, retreating a bit, as if on uncertain ground. Into his voice sprang an unhesitating pompousness, as if he must impress his sincerity upon Boone. "Some of the biggest in the whole county. I always handle arrangements just the way the Indians want 'em. Always with integrity, dignity, and beauty. Why, that little cemetery out there at Gray Horse has the finest collection of stones in the whole state of Oklahoma, bar none. The most beautiful."

"And the most expensive, bar none."

"You get what you pay for, Boone. Marble's expensive."

Their talk was drifting, Boone saw, far from where he intended. He said, abruptly, "Mr. Oliver, I know what the coroner's jury reported. I read it in Judge Pyle's office. But it doesn't satisfy me. I want to know more about what happened to Acey. I have reasons which go way back. We grew up together. He was like an older brother to me. If anybody would notice anything wrong or suspicious, you would. I mean bruises or marks or wounds the other jurymen might miss."

Lester Oliver's steepled hands fell apart. He looked keenly at Boone, rather shocked. There was total silence save for the monotonous whirring of the fan. Oliver said, "You're invading my ethical province. I never discuss such matters." Picking up a fan, he cooled himself with rapid strokes.

"Wouldn't you, if the county attorney asked you?"

"That would be different. But the inquest is over."

"You could tell me — Acey's best friend." It had required some time, but he was learning how to frame direct questions. "Did you find anything suspicious?"

"Nothing." The hush had gone out of Oliver's voice. "I found nothing whatever suspicious."

Boone heaved to his feet. "I have the feeling I'm rocking the boat a little too much around here — and there's no reason for that unless something is wrong." He waited for Oliver's rebuttal; there was none. Without thinking, Boone heard his voice spilling the words: "I think you ought to know what's being said around town."

"What's that?" Oliver asked, jarred out of his composure.

"That Acey had a knot on the back of his head as big as a goose egg."

"A knot?" Oliver had quit fanning himself. His eyes bored into Boone.

"Yeah — a knot."

"Now who said that?"

"It's common talk. I heard it at the Goodtime and I heard it on the street."

Oliver was fingering the buttonhole carnation. A leaf fluttered flakelike to the desk.

"It didn't come from here," he said. "Neither did I find a knot."

"Just thought you ought to know." Boone, starting toward the doorway, paused once more. "Mr. Oliver, I've talked to a lot of people about Acey, and I've heard him called a drunk and a rich Osage. Not once have I heard him referred to as a human being." He let that float through the silence of the room as he went out into the hallway,

135

welcoming the familiar street smells of tobacco and dust and fried foods, his mind lodged on the lie he had hurled out of pure frustration and angry bitterness.

He came down the wooden stairs and stood in front of the Rexall, hoping to God that when he died there would be no ghoulish Lester Oliver around to work on him.

Dane Horn crossed from the Packard place to the bank corner, heading for his office, as usual nodding and waving and speaking. He nodded to Boone and was turning into the stairway entrance when Boone said, "Dane."

Horn held up.

"Can we talk?"

"You still frettin' about that?"

"There's something that bothers me," Boone said.

Boone had never seen him show annoyed reluctance at such a request. He did now as he pulled a gold watch from his vest, eyed it, and said explicitly, "I've got a cattle deal on the fire, but come up."

Boone joined him in stride up the stairs, thinking that Dane Horn never turned you down, even when pressed for time, as evidently he was now. That Dane always had time for you, maybe not much, but enough. That the most unforgivable affront in the free-and-easy Osage was to turn your back on a man when he wanted to talk to you.

Miss Opal Whipple, Dane Horn's secretary of many years, greeted them. A staunch churchworker, a rather prim brunette in her early forties, obviously unaware of her supple body curving against the austere restrictions of her dark business dress. Her avowed stand against whiskey and gambling and dancing had discouraged suitors in a town short of eligible women. Likewise, her abstemious life provided an additional air of trustworthiness to Dan Horn's operations. One of eleven children, the eldest daughter of an honest but impoverished house painter and odd-jobs man, Miss Whipple was pointed to with pride in Paradise as an example of home-town backbone. After finishing high school with honors, she had clerked days in a Tulsa variety store, then attended night business college. Following graduation and a stint in the Salt Creek Trading Company's bookkeeping department, she moved to Dane Horn's office and had been there since. She was very polite, very businesslike. Her plain face, devoid of even the faintest trace of make-up, was not unattractive despite its severity.

"You remember Boone Terrell," Horn said to her as they came in.

"Oh yes. Hello, Boone."

Boone removed his hat and inclined his head.

"Oh, Mr. Horn," she said, "Mrs. Horn called. She'll be at a meeting of the Gladiolus Club most of the afternoon . . . And Preacher Smythe was by a little while ago."

"Reckon the church needs a helping hand?" Horn divined, flashing his even-toothed smile.

"Well, yes."

"Make out a check for the same amount the office gave last time. I'll sign it later."

Miss Whipple's businesslike blue eyes softened perceptibly. "Thank you, Mr. Horn. Preacher Smythe will appreciate it so much. All of us will. We're building onto our Sunday-school room."

"You should have told me sooner."

"But you always give so much."

"Just a little stewardship, Opal. You take care of that now. Keep me in good standing."

"I should say that's hardly necessary, Mr. Horn," said Miss Whipple. Her eyes followed him as he went by.

Boone gathered that she worshiped Dane Horn; that his success as the county's leading cowman and the principal builder of Paradise, plus his influence in Democratic circles, provided a needful glow in the otherwise dull and dimly lighted corridor of her existence.

They entered Horn's private office. Only once had Boone come here — that years ago, in high school, when Acey was short of spending money. Now, as then, the high windows were as a vantage peak from which Dane Horn might survey the fruits of his labors. A bustling trade town. The Cattlemen's Bank on the corner. Across the street the Salt Creek Trading Company, that "bird nest on the ground," and, more recently, the Packard agency.

Rows of thick law books, presiding impressively behind glassed cases, filled one wall from floor to ceiling. Once, Dane Horn had studied law. His burly iron safe still occupied its corner like a bulldog on guard. The object embedded deepest in Boone's memory — because it was symbolical of the man's driving life — was the single spur on the scarred rawhide strap there against the plain wall where Dane Horn could see it when he sat at his desk. As a young cowboy, Dane Horn had drifted out of Texas into the grass-rich Osage, down to the one spur, a "ten-dollar horse and thirty-dollar saddle," and his gut "shrunk against my backbone." On that long ago afternoon he had told the two Indian boys of his youth and lectured them at length on the virtues of hard work and thrift. Dane Horn liked to point to the spur as a tangible token of his hardscrabble beginning in the Osage, of his rise from improvidence to his current prominence. Now in his fifties, Dane Horn was at the peak of his career.

He closed the door, hooked his big hat on the buffalo-horn rack, went to his desk and opened a mahogany cigar box, offered to Boone, who shook his head, dug out a cigar for himself, bit off the end, phutted it on the rug, clamped the cigar between his strong teeth, planted himself behind the desk, and said, "Shoot."

"Why would Acey try to cross the creek when it was up?"

"You never know what a drunk will do. Maybe he didn't care." Horn himself did not drink, an unusual abstention in the hard-drinking Osage. That came to Boone's mind.

"I can think of easier ways for a man to take his own life. Was there a lump on his head? A bruise or mark on his face?"

"I didn't notice any, and I tell you we took a pretty thorough look at the funeral parlor. It's like I told you and Newt. I think he fell outa the saddle — dead drunk — took in a lot of water . . . and that was it. Donna told the boys Acey was drinking that morning, which was nothing new. Been new if he wasn't."

Boone sat awhile in thought. He guessed, most of all, he wanted further assurance of Dane Horn's opinion. He could think of nothing more to ask.

Horn glanced meaningfully at his watch. "Don't know what else to tell you, Boone," he said and stood, yanking at his vest riding high on the pronounced bulge of his paunch.

As Boone rose to leave, the question seemed to leap out of the past:

"Did Acey owe you when he died?"

A flicker of surprise scuttled across the moon face, a reaction bordering on offense; then Dane Horn gave a reminiscent nod. "Didn't he always?"

"I mean a lot?"

"He's always owed me, Boone. You know that. I'm to blame. I'm too easy. Guess I'll get it all eventually when the estate is settled."

Boone wasn't surprised and his mind wasn't clear as to why he had asked. Acey's being in debt was just a continuation of the old cycle, one in which an Osage seldom, if ever, seemed to extricate himself, once in.

And it pointed to no motive on Horn's part; to the contrary, Dane Horn stood to lose money with Acey gone. Neither could Boone see Acey taking his own life because of debts.

Murmuring his thanks, Boone opened the door and, nodding to Miss Whipple, walked out. He was at the bottom of the stairs when he grasped that Horn had evaded his question of how much. His frustration became a prod, urging him along the dusty street to the telephone exchange, where he put in a call to Tan Labeau at the Osage agency in Pawhuska.

CHAPTER 6

After a ten-minute delay, a man's steady voice came on the line. "Howdy. This is Tan Labeau."

"This is Boone Terrell. Will you be there awhile?"

"What's it about?"

"Acey Standing Elk."

A dead silence. Then Labeau said, "Come on. I'll be here . . . Let's see. You're Egan Terrell's son?"

"Yes, I am."

"All right, Boone. I'll be on the lookout for you."

Boone's pulse jumped. Did Tan Labeau know something?

Moments later, driving the red Stutz roadster north on Main, he saw that Judge Pyle's office was closed. Not that it meant anything. But damned if he wasn't getting suspicious of any variation from the normal in Paradise.

Letting the Stutz roll, once across the Salt Creek bridge, he drove north toward the highway that ran between Ponca City and Pawhuska. There was no traffic. Reaching the first stand of hills, he could view the country speading out and undulating, wave after wave of grassy sea, made green by the late-summer rains, a bounty of feed and of stock water in the man-made ponds shining like handmirrors, so vital when searing winds cooked the prairies. Whiteface cattle looked rolling fat. On north, wooden oil derricks spiked the sky, intrusions on the gentle scene. The air smelled of sulphur, the stink of crude oil, the smell of power — another bounty. In the distance he caught the toiling *clank-clunk* of cable drilling tools.

Turning east for Pawhuska, he turned to look at his disintegrating wake of dust. Some distance behind it boiled the dusty passage of another car. Probably somebody like himself headed for the agency on business, or "goin' to Ponca," as the saying was. Slowing down to enjoy the view, he thought no more of the car.

Nate was right. He had an obligation to his heritage. He ought to come back and settle down to ranching. With Nate to guide him, they could build up the ranch and make it pay. Way it was now, the operation was hardly more than a token thing, barely out of the "drugstore cowboy" class, which Nate scorned: a townsman running a few head so he could wear a big hat and boots and drop the remark around the Rexall that he was in the "cow business," when the truth was the only time he got dung on his boots was when somebody saddled a horse for him and he had to stroll across the corral to pull his lard into a squeaky new rig. In the back of his mind, Boone knew that he would come back. But when? In a few years? Trouble with that, Nate was getting on in years. But not yet. There were too many big races he hadn't won, too many fast cars he hadn't driven.

At times, when soul-searching like this, he suspected that for him racing was a substitute for the warring and horse-taking and game-chasing that occupied young Indians of buffalo days. Racing possessed him. Racing was his hot-blooded outlet, his need, his expression of fulfillment, his road to follow, although a white man's road.

As he loafed along, an unusual keenness seemed to alert him from behind, more sense than actual awareness, and yet a sense of uneasiness, as you might feel when someone stared hard at your back. He turned his head.

A black sedan was creeping down the last slope, remindful of a long black cat, following at the edge of Boone's dust. Boone was doing a lazy forty. He sped up, figuring the other driver wanted to go faster and declined to pass because of the dust, as Boone might not were he trailing a slower-moving car.

Looking over his shoulder, he saw the sedan also speed up. On the precipitate hope that the other might like to race, he shot the Stutz out faster, much faster, and when he glanced again through the dusty veil, the sedan also had increased speed. Not enough, however, to come on challenging. Was the driver deliberately hanging back to trail him? It was a little puzzling. Was it a game? If so, why not play it?

Boone cut his speed abruptly, and saw the sedan let up as well. Boone further reduced speed, down to fifty-five . . . to fifty . . . now forty-five. The sedan dropped back likewise and maintained the same careful interval, barely beyond the track of Boone's dust. Boone cut down to forty, now thirty-five. He looked back. The sedan was no nearer.

So it was some sort of trailing game, one that didn't make sense. And too slow, with Tan Labeau waiting for him at the agency.

Suddenly Boone roared ahead and settled on the consistent gait he preferred over these rough and dusty roads, between fifty and fifty-five, bouncing now and then, dodging rocks and ruts. Whenever he took his look, the black cat sedan was there, gulping the turbulence of Boone's dust. Who? Sammy, maybe? But Sammy, if he even had a car now, would be coming hell-bent Osage long before now, swaying from one side the road to the other as he steered for the smooth places. No, it wasn't Sammy. He was being followed. He thought of hijackers.

Hence, he concentrated on the road, which he knew almost as well as he did the stretch from Paradise home, and forced his mind to reconstruct the stretch between him and Pawhuska. He thought he had it now. There was a wooded place not far ahead, close to the highway.

He gave the Stutz its head. When the needle hit seventy, he knew that he had reached the point of damned foolishness. There was no need to look back yet. He was churning up a vast cloud of dust and the dust hid the sedan, the cover he wanted, because he was going to play the trick he used to with Sammy and Acey.

In a short time he saw the road peeling off into the blackjacks on his right, very close to the highway. Slowing, braking, letting up when on the verge of skidding, then braking again, he whipped off onto the side road, braking harder, the roadster swaying violently for a moment, then taking the square turn under control. He made another whipping turn, shifting gears and rushing under the trees, and cut around where he could observe the main road, and stopped, leaving the motor running. He was sweating furiously, his heart pumping fast against the drum of his chest. There was a tire tool under the seat. He picked it up.

He waited. His dust still hung heavily over the road in the windless heat, a yellowish fog that was beginning to drift a little and settle. He could hear the sedan's roar, coming fast. Suddenly he saw it. Like a long black hearse, it broke through the powdery haze, ominous, deliberate. A Packard sedan. A burly white man wearing a white hat behind the wheel, eyes glued ahead. Boone got that glimpse of him, and of the battered face as the sedan roared past.

Boone sat there a spell, watching the dust clear and hearing the fading roar. When it was gone, he drove out on the highway and idled on toward Pawhuska. Some miles ahead he drove over the Bird Creek bridge; by then he concluded that he was mistaken, that he was just getting jumpy. Nonetheless, instead of driving straight to the agency on the hill, he entered the business area and circled back. He passed a building where many leading lawyers had offices, where he remembered going with his mother, and which the Osages, when driving by, would point to and mutter *"pi-zhi,"* which meant bad. As he drove along the streets, the flame-colored Stutz attracted the usual sidewalk stares; even here in the Osage capital, where flashy cars were common.

He made the circle a second time, and saw no black Packard.

Shifting into second gear, he took the steep hill leading to the agency and turned left along the spine of the high, prominent ridge. Looking downhill, he felt a jolt. The sedan was emerging from a side street at the base of the hill; now it began climbing the hill.

Boone drove past the grim sandstone

buildings where his mother had gone to school as a child to the prim, well-meaning teachers from Back East, and came to the smaller stone building that housed the agency offices and got out. He did not look back. That wasn't necessary. From the edge of his eyes he could see the dark bulk of the sedan catting along the graveled road. Up the steps and inside, he whirled and looked.

It was the same sedan, all right, and the same battered-faced man behind the wheel. Boone saw him look the Stutz over, pause and shift gears, then drive on, passing slowly from sight downhill toward the county courthouse. Who?

Tan Labeau's office was down the hall on the main floor — a single room, a single desk, a single chair before it, bare of other furnishings except for a framed photograph of Chief Lookout, the revered leader of the Osages. Gazing up at the proud, calm features of the great man, Boone could not but feel moved and humble. Chief Lookout also had made the long walk from the Kansas lands.

Labeau came in from the hall. He shook hands ceremoniously, lax-fingered, Indian fashion, a short, soft-bodied man in his early fifties, growing gray at the temples. Labeau's weariness conveyed some of the frustration and failures of attempting to protect the rights of tribesmen scattered across the largest county in Oklahoma. He was Osage and French, the dark confluence that produced a more Indian-looking man than he was by blood. Boone hadn't seen him since he was a boy. In those days Tan Labeau wore a revolver on his hip and his dark eyes were keen. He had loomed big then, Boone's picture of a hero. Today he looked tired and paunchy, old and ineffective, if not cynical, and he was unarmed. Fatigue lines creased his face; there were dark pouches under his eyes. And yet, Boone's judgment told him, here was a man wholly in charge of himself.

When Boone had finished his story, Labeau did not change expression. "So you think something's wrong?" And when Boone nodded, Labeau said, "What you think doesn't mean much. You don't know that anything's wrong. There's nothing to file charges on. The county attorney won't act without evidence. Got a suspect in mind?"

"None," Boone admitted. "I just don't think Acey would try to cross that creek."

"Listen," Labeau said, canting his head at Boone, "when you called I'd just come in from Wynona. A dead Indian in a ditch north of town. Somebody knocked him in the head and robbed him. One of the Blue

Wing boys. Nothin' to go on. Nobody saw him with anybody. Yesterday it was a knifing at Nelogoney. Nothin' to go on." He rolled a lumpy, brown-paper cigarette, let it hang from his lips unlighted. "Now you tell me this. Which is nothin' more than I found out at the inquest."

"Did you examine the body?"

"Yes. With the jury."

"See any lumps or marks?"

"Nothing that made me suspicious. No wound caused by a blow on the head, if that's what you're thinking."

Boone took that in and felt his hopes flatten. But a stubborn persistence welled up in him. He said, "I was followed over here."

"You sure?" Labeau struck a match on his boot heel.

"I am. Positive."

"Maybe somebody just comin' to Pawhuska too."

"You forget I've been asking questions in Paradise. Would he follow me to the agency, look my car over, and not get out?"

"What're you drivin'?"

"A Stutz Bearcat."

"There's your reason. He was curious."

"Curious, maybe, but not about the car. He wanted to know where I was going."

"Naturally you didn't know who it was,"

said Labeau, his tone trailing sarcasm.

"It was a white man — that's all I know."

"My advice to you is forget it. Sounds like a coincidence."

Boone could hardly believe his ears. Tan Labeau was giving him the brush off like the others, telling him to go about his business and forget that a friend had lost his life. "I thought you might help," Boone said, let down.

Labeau was so unmoving he might not have heard. He went on smoking, relishing that small comfort, letting the smoke curl from his mouth and nostrils, a man past his physical prime dragging on the reserve of his experience.

"Newt Chapman suggested I see you."

"What does that mean?"

Boone felt an angry flush heating his face. "Maybe he thought you knew something?"

"If I were you, I'd go back to Paradise and quit this detective stuff."

"You didn't answer my question."

"I don't have to."

Triggered, the hot, unthinking response exploded within Boone. "You're just like the rest. You don't want to look. You don't want to know. You're afraid you might find something." He wheeled and stalked out to the hall and down it past the offices, and the eyes of the startled clerks, and out to his car, there to pause over the consequence of what he had said. As he slid in behind the wheel, he saw Labeau coming down the agency steps. Labeau came unhurriedly to the driver's side. Boone was surprised to see that if the full, dark face showed any feeling at all, it was one of calm refraining.

Resting his hand on the car door, Labeau said, "You've been asking questions. That could be dangerous."

"Why would I ask any more? You said forget it."

"I don't want to find you rolled in a ditch like that Blue Wing boy."

"What if I find out there was foul play?"

"Likely you won't. Everybody gets lockjaw when a dead Indian is found in Osage County. I know . . . I've been at this for twenty-five years." He lifted his hand from the car door and brought it down with a thump. "In the eyes of some people, killin' an Indian is not the same as killin' a white man. It's like killin' a varmint."

He stepped back, the dark brown eyes as enigmatic as if nothing had been said.

Boone hardly knew what to think. He was outside of town, driving west, when he remembered the doll in the box on the seat. By taking the cutoff to Paradise, he could drop it off for Mary Elizabeth, then go on into town and look up Snipe Murray and Herb Staley.

Donna Standing Elk's yellow sedan was in the drive, but Boone knocked four times before she came to the door. He received the instant impression that he wasn't welcome. Her blond hair was combed straight back, she wore no make-up, and she had on a rose-colored robe, tied at the waist, which hung loosely in front, revealing a loose-fitting slip baring in part the whiteness of her breasts. As if just now aware of her appearance, she tucked in the folds of the robe, which fell open again when she let go. Boone wondered if she was in the habit of not wearing a dress around the house.

"You . . . Boone." Her green eyes were neither friendly nor hostile.

"I brought something for Mary Elizabeth. Hope you don't mind?"

"Why should I? That's nice. Maybe it will cheer her up."

"I won't come in."

"You must. So you can give it to her. She needs that." As Boone went in, she turned and called, "Mary, come down. There's someone here to see you." When the child did not reply or appear after some moments, the woman's aggravation showed.

"That child!" she said and called again.

This time Mary Elizabeth came at once to the head of the stairs. Tentatively, halting on each step, she edged down the carpeted staircase. As before, her face was flour-white. Boone, pretending not to notice, smiled at her and held out the box. "This is for you."

The smoky eyes became enormous. She did not move from the foot of the staircase.

He had never looked upon a face so sensitive and delicately made, so flower-like with beauty. And he kept seeing something of Acey, in the nose slightly arched and proud, in the expression about the mouth as if masking a smile. And the warning sounded in his mind that, above all, he must speak to her carefully and gently, for he longed very much to please her, this haunted full-blood child.

He came a little closer and said, "It's for you."

Shyly, she took the box (for a heartbeat he feared she would not), yet made no effort to open it.

"What do you say?" her stepmother coached her.

"Thank you."

Boone smiled at her. "Why don't you take

it upstairs and open it? I think you'll like it."

She whirled away, bounding up the stairs two at a time, nimble and eager.

"She likes you," the Standing Elk woman said. "She's so shy — and afraid."

"Afraid of what?"

"I wish I knew. She won't tell me."

"When did this start?"

"About the time Acey died."

"Guess that's understandable."

"It's strange. Very strange."

"How long has she been putting flour on her face?"

"This summer. I've tried not to make a big fuss about it, but she still does it. Maybe when school starts, she'll stop."

Boone didn't trust the woman, mainly he admitted to himself, because he trusted no white woman married to an Osage, having yet to know of one who hadn't done so for money. But if her concern for the child wasn't sincere, she cloaked it convincingly.

"Won't you sit down?" she invited, her detachment fading. "I would offer you a drink, but there's none in the house. Acey saw to that the morning before he rode off to the pasture on Salt Creek. He was getting pretty drunk and abusive, so I drove into town to get away for a while."

"Mary Elizabeth was here when you left?"

She nodded. "School hasn't started yet. Acey never abused her. Just me. He never got over losing his Indian wife, Annie. He'd start drinking, then commence brooding about her. He used to beat me." Seeing Boone's doubt, she drew up the sleeve of her robe. He saw a dark bruise on her forearm.

"That," she said, "he gave me the morning of the day he died."

"Doesn't sound like the old Acey," he said skeptically.

"He wasn't the old Acey."

"Did Mary Elizabeth see Acey ride off with anybody?"

Contempt filled her eyes, that and resentment. "Don't think you're the first person to ask that. As soon as I found out what had happened, when the searching party came to the house with the body, I asked Mary. Later Tan Labeau asked me that and a lot of other questions. Mary said she didn't see Acey ride off with anyone. Said she was upstairs playing when he left." Donna Standing Elk clasped her hands tightly. She looked pale and unhappy. "I've asked her several times. She always tells the same story."

Boone was thinking: If Tan Labeau's been

157

here, he knows a great deal more about the case than he's let on.

"But Mary Elizabeth is afraid," Boone said.

"She's always been shy. It's her nature. This has made it worse. She doesn't sleep well. She has bad dreams. She's jumpy." Donna Standing Elk's self-reliance seemed to leave her all at once. She rose and crossed the room to Boone, an appeal intensifying in her eyes. As she sat beside him, the loose-fitting robe fell apart again and there was a flash of bare thigh he couldn't miss. He got the heaviness of her perfume, though it was not unpleasant. "I don't know what to do for Mary," she said, making a vain attempt to cover herself.

"She needs time," Boone said. "What about your hired help that day? They see anybody?"

"We don't have help now. Acey got to where he couldn't pay them. He was always in debt."

"It was that bad?" Boone asked, surprised; in another way he was not, for endless debt was part of the cycle.

"An Osage can drink up a lot of money, besides what he spends on his friends and just gives away. I have to charge everything in town. We trade at the big store. Mr.

Chapman's been very understanding. I hope he gets his money."

"Don't worry. They'll get it and then some."

"The way the store has to wait for its money sometimes, I don't mind."

"Acey wasn't restricted, I remember."

"Better if he'd had a guardian, been on an allowance. He blew it all."

"It'll take six months to a year to settle the estate," he said, remembering. "Including weeding out a batch of claims filed by people you never heard of."

"You mean false claims?"

"I went through that when my mother passed away. It's an old game. You'd be surprised at what some people will think up. To the extent of using witnesses to swear that the lien was owed."

Without pausing, she said, "It's been lonesome out here. So few people to talk to. Acey's fullblood friends didn't come by much. When we did see them, which was generally in town, they were polite but cool. They thought I married him for his money."

"Did you?"

She laughed bitterly. "Of course, I did! No woman ever married an Osage except for his money. No white woman ever loved an Indian. Listen to me, Boone. I loved that big guy in the beginning." The harshness left her face; altered, it grew soft and appealing. Her voice softened to a reminiscent tone. "He brought a load of cattle to Kansas City. I met him at a night club where I was singing. He was good-looking and loads of fun. A marvelous dancer. He looked strong and clean, and he was, then. He threw money around like it was chicken feed. He was exciting. He was different. In three days we were married. My folks had a fit. All they could see in Acey was a wild Indian from Oklahoma. They said I'd disgraced them. I haven't seen them in over two years."

How much of this could he believe? But despite his built-in prejudice, he found himself listening with sympathetic understanding.

"Of course," she said, lapsing into mockery, "I married him for his money. I thought it would be nice to have everything I wanted. To live on a ranch. And it was nice — until he kept on drinking and drinking, and brooding about his first wife, and seldom coming home, and drunk when he did, and getting deeper into debt." She shrugged off her bitterness. "Yet it was harder on Mary than me. For her to see her father dead drunk, to hear him cussing me. Once he knocked me downstairs when I hid his bottle. No wonder Mary puts flour on her face, poor little thing. No wonder she's ashamed . . . So it's been a bed of roses every minute, Boone Terrell, my late husband's very best friend — love, money, respect, peace of mind, security," she summed up, flinging her blond head overdramatically. The trembling of her throaty voice affected him, weakening his resolve to show her no sympathy.

"Why didn't you leave or get a divorce?" he asked her.

"You won't believe me," she said, looking up, suddenly near tears, "because I see that you don't believe anything I've told you. You don't. It's in your eyes. I didn't leave because of Mary — she needs a mother. I really feel for that poor kid." She shrugged. "Besides, Acey wouldn't divorce me. He was Catholic." She daubed at her eyes and rearranged her sagging robe, which fell open again when she leaned forward to take a cigarette from the silver box on the table. She lit up and sat back, inhaling deeply. He saw her regain her self-possession. Her cool eyes seemed to place him at a distance.

"Any more questions?" she asked. "For some reason, I feel much better. Outside of Lester Oliver and the others asking me questions, you're the only person I've really talked with since it happened."

He disliked the interrogator's role he was playing; nevertheless, he pushed ahead. "Did Acey leave any insurance?"

"Insurance?" She was being sarcastic again. "That would take away from whiskey money."

"Was he having trouble over cattle? Nate Robb says rustling is back in style."

"If he was, he never mentioned it to me. Acey was so agreeable outside the family, so well-liked." Briefly, it seemed, her voice changed and there was only regret, no resentment, no bitterness. "A war hero. A football star."

"How about your neighbors? Any squabbles?"

She laughed outright, an acrid laugh. "Why should there be any when, drunk, he didn't know whether he was being cheated or not? . . . You Osages are too naïve and trusting. You know that don't you, Boone? You're all suckers."

The front of her robe had fallen open again, making it difficult for him to ignore her nearness.

"I know that all too well," he said. "I'm like that too, but not as much as I used to be."

"Why don't you call me Donna? After all,

162

we're discussing some pretty personal matters."

Boone said nothing.

She said, "You wouldn't be asking me these questions if you weren't part white," and he did not miss her suggestion of intimacy, that they were exchanging confidences. "A fullblood wouldn't. He'd be afraid he'd hurt my feelings or invade my privacy."

"I happen to like those virtues. But you're right. And I think it's time Osages started asking questions about what's going on in Osage County."

"That day will never come."

"You're wrong there. It's here. I'm asking."

"You're not a fullblood."

"Donna," he said, and he had spoken her name while not meaning to, not meaning to give her that edge, "you don't have to be a fullblood to be an Indian at heart."

Her belittling retreated, first from her mouth, then her eyes. "I believe you mean that, Boone."

"I do. It's true. So tell me who's your nearest neighbor?"

"The DeVores — Buck and Rose. He's white. Their place is across Salt Creek. Rose is a cousin of Acey's. Guess you knew that?"

Boone nodded. "Acey have any trouble with Buck?"

"I never knew of any. Not that I like the man — I don't. He's arrogant, he's common, he's ambitious. He treats Rose like dirt, and being Indian she takes it. Frankly, Boone, Acey didn't confide in me much the last two years. He was generally drunk."

"Who'd Acey do most of his drinking with?"

"Sammy Buffalo Killer . . . they're cousins, you know . . . and sometimes Buck. Mostly Sammy."

"Did Acey have a will?"

"That's one thing he did get done," she said, speaking faster, with a freshening hurt. "It's on file at the agency."

"What does it say?"

He saw her sense the drift at once. Her face crimsoned, and her voice, no longer controlled, hurled a knifing edge. "You don't trust me at all, do you, Boone? You don't think Acey drowned. You think I had him killed and tossed in the creek to look like drowning. Don't you? Well, think what you like!"

"I haven't accused you."

"Not yet — with words. I keep seeing it in your eyes. You're leading up to it. You don't trust me because I'm a white woman."

"Hold on." He found his hand resting on her shoulder, feeling the silk of her skin beneath the thin robe. "I'm just trying to get things straight in my mind." She calmed down at that, and he felt a genuine sympathy for her as he said, "Let's see. I remember Acey had six headrights." Still, while saying so, he could not but liken himself to a white man counting off an Osage's headrights in public, like Dane Horn, or others he'd heard, or Newt Chapman relishing the prospects of next payment.

"Yes — six." Her voice had a slapping ferocity and hurt. "Six whole headrights — at the present rate of income that figures seventy-two thousand a year. All going to Mary Elizabeth. None to me — his wife."

That was hard to believe. He could not avoid feeling for her, to see her side after what she had been through. On the other hand, she could hire a slick Pawhuska lawyer, or some shyster out of Tulsa or Oklahoma City, and try to break the will, which probably she could and would, as other white women had done before her. She deserved something, if what she had told him was true.

While he pondered in silence, she flared at him. "If you don't believe me, go to the agency or see Boots Gayle."

165

"Boots Gayle? Who's he?"

"Acey's lawyer. He stole us blind on some cattle deals and loans, and I can't prove he took one dime."

"Where is he, Pawhuska?"

"No — Whizzbang. That's closer to Paradise than Pawhuska, and whiskey's easier to get there."

"If he's so crooked, why didn't you take him to court or complain to the agency?"

"Oh, Acey trusted him. He liked Boots Gayle. Acey liked anybody, they could do no wrong. Boots gave him whiskey and robbed him at the same time. How I detest that shyster!"

Boone searched her face for either truth or duplicity. She appeared to read his thoughts. "Now that you know," she challenged him, "would I have had Acey killed . . . would I, if I inherited no head-rights?"

"I haven't accused you of anything," Boone replied and rose and walked to the door. "I'm sorry if it seemed that way, and I'm sorry for what you and Mary Elizabeth have been through." And yet, examining his feelings with honesty, he knew that he still retained reservations about her.

He glanced back, expecting to see her seated on the sofa, displaying self-righteous anger. Instead, she was following him, her slippered feet noiseless on the carpeting. In addition, she had put away her anger, and she was saying, "I wish you'd come back again, Boone. It's so good to talk to someone. And thank you for thinking of Mary Elizabeth. It's a doll, I'm sure. Just what she'd want."

He nodded and was silent, seeing her in a different and most human light. A good-looking woman, troubled and lonely and somewhat frightened, the lovely green eyes extending an invitation that somehow was without boldness. She came closer. She reached out. She stroked his arm; her touch became a caress. She tilted her face a little, an angle which complimented the fullness of her mouth and the pale perfection of her throat and face. Her color deepened. She was waiting.

He held her lightly, his cheek against her cheek, his body stiff to the sudden giving of hers. He felt her hands on his shoulders. That . . . for a moment, and she stepped apart.

His mind was a deluge of shock and surprise, and also a plunging awareness of her that shortened his breathing. Holding her open look, he sensed her dearth of living and her need. He looked at her for so long without moving that at last she turned her eyes away. He saw her waiting and tenseness leave her as she sighed and her shoulders shifted and fell.

She said, "I understand . . . you're Acey's best friend. I just wish he deserved all that loyalty."

He put his hand on the screen door to go.

"There's one more thing," she said, her voice coming back to old matters. "This place — the ranch — the cattle — everything — goes to Mary, too. That lets me off the hook, doesn't it?"

He was ashamed for doubting her. He wanted to believe her. Yet.

He went out.

CHAPTER 7

Driving, he couldn't dislodge Donna Standing Elk from his mind. Nor his reservations about her. One possibility nagged him, and he kept circling back to it again and again. Acey was a Catholic. He wouldn't give her a divorce. What if she had wanted to be free of Acey — that alone — then planned to break the will? And, like a beam of murky light across his gropings, there glared another motivation, ugly and shocking. What if the agency appointed her guardian for Mary Elizabeth? That was possible. In that event Donna would control a fortune of six headrights. One alone was bringing in twelve thousand a year. The more he thought of it, the more it intrigued him. The guardian game ("gar-deens," the Osages called them) was among the most profitable schemes practiced in the Osage; cloaked in legality, a favorite pursuit of lawyers and businessmen. Donna, with her looks and education, could play a convincing role as the concerned stepmother of a rich and lonely little Indian girl.

Nate Robb wasn't around the ranch house when Boone called the agency on the phone, and after the usual delay before Tan Labeau answered, Boone said, "I just talked with Acey's widow, Donna. She claims he left everything to Mary Elizabeth. That right?"

"That's right. It's in his will on file here." Labeau's voice expressed boredom, Boone thought, as if the call had interrupted more important duties.

"So she was telling me the truth?"

"She was. You sound disappointed, Boone."

"Guess that had to check out. But if anybody's got a motive, she has. Even if she's left out of the will, she'll have control of the estate if the agency makes her guardian of the little girl. Which means till Mary Elizabeth comes of age. Think the agency will do that?"

"Why not? She's the little girl's step-mother. Who else would be appointed? We haven't had any complaints on Donna — just on Acey. His drinking. And from his creditors. Donna checks out."

"At least for a while."

"You're hard to convince."

"I'm not finished asking questions."

"All right. But remember what I told you this morning. Stay away from that ditch."

"Much obliged, Tan," Boone said and hung up.

Taking the Paradise road, he found his thoughts drifting once more. This Boots Gayle, this lawyer Donna had told him about. There was time to drive to Whizzbang, if Boone humped it, then back to Paradise to see Herb Staley, who Nate said ran the Packard agency for Dane Horn, and then out to Snipe Murray's. For the second time that day he took the north road.

The oil boom town of Whizzbang was a treeless sprawl of frame houses and shacks and rutted streets and mounds of stacked pipe and heavy equipment. Metal on metal clanged nearby and, like background accompaniment to this wild dissonance, there pounded in the distance the rhythmic *clank-clunk* of cable drilling tools and the coughing of pumps, which Boone had been hearing for miles. A mile or so away black smoke billowed up from a burning sludge pit. The smell of raw crude oil rode the air. He sniffed the smell, liking it.

He thought of an ant hill as he entered the town. Outgoing trucks and wagons hauled heavy rig timbers, tools and long sections of pipe. A dusty haze hung over the place.

Looking for Gayle's office, Boone slowed to second gear as he bumped along the crowded street, past the high-fronted store buildings. There was a kind of menace about the town. He sensed it. An undercurrent of violence. A considerable number of men appeared going about work, but as many stood on the street, on the board sidewalks, just watching and waiting, waiting for what? Of all the Osage County oil boom camps, Whizzbang was said to be the toughest; it also had the dubious distinction of having connections with the Kansas City underworld, Nate said.

Not seeing Gayle's office, he made a turn at the end of the street and started back. On this side he spotted the lettering on a dusty window: BOOTS GAYLE, ATTORNEY

171

AT LAW, and pulled over and parked. He got out and stepped to the wooden walk and tried the door. It was locked and green shades covered the window.

He was idling there when a young woman sauntered forth to the next doorway, under an overhead sign which read SLEEPING ROOMS. She beckoned him with her eyes.

"Hope you didn't leave your key in the switch," she said, indulging her attention on the red Stutz. "It'll be gone in a minute."

"It's in my pocket. You happen to know where I might find Boots Gayle?"

She shrugged indifferently, giving him a half smile. She couldn't be more than eighteen, Boone judged. Pretty in a careless way; dark brown hair cut short, flapper style. She had long-lashed gray eyes in a pinched oval face that bore too much rouge and lipstick and suggested an underneath hardness, an apparent discontent.

"Boots Gayle," she repeated, and her lips were heavy with teasing. "You know, he forgot to tell me where he was goin'." She was frankly appraising him, her eyes straying back and forth from him to the roadster. "Might find him at the drug store." She placed an extra emphasis on the last. "Least that's what they call it here. Back in Kansas City we'd call it a joint."

172

"Suppose he'll be back pretty soon?"

"Who knows? Maybe you'd like to come in and wait?" She was rating him again, her eyes relaying unmasked invitation. "You'll hear him when he comes in. You hear everything in this town. Every time somebody slams a door the walls shake." Her eyes hunted down the street, behind Boone. "You won't have to wait after all. He's coming now. The one in the fancy boots. Later you might come next door here. Just ask for Millie."

The middle-aged, florid-faced man clumping toward the office door in yellow boots bore an air of complete confidence. A poseur, Boone tagged him, and immediately thought of an outlandish figure in a Wild West show. Silvery hair flowed beneath his tan Stetson to his plump shoulders. He fancied expensive, fawn-colored trousers tucked inside the splashy boots, a beaded Indian vest of floral design over a bright red shirt, and his belly lapped a silver-studded belt like a sagging feed sack. The man's eyes, like the girl's, alertly sizing up Boone and the Stutz, seemed to say: Here's money. Here's a rich Osage.

"Mr. Gayle?" Boone began.

"Boots Gayle," the other said, as if the name were of unusual note. The flushed jowls quivered as he spoke and extended his hand, which Boone took, and to his surprise received an Indian handshake. "Who are you?" Boots Gayle asked.

"Boone Terrell, from down around Paradise. I'd like to talk to you."

Gayle unlocked the door and held it open for Boone, who entered a room which held one bare desk, three chairs, and a wooden filing cabinet. And, as the girl from Kansas City said, the walls did indeed shake as Gayle shut the door. He waved Boone to a chair and raised the green shades. His tone was anticipatory:

"What's on your mind?"

"Acey Standing Elk. He and I were boyhood friends. I've been gone several years and came back for the funeral."

"He was dead and buried before I heard," said Gayle, choosing the swivel chair behind the desk. He opened a drawer and took out a full pint, and once again Boone saw the self-importance rise to Gayle's overfleshed face and heard the anticipatory tone as Gayle asked, "How about a drink?"

For one part of a moment Boone felt the consuming demand of his old desire for the taste of corn whiskey. His mind seemed to leave him. It lasted only that briefness as, with effort, he had hold of himself and he shook his head, declining, and the insight crashed through him that many times Acey had sat in this same chair and experienced the same wildness, and given in to it; that this was Gayle's way of operating: to open with a drink.

"What you want to know about Acey? We were mighty good friends." (Boots Gayle was sounding like Dane Horn.) "I made him loans. A heap of 'em."

"Get your money?"

"Acey was pretty good about that. However, he owed me when he died. I'll be slow getting it."

"Much?"

Boots Gayle smiled. There was also a vigilance there. "Considerable. But I won't tell you. That's my business."

"Can you tell me anybody who'd have reason to murder Acey?"

"Murder? I thought he drowned?"

"I'm assuming there's more to it than that."

"In that case, I'd nominate his nagging wife. She married him for his money. Everything she could get. Last payment time she drove up here. Gave me hell for making him loans."

Boone hesitated, finding himself in the unforeseen position of defending Donna.

"She told me you furnished Acey whiskey."

"If a man wants a drink, I give it to him."

"Even if he's a known alcoholic?"

Gayle's face flamed higher. "Say, Indian, you on the prod?"

"Call it what you like. Another thing: Would Donna have him killed if she gets nothing from the will?"

"There's more'n one way to skin a cat in the Osage. I know what's in the will. I helped Acey draw it up. Yet she might be able to break it. The grieving widow. Hardship case."

"Were the loans secured?"

"I won't tell you. I told Tan Labeau the same thing when he was here nosing around."

"What about cattle deals?"

"I represented Acey several times when he bought stuff in the Flint Hills. I charged him for the service." All Gayle's geniality was gone. "What the hell? You think I took him?"

"Every time," Boone told him, rising. He had reached another impasse. Why had he even come?

"I'll be filing some liens," Boots Gayle said. "You can bet on that."

"I'm sure you will, all proper and legal." Boone walked out.

Two men were slouched near the Stutz, eying its racy lines. So it seemed. A coolness prickled up Boone's spine. As he watched, one of the pair strolled around to the other side of the car and paused by the front fender, as if to admire the headlight. The other man also drifted toward the front.

Boone stepped to his car, watching the man on his left.

He was hardly inside, quickly starting the motor, when the man on the driver's side spun around. Boone saw the slick shine of a revolver. At the same instant, he shifted into reverse and gunned the motor and cut the wheel hard right. The nimble Stutz made a swift arc to the left. The man yelled as the left front fender knocked him down. He was getting to his feet when Boone braked and shifted into low. He took off roaring, straight for the gunman, firmly resolved to run him down. The man shouted. He dodged and leaped to the walk as Boone shot past. The girl Millie stood in her doorway. Boone thought she was smiling.

He roared around a string of big dapple-grays pulling a wagonload of pipe, and held the Stutz in second gear all the way out of town, feeling better than he had in days.

There were two more jurymen to see — Herb Staley and Snipe Murray. He was going to crowd them.

Although hungry when he reached Paradise, he passed the Blue Bird Cafe and drove to the south end of Main and turned around and came back and parked in front of the Packard agency and sat a bit before going in, recalling what Nate Robb had told him last night about Staley:

"An ex-con on parole out of McAlester. Manslaughter. Happened at Tulsa. Other fella was a store clerk. Staley claimed self-defense, which is kinda odd when they say he's an ex-pug."

Shiny new models crowded the showroom. A steady banging sounded from the garage area. As Boone looked around, a salesman, natty in his striped suit and hair slicked down imitative of actor Rudolph Valentino, came out to wait on him.

"Herb Staley?" Boone asked.

The man hooked a finger rearward. "Back there."

Boone went back. Beyond the open rear door of the garage he could see a clutter of parked cars, including a wrecker. Across, a bulky-shouldered man wearing a big white hat and glossy brown suit chatted with a mechanic tinkering under a hood.

Boone waited. Idly, he glanced outside again and was turning away when a car took his attention. A Packard. A black Packard sedan, coated with dust. Now the mechanic raised up and, seeing Boone, said something and the other man turned and crossed over, a patronizing smile overspreading his battered face.

"Mr. Staley?"

"I'm him. Guess you wanta look at a new car? I've got just what you want, chief."

Boone moved his head from side to side in negation, struck by a stabbing recognition. It was unmistakable. The ruined face he had glimpsed in the dust from the side of the Pawhuska road, then again, full on at the agency when the driver of the black Packard followed him. Now, this close, Boone saw the fighter's crooked nose and crinkled ears and sledge-shaped hands and eyes the color of mustard seed. Staley was as overdressed as a green squawman. His suit had the expensive look of the men's department at the Salt Creek Trading Store ("We're in style — are you?"), his yellow shoes shone like rubbed brass and he wore a candy-striped silk shirt.

"Mind if I ask you some questions?" Boone began.

"Not at all, chief. Let's go up front where it's quieter."

When they entered the showroom, the

parked Stutz stood out like a fire engine through the glassed front. Staley couldn't miss seeing it. But when he turned to Boone, there was no reaction on his face.

"That your red job out there?" And when Boone nodded, Staley, his crushed mouth curling persuasion, said, "I'll make you a good trade. That blue roadster over there is just as fast."

"Or that dusty black Packard sedan back there?" Boone said. By that, Boone knew that Staley knew and Boone continued, "Kinda missed you on the way back from Pawhuska. Lonesome with nobody to follow me."

Staley let go a belly laugh. "So you figured I follered you? Well, I did. I wanted a good look at that red Stutz. It's a beauty. Must be the only one in Osage County."

Boone doubted him; he was too hearty. He "talked from the teeth," the old Indians would say. Boone said, "I went to the agency to see what's being done in the Acey Standing Elk investigation, in case you're interested."

"Why should I be?"

"You were on the coroner's jury."

"Just doing my civic duty, chief. An investigation, you say? I thought the inquest settled that."

180

"It's not over by any means."

"That's news to me, chief. You a friend of his?"

The "chief" thing was galling Boone no little. Suppressing it, he said, "An old friend. Maybe you can help. Did Acey have trouble with anybody in Paradise?"

"How would I know? I didn't run around with that sot."

A hot wind whirled up through Boone. He beat down the feeling and said, "Acey Standing Elk was a brave man. A national war hero. They had a parade for him here in Paradise. The Osages honored him. He was also a great athlete."

Staley gave a twisted grin of indifference. Their eyes met and clashed, deadlocked. Boone heard a voice, distinct and hard: "They're saying around town that Acey was murdered." And he was shocked. The voice was his own. He had spoken to break the man's cocksureness.

"Murder?" The yellow eyes did not alter, and Boone saw that startling Staley wasn't easy. Staley's lone response was a little wave of combativeness that washed across the muscles of the ruined features. With the heel of his left hand, he cracked the knuckles of his right; an instinctive gesture.

"Hadn't heard that," he said, shrugging.

"Guess I don't hear much here. Too busy to listen to rumors."

Boone, his voice as casual as he could make it, said, "That was a long drive just to look at a new Stutz." Turning to go, he saw the crushed smile again and he heard the knuckle-crackling as Staley's indifference followed him:

"Whatever you say, chief."

Boone had a quick meal at the Blue Bird Cafe and returned to his car. If he intended to question Snipe Murray, the last juryman on the list, now was the time, before Snipe's regular customers started showing up about dark. Once his trade started coming in, he would shoo Boone on without talk.

Not seeing Marshal Sid Criner, Boone backed to the center of the empty street and took off north, doing fifty in second gear by the time he crossed the Santa Fe tracks. At the edge of town, he cut left onto a narrow dirt road winding up Salt Creek, a stretch so known to him that he could drive it after dark without the car lights on and never miss a turn.

And so, shortly, a rope's throw beyond the city limits of Paradise, he rolled up to the place where he used to come with Acey and Sammy and others; to the paintless frame house, squatting like an inert toad off the rim of the road, in perpetual deep shadow among the elms and sycamores under which it stood, its lacework of honeysuckle further darkening the porch. Boone raced the motor three times before he cut the switch, thinking wryly: Just like old times. Wild Indian Boone Terrell come for his drinkin' whiskey, by God.

A little bell tinkled in signal as he opened the wooden gate, which a high, hot-tight wire fence flanked and encircled the house; that way, Boone remembered, no one could sneak in on Murray.

Boone was whistling as he walked upon the porch and knocked, waiting as he used to wait, knowing that Murray wouldn't show himself immediately, not until he had eyeballed the customer through a slit in the front-room curtain. As the town's most long-lasting bootlegger, Snipe Murray survived by being careful and screening his customers, among them Paradise's leading businessmen, and selling only to those Osages who wouldn't get him in trouble; that meant no whiskey if you were too drunk to drive, absolutely no drinking on or near the premises and leaving quietly.

Thus, operating discreetly, Murray stayed in business year after year, a town fixture, accepted as a legitimate tradesman supplying a vital local need. An indication of his status was that he had served on the coroner's jury.

From habit, Boone glanced back up the road toward town. No one was coming. A breeze flowed through the creek timber. Evening haze was gathering. And without warning, Boone experienced an awakening hot thirst for whiskey; at that instant he knew a sharp-cut self-truth that unsettled him: He hadn't killed his want, he'd merely buried it by a frenzy of action on the tracks and demanding self-control; it still seethed inside him, deep down, as alive as the coals of an ashes-banked campfire, now uncovered, ready to consume him again. Just coming here was dangerous for him.

Someone was stirring inside the house, the old sign that all was well. A voice whined like old times, "Who is it?"

"Don't tell me you don't know — it's Boone Terrell!" Laughter laced Boone's voice.

The door opened a cautious inch at a time. "Kinda figured it was you," Snipe Murray said, showing a drawn-in face, his voice gaining confidence. "Had to be sure. The Feds been watchin' me lately. I closed up two days last week. Come in." And when Boone had entered: "Same old Boone, racin' his motor. Well, I got some extra good stuff. Just hauled in last night from Coalgate."

Boone grinned. Snipe's stuff was always "extra good," when, in fact, it was never good, always hot. "I want to talk to you about Acey, since you were on the coroner's jury."

"What about 'im — he's dead." The whine had re-entered the careful voice, at once suspicious.

"Just a few questions, Snipe."

Boone saw that Murray had changed very little. Grayer, maybe, that was all. Still a catlike, colorless, drab little guy, still needing a shave, his movements as jumpy as ever, his black eyes constantly shifting, constantly turning his head as he listened for cars coming along the creek road. The room likewise drab and unchanged, from the brownish rug to the bare brown walls and the dull brown table and the canebottom chairs; brown curtains, which looked like gunny sack, covered the windows and shut off the doorway opening on the back part of the house.

Boone began going over the usual questions, and to each Murray replied with a vigorous head-shaking denial. "I didn't see a thing that looked wrong. Honest to God,

Boone. And I never heard that anybody threatened him or of any fights he got into. Acey was a peaceful fella. All I know is he was always drunk." He shook his head. "Just drunk. But drunk he could drive better'n most sober folks. You know I like you Osage boys. Many's the time I told Acey I'se out when he was drunk an' I had plenty of extra good stuff. Many's the time. That boy never harmed a soul in his life. He was always courteous. I'm mighty sorry he's dead."

"Glad to hear you say that, Snipe."

Murray wasn't used to approval; his voice grew stronger, imparting a rare warmth of feeling. "I used to close up Sundays, drive to Hominy . . . watch him play with the Hominy Indians. That was before he started hittin' the bottle so hard. God, he could kick a football, couldn't he? Folks forget too soon. Him a war hero too. All by himself, knockin' out that German machine gun nest." Murray's eyes glinted as he imagined the deed; he made a sudden lunge. "Him goin' in there to wipe 'em out, hand-to-hand. An' when he drowned, all they said was another drunk Osage gone."

True, Boone agreed in silence. People forgot. But he also remembered that you couldn't always tell about Snipe. He was sly, quick to sway with the wind, ready to second your opinions if that kept the situation calm. In short, he wanted no trouble.

"No, sir, Boone, I didn't see a thing that looked wrong, honest. I'll tell you this: Lester Oliver had Acey lookin' mighty nice. I went to the church."

"No dead person ever looks nice, Snipe."

"What you're gettin' at is, you think maybe somebody done Acey in?"

"That's a possibility."

"No wounds on him that I could see," Murray disagreed, his ferret's eyes getting big.

"So I'm told," Boone said wearily.

"He never brought strangers here," Murray said. "Generally, just him an' Sammy. A few times with Buck DeVore. Never was any trouble."

Boone rammed his hands into his pockets and stared at an old spot on the brown rug. He'd always held a liking for the little guy. Maybe because Boone felt sorry for him and the world of fear in which he lived, maybe because he was so pathetic-looking. Boone said, "If you're afraid like Judge Pyle and Smiley Kemp, I understand. But if you do know something, tell me. I swear I won't say you told me. I give you my word, Snipe."

"Jesus, I'm always afraid. You know how it is. One stretch at Big Mac was enough for me." Boone nodded in understanding. He could feel only sympathy, then weariness as Murray continued in the familiar evasive vein: "I didn't see anything wrong. I didn't hear anything. Honest to God."

"OK, Snipe," Boone said, giving up. He was opening the door to step out on the porch when Murray, his whining voice changing abruptly, blurted, "Come to think of it, there was something. Acey told me right here in this room."

Boone jerked around. "What was it?"

Murray's little eyes seemed about to jump out of their sockets. He was blinking furiously. He rushed the words out. "Four or five months ago — back in April, guess it was — Acey came in for a coupla pints. He was loaded as usual; not that you could tell it by lookin' at him. You know how he always walked, straight an' sure on his feet, head up, like he was a chief or something."

"Yeah," Boone hurried him. "Yeah."

"Acey kept laughin' to himself. I said, 'What's so funny?' He laughed again. Said he'd just been insured for twenty-five thousand. He thought it was funny. A big joke. That's about all he said. I remember he kept laughin'."

"Exactly what did he say, Snipe? Remember?"

Snipe Murray pressed a hand to his forehead. "He said, 'Snipe, imagine a drunk Eendin bein' insured for twenty-five thousand dollars. Funny, ain't it?' That's all he said, honest. About that time I heard a car comin'."

"Did he say who got the twenty-five thousand if he died?"

"He didn't say — I didn't ask."

Boone took a firm hold of the little man's shoulder. "Are you sure?"

"Didn't have to tell you that much." A stark fear flared in Murray's eyes. "You won't let on to anybody I ever breathed a word about Acey, will you, Boone?"

"No — hell, no — I promise," Boone said, dropping his hand, nauseated by the beseeching face, and thinking: Donna, though she had denied there was any insurance, thinking Donna or Boots Gayle.

The roar of a car on the creek road broke his concentration.

"Better git," Murray cautioned.

Boone, nodding, moved toward the door. Before he reached it he felt himself turning, obeying an impelling force beyond his control, and as if it were the most normal of requests, saying, "Get me a pint, Snipe."

Surprise shuttled over Murray's face, wiping off his fearful look. "Thought maybe you'd quit?"

"Just one for old times."

Catlike, Murray disappeared through the curtains; within seconds he was back, shoving a pint at Boone. The murky light laid a dull shine on the corked bottle, which felt cool in Boone's hands, just right.

"That's five bucks," Murray said fast. The roar of the car on the creek road was getting louder. "Git along, Boone. No tellin' who that might be. Maybe the Feds."

"OK. And you didn't tell me a thing. Not a thing."

And just like old times, Boone paid him, slipped the bottle inside his shirt and under his belt, and went quickly out. Driving off, he groped within himself to find what had caused him to break over back there; to let three years go down the drain. Why? Why? It was too deep, too uncalculated for him to understand; it had come over him in an instant; it had just happened, triggered maybe by returning to a familiar haunt as the present, in reverse, became the past . . . What shook him was that he hadn't known he was going to buy a pint until he heard his voice, the voice of his younger, reckless self, his other stranger self, expressing his sudden and overpowering craving for whiskey. He'd take a drink right now if that car wasn't coming, that black Packard sedan. It passed. He glimpsed the face of Herb Staley, who gave no sign of recognition, who looked straight ahead.

Why, Boone pondered, did white men coming to the Osage think they needed a big hat as a symbol of status, when, actually, it merely made them look like squawmen or other newcomers?

He was nearing the main road before he thought again of whiskey, and by then another car was making dust on the creek road. The young Osage he'd seen in the doctor's office whipped past in a purple Cadillac. With the cover of dusk, Snipe Murray's business was picking up.

Boone, thinking he might find Sammy there, drove to the Blue Bird Cafe and parked.

Sid Criner stood slouched on the curb, left thumb hooked in his gunbelt. He appeared to be waiting for someone. Boone was getting out of the roadster when Criner, suddenly, stepped down the curb to him.

"Come along," he ordered, jerking his head. The emotionless quality of his voice, as perfunctory as a casual greeting, added an unmistakable meaning to his words.

Boone was too astonished to reply for a

moment. "What for?"

"For one — making an illegal turn on Main Street. You backed across the center."

"I didn't back across the center."

"I saw you from the bank corner," Criner said, shifting his shoulders. "Not only that — exceeding the speed limit. I saw you tear ass for the tracks on your way to Snipe Murray's."

"Now hold on, Mr. Criner."

"What you think Main Street is — a race track? Put up your hands. I'm gonna search you."

"I don't carry a gun," Boone said.

"I said: PUT UP YOUR HANDS."

Before Boone could protest more, Criner was slapping at Boone's shirt and pockets. He discovered the bottle; Boone could feel Criner's instant jerk.

"Hand it over," he said.

Boone complied, unable to believe what was happening to him. He found his voice. "I want to post bond. How much is it?"

"Too late tonight."

"I asked you how much?"

"Illegal turn's fifty bucks. Speeding's a hundred. Possession is a felony. Judge Pyle'll have to see about that. Come along."

"Call the judge. Tell him I'll post bond tonight. I've got enough on me for the first two. I can put up my car on the other charge."

"His honor is never disturbed at night."

"All you have to do is call him. It's early."

"You gonna come along, goddamnit, or am I gonna have to lay my pistol across that thick Osage skull of yours?"

Boone came along, shaken and humiliated and intensely angered. Reckless Boone Terrell of earlier years would have resisted and got pistol-whipped and charged with resisting an officer. Tonight's older self said wait, tighten up on your temper. If he made trouble and fought the charges, there'd be a trial just when he needed time to continue asking about Acey, futile as it was so far; and if he went to trial he'd need a lawyer and he didn't know one he trusted. The sensible way out was to forfeit the bonds tomorrow and go free.

Paradise's city jail, a one-story sandstone building constructed at the turn of the century, smelled of years of unwashed floors and foul mattresses and the heavings of sick drunks and stale tobacco. In the dingy office, Criner took Boone's car keys and money and pocket watch and deposited them in a brown envelope.

"You get these back when you're released," Criner said, the epitome of official

193

solicitude.

"I want to see Judge Pyle first thing in the morning," Boone reminded Criner as the marshal locked him in a cell.

"I can't promise that. He was feelin' poorly today. You might have to stay with us a spell."

"You can call him on the phone in the morning."

"We don't conduct the court's business like that. In this town the culprit appears before his honor in person, even if Judge Pyle is under the weather and it means a little holdup, say, of a week or so."

"A week!" Boone shouted, incensed. "You can't hold me that long. Not over twenty-four hours. That's the law."

"Now ain't you the one to be remindin' me of what the law provides? You with two traffic violations and a mighty serious felony already?"

"Let me use your phone. I want to call Tan Labeau at Pawhuska."

"Labeau don't run this town. I do. I'm the law. Now you just tuck yourself in and get some beauty sleep like a good little In-jun."

Boone slumped down on the smelly cot, his anger boiling. He had been in and out of Paradise all his life, gone to school here and played football and helped bring the town statewide athletic honors, and now he was seeing it unmasked, the glint of the cesspool underneath, dominated by a few men. Well, he could thank Criner for unintentionally doing him one favor, for saving him from taking his first drink in three years. Boone shuddered. Why had he bought that rotten stuff? He didn't understand, he didn't understand himself. Was it defiance on his part, a rebellion against the existing order? Was it frustration? Or, instead, was he slipping back into the old futility and self-destruction? Like Acey? Like Sammy? Once he had fallen into an abyss of drinking, to stay there a long time; crawling out on his own, he had reached the edge and clung there, weary of mind and body, and there he was yet, holding fast, so as not to drop back into the darkness.

He dozed, conscious of evening passing into night, of the muffled hum of the town; finally there were no sounds.

Sometime later he heard low voices and the rattle of keys; although he recognized Criner's flat voice, he couldn't see him because the light in the office was out.

Footsteps sounded outside Boone's cell. He could make out two, three dim figures.

"Who's there?" Boone called. When no

one answered, he called again. He heard a key turn in the lock and he heard the door grate back.

Two figures entered. The door clanged behind them. A man went away, boot heels clumping. That Criner?

Boone's senses jumped alive. Why put them in here when other cells were empty?

"Who are you?" he asked, trying to keep his voice calm.

Silence.

He stood up, sensing the wrongness. A cold sweat began to stand out on his face. He backed up against the wall by the cot and raised his fists.

The formless dark erupted suddenly, becoming two advancing shapes. He felt a numbing blow across his left shoulder. He swung back, missing, and then they were upon him and he was fighting back, blindly, desperately, now and then feeling his blows landing. There was a moment when he thought he was driving them back, for one of them cried out. That was just before his head seemed to explode. After that he remembered no more.

CHAPTER 8

He saw light. Dim light. Distorted light.
Light that was curtained off as a tide of pain
smashed over him and his senses reeled,
spinning him to the edge of blackness again.
He lay motionless, groaning. Clamping
hands to his thundering head, he thus
learned that he was on a cot, which kept
lifting and settling and swaying. When
finally it steadied, he mustered all his
strength and pushed up on his right elbow
and opened his eyes again and saw daylight,
full daylight, through a barred window.
Teeth set, he examined the puffiness of his
lips and the swollen knobs of his cheekbones
and the spongy mass of his left eye, shuttered to a mere slit. He ached all over.

Slumped on the edge of the cot, he
struggled to pull himself together. A cigarette helped; Criner had left him tobacco
and matches. Because he hurt more when
he looked up, he kept his head bowed and
had another cigarette.

He must have stared unseeing at the floor
several minutes before he noticed something
shiny amid the dust and the litter of cigarette stubs and burned matches and soiled
magazines. Groaning softly, begrudging the
effort, he reached down and picked up a

silver cuff link. He examined it without particular interest: expensive-looking, the size of a half dollar, a bronze horse's head decorating it. Something that would come from the men's department at the big store. Probably the property of some drunk Osage Criner had brought in.

Down the corridor at the moment, he heard voices in the jail office. One sounded familiar, resonant with authority, but he couldn't be certain. The voices grew more distinct. Next he saw Criner pigeon-toeing down the corridor, followed by Dane Horn. Boone dropped the cuff link in his shirt pocket. Criner unlocked the cell.

Boone sprang up. "Where are they?"

"Where's who?"

"The two you put in here last night who beat me up."

"Oh, them two." Criner didn't bat an eye. "I didn't hear no ruckus."

"Look at me," Boone protested. "Does that convince you? Where are they?"

"Vamoosed. Made bond this morning while you snoozed."

"Made bond this early — with Judge Pyle sick last night, you said? You put that pair in here on purpose to beat me up."

"Making bond is why I'm here, Boone," Horn broke in. "Sid, I don't like the way

this was handled. Boone's got a good reputation around here. He's never been in
trouble before. I've known him all his life.
Knew his folks well. Good friends. I want
to see him alone. Understand?"

If the reprimand bothered Criner, he
failed to let it show. He turned to Horn,
shrugged and said, "Take all the time you
need, Mr. Horn," and left them.

Horn's boot heels rang on the stone floor
as he entered the cell. He ran a scouring
look over the littered floor and shook his
head. "I didn't hear about this till a few
minutes ago when I saw Sid on the street.
Came right over."

"Thanks," Boone murmured gratefully,
head lowered against the constant pounding.

"Sid said those two were oil-field toughs
he threw in for disturbing the peace. From
up around Whizzbang. They were drinking
pretty heavy."

"That's funny. I didn't smell whiskey on
'em. And they started in on me right after
he let 'em in. They sure knew what they
came for."

"Now, Boone, don't go to jumping to
conclusions," Horn said, smiling his tolerance. "You've had a hard night. I figure
you'll forget that when you hear the good

199

news . . . I've arranged for your bond. You're free on your own recognizance. I talked to Judge Pyle. He's sick, just as Sid told you. So you can go now. Doesn't that make things look a little better this morning?"

Boone got his head up. The cell spun crazily. He swayed and righted himself, slowly absorbing Horn's meaning. He could go. He was free. He rubbed his thundering head, thinking how easy it was now, almost too easy, when last night, stone sober, he couldn't post a dime. Just a few words from Dane Horn opened the door.

"I'm sure much obliged, Dane," he said and weaved forward to go.

Horn cleared his throat. "Uh . . . I want to make a little suggestion, Boone. One I hope you'll follow for your own good."

"Yeah?" Boone, head down, held on to the cell door for support.

"It's this: I think you'd be wise to leave town."

That required a moment to filter past the constant barrage of Boone's pain. Had he heard Dane Horn right? "Leave? Why?"

"As I said, I had a little talk with Judge Pyle," Horn said. At this moment, he could be counseling young Indian men on the streets of Paradise, reasoning, suggesting, chiding them for their wasteful ways, but never ordering. Boone saw that as vividly as a familiar scene viewed over and over. "Judge Pyle said if you left the county for a year, he'd forget about the charges, including the whiskey possession."

Boone was lost for understanding. "Why does he want me to leave?"

"So you'll stay out of trouble. He's afraid that coming back home is leading you into your old ways. So am I. Last night you bought whiskey. Before you know it you'll be hitting the bottle hard again, driving like crazy. You'll end up a drunk — dead like Acey."

There was truth in that, Boone admitted to himself. Dane Horn knew Indians. He knew. Still, Boone asked, "Did the judge tell you I asked about the inquest? He didn't like that."

"As a matter of fact, he didn't say. What if you did? You asked me too. That's your right. Anybody's. Acey was your friend. However, in this situation, considering that you have a possession case against you — and which could lead to a sentence in the county jail — I think you'd be wise to follow the judge's recommendation. He's being mighty lenient."

Closing his eyes, Boone pictured Judge Pyle's ruffled dignity, his affront at the questions, his guardedness and his fear. Boone's head was clearing. "Let me think about it," he parried.

"If this goes to trial, you'll get thirty days — maybe more," Horn warned. "Why not leave town till it blows over?" The moon face wore a fatherly expression, and the bluish gray eyes seemed to project a hypnotic quality. The impression passed, so fleetingly that Boone questioned his punished senses. In the next moment Dane Horn was saying genially, "Think it over, then," and gesturing to the open cell door.

Criner waited in the office. While Boone looked on, Horn beside him in the role of his protector, the marshal emptied the contents of the brown envelope on the desk. "Count it," he told Boone.

Boone thumbed through the greenbacks and retrieved the pocket watch and car keys and coins. Everything was there. He threw Criner a stubborn look. "Mind telling me who the two bruisers are, Marshal?"

"Couple of drunks."

"No names? You just tossed 'em in the jug?"

"That's right. Get 'em off the streets and out of town — that's my job. If they make bond or come to trial, Judge Pyle worries about names."

"So he took their names early this morning, even though he's sick, and let 'em make bond? Or did they make bond at all? Did you let 'em out as soon as they'd worked me over?"

Criner did not reply. He stood there slouched, thumbs hooked in the wide gunbelt, mouth ajar over tobacco-blackened teeth, his expressionless face telling Boone he could believe the story or not, that it didn't matter.

A wildness seared Boone. He was about to protest further when he felt Horn lay a hand on his shoulder and he heard Horn's pacifying voice, "We've talked enough. Boone's a sensible boy. He's going to let well enough alone. He's going to obey Judge Pyle's order and get out of Osage County so he won't have to go to jail. Aren't you, boy?"

Unconsciously, Boone shifted his shoulder. Horn's hand dropped. Their faces, Boone saw, were as from the same mold, each bearing the same waiting, the same expectancy, for him to give in as an Indian would. Through the mist of his pain the faces began to acquire a distortion, looming larger and larger, assuming grotesque proportions, disembodied, like masks, and when Boone remained silent, their eyes seemed to bore straight into him with peculiar power, particularly Dane Horn's, and once more Boone experienced the odd hypnotic sensation.

A coldness brushed him. Shaken, he turned his back and walked out.

A single purpose drove him now: to reach his car on Main and race home and rest, rest, rest. He felt hunger as well, but his battered appearance barred going into the Blue Bird; he'd be at the ranch shortly.

He was getting into the Stutz when Andrew Horn, coming out of the cafe, waved a greeting and hastened on toward the bank. He hauled up abruptly and flung around, eyes narrowing on Boone. His hesitation was brief. He stepped down the curb to the driver's side. "You all right?" His brows contracted as he scanned Boone's face.

Boone bobbed his head.

"I think you'd better see Doc Mears."

Boone's curt headshake rejected that. "I'm all right. I'm headed home."

"You look like a trip to the hospital."

Shaking his head, Boone started the motor.

"Wait a minute, Boone. Tell me what happened. Maybe I can help."

"Just got beat up in jail."

"Who?"

"Don't know. Happened last night. Couple guys. They're gone. Criner let 'em out. He had me in for possession."

"Criner?" Andrew's tone did not indicate surprise. "Let me get this straight. He released them after they beat you up last night?"

Boone nodded, shuttering his eyes against the waves of pain smashing through his head, and warmed up the motor.

"Criner's going to hear about this," young Horn said. His indignant eyes kept going to Boone's face. "I've been telling Dad that Criner's too tough for our town. This is no Shamrock or Whizzbang. Boone, you could prefer charges and we'll stop some of this rough stuff."

"Never mind now, Andy. Dane got me out — else I'd rot there." Boone shifted into reverse. The car's motion seemed to release a reminder echoing through the blurred and painful corridors of his mind, something he must pass on to Andy: "Listen, I found out something. Acey took out a twenty-five-thousand-dollar life insurance policy last spring. Gotta go now."

Boone had told him in a guarded voice, which he just now realized. Was the fear getting to him too? By God, he wasn't giving in.

"We can do something about this," Andrew said.

Boone didn't stop. Backing out, he noticed the closed door of Judge Pyle's office, which usually was open at this time. Very convenient, he thought. He drove to the bank corner, turned right and circled back to Main and north, roaring over the rumbling Salt Creek bridge.

As he rushed away, the eye of his mind tracked back to the jail and Sid Criner and Dane Horn and Judge Pyle. And he knew that he was hurrying for a reason other than the food and rest at the haven of the ranch: because he hadn't much time left. One day, maybe two, before Judge Pyle brought him to trial for failing to obey the court's order. If he left the county, nothing more would be said, and if he returned, months later, or a year, nothing would be said. But likewise, if he left, he knew that the questions surrounding Acey's death would haunt him the rest of his life because he hadn't stuck it out.

There was no warning. It happened more suddenly and unaccountably than the two figures in the dark cell advancing upon him, just as he shot around a curve a few miles from the ranch. He heard something metallic snap as he turned the wheel. Instantly he felt its looseness as the car, instead of straightening out, continued to barrel ahead, out of control.

He saw the ditch coming fast. On instinct, without thinking, he leaped from the seat. Just before he struck the road sprawling, he heard the Stutz slam into the ditch with a bending and ripping of metal. He quit tumbling and rolling and flopped around, dazed, seeing the roadster nose up, then crash downward like a wounded animal.

Dust and grit bloomed, a brownish shower that made him cough. As if in a trance, he watched it settle.

Too stunned to rise, he gazed dully at the crumpled and broken mass of his car. It was smoking and the fan was shrieking like a mad cat and the motor was racing as if the accelerator were stuck. Swaying up, he stumbled down into the ditch and turned off the ignition. To make certain, because by this time he didn't trust his senses, he tested the wheel. It spun loosely in his hand.

The backwater of his rage burst. He tore forward and fought to unlatch the misshapen hood. It was jammed tight, bent backward. Pounding didn't help. Mounting the fender, he stamped with his foot, beating the metal down; then, tugging with both hands, he freed the latches and looked down.

A slim brightness shone where the steering column hung disjointed.

Bright metal filings clung to the stub of the severed column, bright and new.

A gathering clarity stormed across his mind. Someone had sawed it while he was in jail. He slammed the hood down and stood back, outraged and not without fear, thinking, Somebody wants me dead.

Trembling and sick over his loss, he circled the wreck to form an idea of the damage. The whole front end was smashed, the radiator was gurgling and coughing up its life's blood, the front axle was twisted and the right front wire wheel was buckled.

Low-cut and sleek, beautiful and different, as fast and free as the wind, the Stutz had been a large part of him and his new life; he had tuned it and cared for it as if it were a living thing. Now, seeing it this way, he could think only of a rare and flame-colored bird shot down in flight.

Unable to bear the sight any further, he plunged out of the ditch and started walking for the ranch.

CHAPTER 9

Nate Robb was fixing the noon meal when Boone limped into the kitchen and slumped down in a chair. The old ranch hand took one look at him and roared, "Who the hell plowed you under?"

"I want to wash up first," Boone panted. "Get rid of this jailhouse stink." The warm soapy water stung. He scrubbed to his waist. Coming in from the porch, he began to fill out the story in terse detail; as he talked he saw Nate's anger mounting.

"What this simmers down to," the older man said, "is somebody figures you've stumbled onto something."

"When the truth is, I haven't. Maybe the insurance policy; maybe it doesn't mean a thing." Boone felt a little guilty. Now, in retrospect, he was less eager to connect Donna. Neither had he told Nate where he learned about the policy.

"I'll have to agree with Dane Horn about one thing," Nate said grimly. "You'll be a damned sight safer out of the county."

"I won't run, Nate. That's exactly what somebody wants me to do. It's not what I've found out, but what they're afraid I will."

"Sid Criner could be in on this. Else why'd he let them two in the cell?"

"Hard to say. But he's never liked Indians. He's roughed up Sammy. Maybe that makes him feel superior."

"How do you figure Judge Pyle?" Nate asked, setting a place at the table for Boone.

"Scared. Same as Smiley Kemp and Newt Chapman. They've all got lockjaw. All the jury members."

"What about Dane Horn?"

"He got me out of jail. I can't forget that." Boone sat down, suddenly weak. "When do we eat?"

"Be a minute yet. Biscuits not quite ready."

Boone went down the hall and rang the Paradise operator and placed a call to Tan Labeau at the agency, and after an interval was told that he was expected back early afternoon; whereupon Boone left word for Labeau to return the call.

He gorged and drank hot coffee. Upstairs in his room he lay down for a nap. A cool breeze stirring the window curtains fanned his bruised face. Little by little his mind ceased spinning. He jerked awake to Nate's voice calling him, "Tan Labeau's on the phone."

"What're you up to now?" Labeau asked wearily when Boone answered.

"Did Acey have a twenty-five-thousand-dollar life insurance policy?"

"Not that we know about here. Who said so?"

"I can't tell you yet. But Acey told him back in April. Now find out the beneficiary and we have a motive for murder. Boots Gayle for one."

"Hold on," Labeau cautioned. "Guess you don't know it, but insurance is getting to be a pretty common way to secure Osage debts. Bankers, lawyers, and other businessmen do it all the time."

"Twenty-five thousand is an extra large debt, don't you think?"

"Is. But it doesn't prove murder."

"Least I've run across a lead that's news to you. On top of that, Sid Criner threw me in jail and I was beaten up. Judge Pyle says if I don't leave the county I'll face whiskey possession, which is true. Criner took a pint off me. Dane Horn got me out. Then somebody sawed the steering column on my car and I ended up in a ditch, my car wrecked."

"Stay away from Paradise." Labeau's blunt voice flung a chill through Boone.

"Have to have my car hauled in. Have to talk to Sammy Buffalo Killer. He was Acey's main drinking partner. He's scared. He hasn't told me everything, I know."

"Forget the car for now. Forget Sammy.

Just stay out of Paradise. Hear me?"

"I'll keep in touch," Boone said, his tone evasive.

Labeau hung on. "Don't get too excited about that policy. Sounds like somebody just backed up a big debt."

"What if the insurance goes to Donna? She told me there wasn't any."

"Don't husbands and wives usually take out insurance with the other as beneficiary?" Labeau was continually shooting holes in murder theories, it seemed.

That ended the conversation. Boone stood awhile in thought. He had to go back to Paradise. He had to rent a car. He had to see Sammy again. Threat of the whiskey possession charge and Judge Pyle's get-out order made delay impossible. He rang the operator again and called Sammy's house in town. No one answered. Next Boone tried the Goodtime Billiards for Sammy.

"He's here," a voice said. "Hold on."

After some moments, Sammy's uncertain voice asked, "Who's this?"

"Boone. My car went haywire. Get a wrecker and pick me up here at the ranch. I need to rent a car in town."

"I dunno." Sammy's voice had an unnatural sound to Boone, a faintness. "Where'll I get a wrecker?"

"There's one at Staley's garage."

"I'm broke." Boone could hear him sniffling.

"Tell 'em I'll pay for it here. Hurry."

"OK, *Wah-Sha-She.* I'll try. Pretty soon. Gotta go by Great White Medicine Man's first."

About an hour later a wrecker lumbered into the ranch yard and Sammy, sitting beside the driver, jumped out and performed a clowning bow for Boone.

"You must feel better," Boone said, grinning.

"All time feel good, you betcha, *Wah-Sha-She.*" Sammy stuck out his lower lip and rolled his dark eyes. "Heap big Eendin, ain't it?" He wasn't sniffling now. His eyes were very bright.

Boone had to laugh. "You didn't sound that good over the phone. How come?"

"It's the fresh air out here," Sammy said, making a face and coming erect and thumping his chest. "Passed your car down the road. Looks like a kicked-in tomato can."

"I'm sick about it. Let's go." Why tell Sammy about the steering column now? When Boone offered to pay for the wrecker service, the driver said, "You'll have to see Herb Staley about that."

Boone sickened anew when he saw his car.

213

While Sammy stood by joking, Boone helped the driver hook on a chain. Afterward, they pulled the Stutz out on the road, tied to the front end and raised it and crawled into Paradise and on to Staley's garage.

"How'd it happen?" a mechanic asked Boone.

"Steering column."

"You'd think a Stutz was made better, wouldn't you?"

"You would," Boone agreed humorlessly, and found Staley nearby. Staley said, "Looks like you busted her up good, chief. Yourself too."

"I didn't get that in the wreck. How much do I owe you for the wrecker?"

"Fifty bucks."

Boone raised a low whistle. Nevertheless, he took fifty from his wallet and paid, adding, "I want to rent a car for a couple of days."

"That's a hundred more."

Although the amount was outrageous alone, Staley's manner more than the money kindled Boone's resistance. Before leaving the Osage and making his own way, he would have grinned, more surprised than angry, and paid without protest, following the ingrained giving in; for an Osage wasn't supposed to haggle or protest.

"That's too high," Boone said, distinct about it.

"That's the rate — fifty dollars a day. And there'll be ten-bucks-a-day rent on your wreck till we get the parts in here to put it back together."

A springy feeling started up in Boone, akin to the feathery lightness he felt just moments before a race as he sat in the Miller Special, tensed for the flag to drop. And he heard himself, almost drawling, "That the same rate you charge everybody? Or is it . . . sorta special for Osages?"

"I said that's the rate," Staley said, raising his right hand to rake a forefinger along his smooth-shaven jaw. The sleeve of his candy-striped shirt extended beyond the arm of his coat and bore the shine of a big silver cuff link.

"Used to be twenty dollars a day," Boone said. "Of course, we paid for the gas."

"Times have changed, chief."

Boone said, "I'd say it's more like highway robbery," and the feathery sensation danced through him again, releasing an unlimited vitality and recklessness as well.

"Take it or leave it," Staley said, and keenly Boone became aware that Staley was enjoying the exchange. He saw Staley, obeying old processes, shuffle his feet and bring up his left hand and crack the knuckles of his right.

Boone remembered, and as Staley continued to knead his knuckles, Boone noticed that a bronze horse's head decorated the right sleeve cuff link, but the other sleeve had no link. In response, he touched his breast pocket and felt the clump of metal there, his brain grasping and connecting as he saw again the dimness of the cell and the two figures barging toward him. He was not afraid and his tingling body seemed to fill out as he asked, "Like at the city jail last night?"

The smooth jaws sagged. "What d'you mean?"

"You lost this last night," said Boone. Reaching inside his shirt pocket, he pitched the cuff link at him.

Staley caught it, glanced down, and a momentary recognition crossed his battered features. He flushed. He recovered, his face straight again.

"I believe," Boone said, "it matches the horse's head of the one you're wearing."

Staley pocketed the cuff link.

"You lost it last night when you and your helper beat me up at the city jail. Now," Boone said, "we'll see what you can do in daylight with nobody to help you."

Staley stared at him in surprise. He rammed his right fist into his left palm and the irregular smile unfolded across his ruined mouth. "Remember," he said, "you asked for it. Never saw a red ass yet that could fight."

"Ever take on a sober one?" Boone taunted him.

Staley sprang in swiftly on the balls of his feet, his left fist extended, his right cocked.

Boone had a flash of misgiving as he saw the professional stance. He raised his fists and moved to meet him. Staley weaved a little, shuffling. Boone saw the left hand flicking out. Too late, he recognized the feint, at the same instant taking a blow on the jaw that hurled him backward.

Boone landed on his buttocks. Odd, but he felt no pain, no weakness. He was stronger and lighter than before. Jumping up, he was aware of men rushing from the garage. He tore in. But Boone dodged the right and ducked under it. He drove his right to Staley's belly, then his left, feeling the softness there like mush. He heard Staley grunt and gulp for air, mouthing, "You red ass — I'll beat your goddamn head in!"

Staley rushed and Boone gave ground, seeking to maintain a gap between them.

He missed a swing at Staley's face, but landed the next into Staley's gut, meantime taking blows to the chest and head. Hurt, he clinched and held on. Staley broke the hold and thrust Boone away and charged after him.

Driving his shoulder into the belly, Boone heard the big man hack for wind. Boone, overanxious, drew back to throw a right at Staley's face. The other caught him coming in and Boone, knocked backward, saw the sky spinning as his head rang. But Staley's wind was going. Boone could hear him blowing like a workhorse as he advanced, this time with caution.

Boone's chest burned. He dragged himself up. Objects danced before his eyes. A moment and the shifting shape righted itself. Boone crouched, head low. Lunging suddenly, he left his feet in a flying tackle. He broke through Staley's guard and smashed the point of his left shoulder into the mushy middle.

Boone heard a grunt of pain as he felt Staley break down under him. Scrambling to his feet, Boone lashed out with his right foot. Staley's head snapped back as if on a spring. Blood flew.

"That's for the sawed steering column,"

Boone burst out. "When you tried to kill me."

Hands pinned his arms from behind before he could kick the bloody face again; a man on each side. He struggled, he couldn't break free. And his left arm was being shoved up between his shoulder blades, higher, higher. He yelled his pain. Through a reddish haze he saw Staley getting up, saw the wild cast on his smeared face.

Staley slugged Boone below the ribs. Then he swung for Boone's jaw. Boone, ducking, felt the fist skid off his skull. His brain flashed: Sammy! Where was he? Twisting to locate Sammy and yelling for him at the same instant, he saw his friend standing by the wrecked Stutz. Sammy appeared grafted there, mired in fear. Boone yelled for him again and saw, for a breath, the torture in Sammy's eyes as he stayed rooted.

Boone heard shouts of "Fight! Fight!" Men came running in from the street. Staley's shape loomed. Boone took a rain of blows as Staley punished his stomach and ribs and chest while Boone kept twisting. Methodical blows. Right. Left. Right. Left.

Boone caught the pounding rush of someone running and a voice shouting, "Stop it!" and the next he knew a man rammed into Staley, throwing a clumsy shoulder block that knocked Staley away.

Through glassy eyes Boone saw Andrew Horn floundering up awkwardly. Staley, who hadn't gone down, gaped at him. "Stay outa this," he grunted and charged Boone as young Horn yelled, "Stop it — I say!"

A distant, heavy voice broke across Boone's consciousness. But nothing changed. The arms gripped him yet and Staley drew back. Boone, seeing the coming blow, kicked out in desperation, using the arms holding him as a springboard. His right foot glanced off Staley's chest, slowing him, but Staley bored in again. Andrew crashed into him and bounced off. Andrew was gathering himself with determination for another charge when the voice rose again.

Andrew stopped. So did Staley, heaving for wind, his battered face jerking in guilty recognition, and the hands gripping Boone suddenly let go. He dropped to the ground.

To Boone, the voice went on shouting for some time before he got his focus back and braced up and saw Dane Horn. It was he whose shouting had stopped the brawl, and he was talking now, his voice both placating and questioning:

"What's going on here, boys?" (It was

always "boys" with Dane Horn.) "What're you doing in this, Andrew? And you, Herb — and you, Boone?" And when Boone couldn't answer: "What's the meaning of this, Herb?"

Staley, nursing his jaw and bleeding mouth, spoke around his hand, his voice muffled. "Terrell got smart over renting a car." Staley's bluster had vanished before the elder Horn. Andrew Horn stood aside, his angry eyes accusing Staley.

"A car?" echoed Dane Horn, as if that were indeed a small matter over which to start a fight. His disapproval flicked over his son at the same moment. "If there's any question about Boone's credit, I'll vouch for him. Let him have the car. I'll stand good for it." Horn's forcible tone was that of a prominent man accustomed to being obeyed in his own town. He glanced around at the crowd and moved his head from side to side, censuring, yet tolerant, yet understanding, much as an elder would after breaking up a scrap between small boys. To Boone he said, "Take the car."

"Not for fifty bucks a day, even if mine is wrecked."

Horn's brows flew up.

"That's the new rate," Staley explained a bit lamely.

"Let Boone have it at the old rate," Horn said, stressing the point. "Boone needs to tend to business out of town. He's leaving the county. He can settle up later. Whatever's necessary. Which one can he take?"

Staley, his reluctance ill-concealed, indicated a Hudson sedan.

Seeing Sid Criner pigeon-toeing up on the double, Horn called out, "It's all right, Sid. Just a little misunderstanding between the boys. It's all settled."

Criner halted, his deadpan stare split between Boone and Staley. He proceeded to roll a brown-paper cigarette.

And then, as Dane Horn turned to his son, his geniality faded and evident annoyance clouded his moon face. "I don't know what you're doing in this, Andrew. Wasn't your concern."

Andrew Horn had not moved. "It's my concern when a man is being beaten to a pulp, while his hands are held, and a crowd stands by doing nothing. What sort of town are we building here, another Whizzbang?"

"I think you're being a little hasty in your judgment, Andrew. Nothing wrong with Paradise."

Boone was conscious of a hush settling over the crowd. Not in his memory had anyone bucked Dane Horn in public; never

222

had Andy. Watching through the haze of his pain, Boone was struck by the differences between father and son. Dane: beefy and round-faced, big hands, big shoulders (his expensive suits from the Salt Creek Trading Company invariably looked too tight), typifying the rugged strength of the vanished southwestern frontier, an aggressive, self-made man who drove hard deals, who, some said, took plenty of hide when he traded. Andy: slim and blond, neat in white shirt and bow tie, the suggestion of a delicate cast to his well-formed features, which some people might mistake for weakness. As his father embodied the old ways, Andy embodied the new. Even so, there was a good deal of the elder's strength in Andy, tempered with reasonableness and the rarity in Paradise of a social conscience.

"Furthermore," said Andrew, keeping his poise, "Boone Terrell was badly beaten in the city jail last night by two thugs, who were then released. Possibly Mr. Criner, since he's the jailkeeper, can explain that?"

"Sure," said Criner. "He just happened to be in the cell where we put 'em. It was dark."

"You have no lights in the jail?"

"In the office. I tell you, Andrew, we don't run no fancy resort hotel with feather beds

223

and maid service. Don't aim to. Don't want the boys to like the place too much." A little ripple of laughter ran through the crowd.

"Would the fact that Boone's an Indian have anything to do with the violent and uncalled-for treatment he received?"

"We treat everybody the same," Criner swore.

"Does that mean everyone gets beaten up?"

(Boone was proud of Andy. Bit by bit, he was tearing down his opponent's defense as he had as a champion high school debater.)

"That's enough, Andrew," Dane Horn broke in.

"I've heard of no drunken cowboys being arrested and man-handled," Andrew persisted, his accusing attention on Criner not wavering. "Had there been, the whole town would've heard about it and you would no longer be city marshal, Mr. Criner."

"All right, Andrew," Dane Horn interrupted. He was beginning to look uncomfortable. "You've had your say. Let's break this up," he added, looking at the crowd.

But as yet no one moved. Everyone, Boone saw, was watching Andy, sensing that he wasn't finished.

Andrew Horn said, "I believe there's yet much to be done in Paradise if we just look at ourselves," and turned his back on his father and Criner, a deliberate gesture, and faced Boone. "If you need anything before you leave town, let me know."

Boone could only thank him with his eyes. As Andrew made his way through the crowd, Boone was of a mind to call him back and accuse Staley of the beating and tampering with the Stutz. But some instinct told him the wiser course was to get out of here now if he intended to persuade Sammy to talk, and that, he suspected, was going to require whiskey. Better go ahead, take the car. Let everyone assume he was leaving the Osage.

Jerking his head at Sammy to follow, Boone got in the sedan and started the motor and backed out. Driving off, he saw the onlookers leaving and Dane Horn and Staley and Criner going inside. What did that mean? Whatever, Dane Horn had made it possible for him to get a car.

The nose of the sedan bucked like a wild horse as Boone gave it the gas and came out on Main Street. He cut sharply to his right, a wind of recklessness howling through his siege of pain, the old wildness multiplied end on end. He needed a drink, lots of drinks. He found himself resisting. But it would take whiskey if he got Sammy to talk. He didn't like it; it was under-handed. But he beat the air with his fist, and as the sedan picked up speed, he yowled, "Sammy, let's go get us some drinkin' whiskey."

"Now, you're talkin', *Wah-Sha-She.*" Sammy's eagerness belied his slumped attitude. He was staring straight ahead as they sped past the Goodtime. "Listen," he said, turning to look at Boone, "I wanted to help you back there, but I couldn't move. I'll swear I couldn't. Dunno why. Afraid . . . maybe. I'm sorry, ol' *Wah-Sha-She.* Sorry as hell." His voice reached Boone as that of a penitent child pleading for forgiveness.

"Forget it," Boone said, trying to make him feel better. Why blame Sammy, who was never a fighter?

"I tell you this thing," Sammy exclaimed. "Andy really went in there, didn't he? And that Dane, he really stopped the show, didn't he? Some big man that Dane, ain't it?"

"He stopped it, all right," Boone said, thinking that Sammy worshiped Dane Horn. Give an Indian something, lend him money and fleece him at the same time, and he was your friend for life.

"Hey, you don't sound like you mean it."

"I don't," Boone said. "It was put on for

everybody to see. Dane Horn owns the garage, the Packard agency. Staley just works for him."

Sammy subsided into silence.

Humped over against his hurts, Boone slammed across the railroad tracks and took the narrow road winding up Salt Creek to Snipe Murray's. Braking with a flourish, he raced the motor three times. The hour was later than he had realized. Already deep shadows cloaked the creek's timber.

"Stay here," he told Sammy. "Be right back."

The bell tinkled its signal, unnecessary now after his noisy arrival, as he opened the gate. He had no more than stepped upon the porch when Murray's scolding voice whined from behind the door. "God sakes, Boone, you'll wake up the dead. Have the Feds down on me."

Boone grinned. Snipe saw a federal officer in every shadow. The door cracked open and Boone entered sideways. Murray waited in the center of the drab little brown room, distress bugging his mournful eyes.

"Don't come in here like that any more," he said. "I like it quiet. No fuss."

"Criner got my pint last night. Get me four."

"Four? Gonna take a bath in the stuff?"

"Sammy's with me."

"Oh . . . well, I got some extra good stuff."

"Just hauled in from Coalgate, huh?"

Murray let the sally pass. There was no room for humor in his business. He went crouching to the window and peeked out, catlike, furtive, and when satisfied turned and darted past Boone through the brown curtains. He slipped back in moments, holding a brown sack. "Twenty bucks," he said. When Boone paid him, he regarded the greenbacks in an abstract way and handed back a five. And when Boone wouldn't take it, Murray pressed the bill firmly into Boone's hand and muttered, "One pint's on me. Sid Criner was here this morning. Threw a bunch of fool questions at me. Wanted to know what you asked me. I said all you wanted was whiskey. Get it?" The little man swallowed visibly. Pleading, he looked old and harassed, ridden down by fright.

"You didn't tell me anything," Boone assured him.

"Hell, I didn't. I blabbed about Acey's insurance." Murray's voice skittered up, a squeak of fear. "Just don't ever let on that I did. Get me?"

"Guess my memory's bad, Snipe. I don't recall a thing."

Snipe Murray expelled an enormous sigh of relief. He smiled gratefully and nudged Boone in the ribs. "Get your ass outa here an' watch your drivin'. I hear a car comin'."

Boone walked fast to the car. By God, Snipe must have the ears of a guard dog, for just now the roar of a car on the creek road was audible.

Driving upcreek at high speed, the wind singing around his ears, Boone sensed the revived wildness surging through him, yet tempered by the knowledge of what he had to do. Like old times, but not quite. Wild Boone Terrell, yet not quite. He'd have to take a few drinks with Sammy to start him talking, if he was going to talk at all, and maybe there was nothing to draw on but old times.

The road narrowed, hemmed in between a barbed-wire fence and the deep-pooled shade of the creek. A mile or so onward he found his objective, a cattle guard that opened on a rutted road wandering off across a broad pasture. Turning and straddling a rut, he drove to the foot of a wooded hill where the trace of an old wagon trail angled dimly away. Shifting to second gear, he left the road and followed the faint tracks, barely visible as dusk moved across the creek valley and purpled the hillsides.

Grass smell rose, sweet and cool. Rocks thumped the sedan's underside. He rounded the hill and drove until, when he looked back, the hill hid the creek road. He braked, turned off the motor, opened the door and walked around. So still now, he thought. So very still.

For this was the place where he and Acey and Sammy and the others used to come and drink. Here you could whoop and holler all you wanted.

Gazing across at the darkening hills, feeling the bluestem grass swishing about his feet as he stirred its sweet scent, haunted by the genial faces that once rendezvoused here, he could not free himself of the depressing admission that he and Sammy were the only ones left of the old bunch. A grievous emptiness fell upon him. Acey, Freddie, Tommy, Charlie, Todd, Joe — they were all gone. If they hadn't drunk themselves to death, they had died in car wrecks or under strange circumstances never quite fully explained or understood.

Walking back to the car, Boone took a pint from the sack and pulled the cork with his teeth. Holding the bottle carelessly, he said, "I been wondering, Sammy. Maybe there's something about Acey you forgot to tell me, huh?"

"I told you."

"Wasn't much."

"I don't know much, *Wah-Sha-She*."

"You know," said Boone, humoring him, "you act like Judge Pyle or Smiley Kemp."

"How's that?"

"Like you're afraid."

After a moment: "Naw, I ain't afraid."

"Did you know that Acey took out a twenty-five-thousand-dollar life insurance policy last spring?"

"Yeah."

"Who's the beneficiary?"

Boone wished he could see Sammy's eyes, but the dingy light, coupled with the dimness within the car, shadowed his face. Sammy answered after a pause: "Acey'd laugh about this thing."

"Who gets the money, Sammy?"

"How'd I know?"

"He told you."

"Hey, let's have a drink."

Boone rubbed the neck of the bottle between thumb and forefinger. "Here," he said and offered the bottle to Sammy, who, quickly, took a long, deep pull and coughed. "God —" he croaked, spluttering. "Gimme cigarette."

Boone held out his pack. Sammy took one and passed the pint back and lit up.

"Why would Acey try to cross Salt Creek at flood stage?" Boone resumed, wondering how many times he had asked that.

"Drinkin', maybe."

"He'd see the danger, wouldn't he? He rode good horses. A smart horse would balk."

"Maybe."

"Have another drink."

"Not till you take one," Sammy said stubbornly.

Gripping the cool roundness of the bottle, the whiskey fumes filling his nostrils, Boone felt the struggle of both revulsion and desire as his taste buds flowed. He delayed so long that Sammy grumbled, "You gonna drink or not? I won't drink alone."

Boone squeezed the bottle harder, conscious of his mind and body jousting, one against the other, longing for a drink although hating it and powerless to deny it.

"Hey, *Wah-Sha-She,* come on."

With a swooping motion, Boone brought the bottle to his lips and tilted it bottom up to the sky and drank, feeling the fire start in his mouth and reach the millrace of his throat and burn his chest and explode in his belly. He tore the bottle away and reached for a cigarette.

"Wheeeee!" Sammy applauded. "Some drink."

After the cigarette, the hot hell within Boone cooled somewhat, and shortly, after Sammy drank, Boone had another. He was beginning to feel grand and exalted, capable of extraordinary deeds. His purpose returned, intensified. He asked:

"Did Acey have any enemies?"

"Naw. Ever'body liked ol' Acey, that man."

"What about Donna? What's she like?"

"She ran me off one time," Sammy said. "Acey raised hell. Said I was his cousin an' frien'."

"What did Donna say?"

"Said I was *pi-zhi* for Acey."

"Maybe she was right," Boone said solemnly.

"Me — his cousin? His frien'?"

Boone passed the bottle, and after Sammy had a shot, Boone had one. He had intended to take only a drink or two to start Sammy talking, but it wasn't working out that way. He could sense his self-control diminishing as they had another, as he began to drink as Wild Boone Terrell used to drink, rapidly, without restraint, and by then he knew that he was going to continue until the last drop was downed.

" 'Nother thing," he mumbled, and his

mind, which seemed disconnected from the rest of him, relayed that the blurred voice belonged to him. "Who'd want Acey dead? Donna? Boots Gayle?"

"Donna, she's . . ."

"She's what?"

Sammy was silent, brooding, perhaps.

"Is she good to Mary Elizabeth?"

"Guess so. Where's that bottle? Good whiskey, ain't it?"

Boone clamped his hand on Sammy's shoulder, rougher than he meant to be. "Answer me this. Did Acey have cattle on the other side of the creek?"

"Naw."

"Then why would he try to cross?"

Suddenly, Sammy was shaking and giggling, his throat gurgling. "To get across th' other side. Like the chicken crossin' the road."

Boone pushed him away, hard. "Get serious. Was Acey in fear of his life? Was he? Goddamnit, Sammy, tell me!"

Sammy fell into another fit of giggling. "How'd I know? Pass the bottle, ol' *Wah-Sha-She.*"

Disgusted, Boone gave up and passed the bottle, and then had his drink. The whiskey hardly burned at all by now. He was changing back, drawn relentlessly into a thick haze of unreality, down, down, into the abyss where he had stayed so long before, where there was no substance, no light.

And so they drank and smoked, watching the sky light alter from late evening to night. Other than a grunted word now and then, for another drink or cigarette, there was no talk. The coolness of approaching fall breathed across the hills. Sometimes Boone imagined that he heard the distant hum of Paradise, or a car roaring up to Snipe Murray's house. All sounds ebbed as the night waned; nothing was distinct except the rasp of a thumbnail on a matchhead or the night-song of insects. Later, Boone and Sammy danced around the car, whooping and stomping, rivulets of sweat pouring down their crouching, whirling bodies. Sometimes they took turns singing brave songs, while the other pounded the side of the sedan like a drum. Spent, they staggered back to the front seat, thirsty again and laughing. The moon, as yellow as tanned buckskin, climbed the great hall of the star-speckled sky as they drank some more.

A sense of guilt stirred within Boone. Long ago he had quit questioning Sammy. He must try again. But when he spoke, his words failed to make sense because he mumbled, and Sammy wasn't there to listen. He was outside the car getting sick. The timid voices of night insects hummed, freed at last to sing with the purring wind, and the world whirling about Boone, and which smelled of night-dampened grass, tilted unexpectedly and he was slipping and sliding, down into the abyss again.

He woke to find Sammy snoring on the seat beside him. Boone moved his right hand and touched a bottle. He picked it up. It was empty. Whiskey fumes rose sourly. Then the first canker of shame bit into him. He was starting to feel terrible. He pushed the bottle away, his head spinning, his stomach pitching. Quite suddenly he had to get out of the car; lurching, frantic, grayishly ill, he pawed for the door, which was open, and fell headlong into the sweet-scented grass and retched, and again and again.

For a while he felt somewhat better. He told himself so. But his legs seemed paralyzed and when he tried to make his way back to the car, his knees buckled and he fell helplessly, flopping across the running board, and his mind fled from him, hurling him into utter darkness.

When consciousness returned, he lay squeezed under the steering wheel, jammed against the seat, half in and half out of the car. He was swimming in green nausea, bathed in cold sweat. Laboriously, painfully, he wormed free and up to the seat, there sinking back groaning and exhausted, too weak to hold up his head. An eternity passed while he lay there, flashing from snatches of tortured sleep to dim wakefulness, when the churning nausea rose again like a green sea.

A time came when he could sleep no more. He was too ill, and a persistent shame flogged him. He must go. Now. Fumbling, he moved the gearshift to neutral and started the motor. At its roar Sammy gave a startled grunt and sat up. "Wha's wrong?"

"We're going home."

Sammy slumped back, uncaring.

It was still night. Boone drove by instinct and memory, calling on a fixed and terrible concentration, grimly steering, bumping over the rocky pasture, thankful for the moonlight. Bouncing across the rutted road, he realized that he hadn't turned on the headlights, and flicking them on he saw the road leading to the cattle guard. Just turning the wheel spent his strength; he rested a bit and went on. When the car bucked, he shifted to second gear and kept it there, not trusting himself to drive faster.

As he passed over the clanging cattle

guard and turned downcreek in the direction of Snipe Murray's, his dull senses registered the faint cough of a car starting up behind him; but when he glanced back he saw no lights. He dismissed the sound as unimportant. He wasn't at all certain that he had heard anything. Shifting to high gear as the road smoothed, he picked up speed. A house jutted out of the gloom. Snipe Murray's. It was dark there.

The wind, singing through the creek timber, fanned his face, bringing cool strength, short-lived as the green nausea churned inside him again. He stopped to hang his head out the door and vomit, and could not, strain as he might; he gagged and drove on, creeping, back in second gear.

That was when, remotely, through the fogginess of his mind, behind him, the low roar of a car pricked at his ears a second time. He lurched around to see. The road was black under the trees. Nothing was visible, and he was too sick to care.

Not far ahead, he blinked at an unaccountable glow, growing more and more distinct. A laggard clarity told him that he was looking at the lights on Main Street, which at the same time seemed out of place; it belonged farther on. But there were the railroad tracks for proof. So he had followed

238

the creek road and turned south toward
Main without realizing it, in his befuddle-
ment thinking he had not yet done so. A
sluggish warning pulsed. Sid Criner would
throw them both in. He braked suddenly.

The abrupt halt threw Sammy against the
dashboard and awake. He looked up, mumbling, "Hey, we're in town. Lemme out."

"Criner'll throw you in. Come on to the
ranch."

To Boone's alarm, Sammy erupted into
violent action, pawing on the door-catch
and snapping it open and tumbling to the
ground and rolling up, to stand, weaving,
clutching the open door for support.

"Sammy — you hear me? Criner'll throw
you in. Come on — get in!"

Sammy was mumbling something. A precipitate earnestness, a guileless pleading,
came forth clearly: "Have t'see Great White
Medicine Man early. Get me a shot."

"A shot?"

"Yeah — a shot. Gotta have it, *Wah-Sha-
She.*"

Meaning charged through Boone, a fright-
ening perception. And suddenly he understood why Sammy was always broke. Why
he was so changed from the old days. So
languid, so indifferent, so often sniffling.
Why he hadn't the will to help, even a little,

even raise his voice at the garage against Herb Staley.

Boone leaned across the seat. "Sammy — you're on dope! Goddamnit — he's got you hooked! Doc Mears — the son of a bitch! Don't go — come with me! I'll take you to a hospital somewhere!" He grabbed for Sammy's arm and caught hold.

Sammy jerked away, ready to run. At the last instant before flight, he hesitated and reeled back to the car, to Boone. He sounded almost sober; he hurried, "I'm afraid, *Wah-Sha-She,* frien'. Dunno why, but I am. Like Acey was . . ."

The low-speed roar of a car swelled out of the blackness behind them.

Sammy looked up and froze.

"What about Acey?" Boone yelled.

Sammy whirled, his movements panicky. He started running. He stumbled deeper into the muddy glow of the lights, and across the railroad tracks, never pausing, never glancing back once, apparently heading for the mouth of a dark alley.

"Sammy — come back! Let me help you. Sammy . . ."

Boone ceased, knowing that calling was futile. He sagged against the wheel. There was a choking in his chest, and now a sobbing. Sammy was gone. Lost forever.

Doomed. Like Acey. Like the others. Boone bowed his head and tears filled his eyes and dropped down his cheeks, splashing like huge raindrops on his wrists.

CHAPTER 10

As Boone turned around to go north, a car with lights off whipped past him south, coming from the creek road. He glimpsed two faces under big hats. Criner and somebody cruising for drunks between Snipe's place and town? The same car Boone had heard back there after turning in from the pasture? Boone was too stupefied and dismayed over Sammy to care.

He drove on. His headlights reminded him of cold yellow fingers as they traced the bony structure of the narrow bridge over Salt Creek, which he now crossed to the din of rumbling plank flooring.

He was still quite drunk and ill, though the shock of pleading with Sammy had cleared his mind somewhat. Seemingly, his bursting head was split into two opposing factions: one his unwell, incoherent self, the other his logical, sane self, saddled with the accusing guilt of taking his first drink in three years and getting drunk. He despised himself completely.

In a breath, and without warning, the nauseous green wave rolled over him and he was sick again. He stopped the car and hung his head out and heaved convulsively and lay back, feeling no better. His weaker self cried out in protest for sleep, anywhere, here in the car, alongside the road, while the other decreed that he must somehow drive on to the ranch.

He continued on, the car in second gear. More than once he remembered slipping into sleep and running off the road, the bumping along the barrow ditch waking him in time to right the car and jerk the wheel and slant back to the road. No longer did he recognize the curves and the black masses of hills. To his straining eyes, every object was distorted. Was that a country road ahead, or was it a sheet of shimmering glass in his headlights, or a mirage, rising and falling, now disappearing, now reappearing? He scrubbed at his eyes.

Long after he had given up deciding where he was, he saw a cattle guard and aimed the nose of the car through the opening and heard the scrape of metal as the front fender and running board on the passenger side grazed the post. Home, he thought, braking, I'm home. A sense of gratefulness overspread him. He turned off the motor, shoved the gear in reverse, and fell sideways on the seat, passed out.

Birdsong, near and insistent, called him awake. He listened at length before he sat up. His eyes opened wider. Beyond the car he saw not the Terrell ranch house, but the quaint and peeled face of his country schoolhouse of old, the Little Chief School. During his stupor last night, he had driven blindly past the ranch. He marveled how he had managed to reach here.

His head throbbed and an overpowering thirst tormented him. He got out on wobbly legs and went around behind the school to the well and pumped furiously. When water gushed, he cupped his hands and gulped, pumped again and drank, cooling the fire that burned his insides. Eased, he bathed his face and wet his hair and removed his shirt and scrubbed. A gradual purged feeling came over him. He felt better physically, although his self-contempt was utter.

He was toweling with his shirt when he heard a car drive up and stop. A door slammed. Light footsteps made haste around the building, and Teresa Chapman burst into view, eyes wildly searching, chestnut hair wind-blown. She had never looked more appealing. She stopped uncertainly when she saw him, brushing a strand of hair from her forehead, then ran over and embraced him for a moment. Concern and relief stood out on her face.

"Boone — what in the world? What's happened to you?"

"Simple," he said, not sparing himself. "I fell off the water wagon last night. I believe that's what you say when you get drunk after three years."

"I mean your face," she said, coming close to him again.

He told her briefly about the beating at the jail, then of the fight with Staley. He pulled on his shirt and buttoned it.

Her hazel eyes deepened, withholding, unwilling. There was a terrible fixation in her eyes. "I've been trying to find you," she said. She looked about ready to cry. She was crying. "It's Sammy, Boone — he's dead. Beaten. A horrible thing."

"Dead?" He stiffened and looked at her as if she were playing a bad joke on him. "Dead? I don't believe it."

"It's true. Beaten to death."

He looked at the ground and then he looked up, mouth trembling, shaking his head, unable to accept emotionally what his mind said was true.

"To make it even worse," she said, "they're looking for you. In town they're saying you did it became you were the last person seen with Sammy."

A muscle jerked in his face. His throat caught. He went on shaking his head. A heavy mist fell across his eyes, blinding him. He pressed fingers to his forehead. Turning away, he closed his eyes and covered his face with his hands and choked out a sob. He tried to swallow and tasted the salt of tears streaking his cheeks. He thought, Gone. Poor, harmless, generous, fun-loving Sammy, who wouldn't hurt a fly.

"Boone," she said, with urgency, "you still don't understand. They're looking for you."

The first stir of retaliation stung him. He wrenched around. "I let him out at the tracks," Boone swore. "Guess it was around midnight. I tried to get him to come with me so Sid Criner wouldn't throw him in for drunk. He wouldn't. Said he had to see Doc Mears early today. Said he had to get a shot . . . *He was on dope, Teresa . . . on dope* . . . I think he was trying to tell me something about Acey when we heard the car."

"What car?"

"There was a car behind us. I think it was trailing us. I saw it after I let Sammy out. It passed me fast with the lights off."

"Who?"

"I'm not sure. I thought it was Criner. There was somebody with him."

She went on, her voice matter-of-fact. "A ranch hand found Sammy early this morning in the pasture past Snipe Murray's. There were empty whiskey bottles around. Snipe told the city authorities you bought whiskey last night. Said he saw Sammy waiting in your car."

"That's true. We went to the pasture. We got drunk. Later, I drove back and let Sammy out at the tracks."

Her voice gravely soft, she said, "Except nobody saw you let Sammy out. Don't you understand?"

"Whoever was in that car did."

"Anyway," she said, spreading her hands in a gesture of helplessness, "a posse's been formed. They're hunting you. Just like in the movies. Feelings are high in town. Everybody liked Sammy. He was, well . . ."

"Harmless," Boone said. "Why would anybody want to kill him?"

"Boone," she said sharply, "you've got to do something. Give yourself up so they won't hunt you down and kill you. That — or get out of the county."

Get out? Why, that was what Dane Horn

had urged him to do. Yet, if he had, Sammy might be alive today. Yet, too, he would never learn the truth about Acey.

She shook her head in understanding. "I know there's little choice, but you can't just stay here."

"If I turn myself in," he said, his bitterness emerging, "they'll pin it on me. Be my word against Criner's and Staley's. If I run away, I'll be admitting I did it — and I did not. If I stay out, I've got a chance."

"Stay where?"

"See those hills?" He pointed south of the schoolhouse, indicating a bank of furry hills, wooded and rocky, too rough to ride a horse through: in there, hidden, jewel-like, a sweet-water spring, and a cave and a lookout knob, which he and Acey had called their "Medicine Hill." There as boys, stripped to crude breechclouts, they had gone on vision quests and lain under the summer sun and through the star-filled nights, denying themselves food and water, while dreaming great dreams that never came true in the white man's world. He had thought of the place instinctively.

Her eyes at once rejected his notion as foolhardy. She flung up a hand. "The posse's armed, Boone," as if he failed to understand. "They'll hunt you down. They'll kill you if you resist or run."

"They'll have to catch me first."

"You can't hide out there indefinitely."

"Hiding beats being framed. I tell you they're framing me."

"Why would anyone frame you?"

"Because they think I know something about Acey's death. More than's been let out. I don't. Or didn't. After what happened to Sammy, I know something's wrong. He was afraid; he admitted it. He said Acey was too."

She only looked bewildered and further troubled. *"They?* You keep saying *they."*

"I should say those who run Paradise. I don't trust 'em any more. I've talked to everyone on the coroner's jury, including your father."

"You think he's involved?" She moistened her lips; in her eyes he saw not anger but concern.

"No. He was just vague, like the rest. He did tell me to see Tan Labeau, which I did."

"Won't Dane Horn help you? He helps everyone."

"I can't go to him."

"So you're going to hide out and keep working," she said, nodding impatiently. "Boone, I think you'd better hire a good lawyer and turn yourself in."

"A good lawyer?" He was mocking her. "Is there an honest one in the whole county?"

Her eyes said she disagreed, that he was being unreasonable because of Sammy. But she reached out and touched his arm, understanding, then touched his face, and the contact went through him. He'd almost forgotten the effect she used to have on him.

"I'm going to help," she said, standing back. "It won't work. But I'm going to help."

"You're going to stay out of this," he said firmly. He was thinking at last. "Now I have to hide that car I rented from Staley. I know I have to do that." He was moving past her. She caught up with him, her long, silk-clad legs matching him stride for stride. When he started the car, she said, "I'll be here every day if you need me. School starts Monday."

"Stay out of this, Teresa. I don't want you involved. Right now I'm bad medicine."

She stood well away from him, arms tightly to her sides, her wooden face still disapproving his decision. An emotion crept into her face when he put the car in gear. "Boone," she said, "be careful."

He spun the wheel and backed out and roared across the cattle guard. Seeing the road was clear, he stepped on the gas in the direction of Paradise, drawing a mental picture of the range country ahead as he had known it all his life.

When a dim wagon trace curled out of a pasture, he turned and bumped across the ditch up to the wire gate, hastened out and pushed up the wire hoop on the gate, flung the gate out of the way and drove through, ran back and fastened the gate and drove ahead.

The little-used road led through a gap which opened into a jumble of broken hills thick with blackjacks. Once past the gap, he left the old trail and drove into the timber, left the keys in the car and returned to the gap. Looking back, he couldn't see the car. A man on horseback would have to find it.

Afoot, he soon realized that by acting on impulse he had handicapped himself. No water, no food. He began to sweat and smell of whiskey. Waves of heat rose from the grass. He flushed a family of quail, which went scudding away. Following them with his eyes, he was caught in the creeping loneliness of a man denied his familiar world. He thought of Sammy with an unremitting depression, and still with disbelief, feeling as never before his affection, too late left unspoken, though he could hope that Sammy was not unaware of it. A lump kept forming deep down and rising to his throat.

The menacing growl of a speeding car threw him headlong into the grass, heart pumping, head cocked for a change in the sound, a letting up and bumping across the ditch and stopping at the gate.

But the car passed, and he relaxed a little.

From there he set a course roughly parallel to the road. In the next half hour he sometimes had stands of blackjacks for cover; more often he was in the open. A risky thing, but he felt that he must be where he could watch the road at all times.

A car was coming from Paradise. He flattened out; it passed. Another roar followed. And suddenly the road came alive. Car after car swept past. He counted them: eight. He lay there some time before the countryside stilled and he moved on.

Belly flat, at noon, he watched the Terrell ranch house from a round wooded hill some hundred yards across the road. Men and cars jammed the yard. There seemed to be a great deal of standing around. Other figures moved in and out of the house. Two cars raced off eastward, boiling dust, sagging to their springs with overloads of possemen, swaying from side to side on the road, gun barrels sticking out like spears. Not one horse could Boone see. And he wondered why the posse didn't comb the hills. But that called for effort and wouldn't come, he supposed, wryly, until the excitement of the hunt had worn off.

Chewing on grass stems to relieve his thirst, he willed himself to lie still and wait. Visualizing what was going on down there lessened his craving for water. They would be questioning Old Nate, and getting nowhere, and using the phone in the hall to call "the law" in other sections of the county and towns in other counties to be on the lookout for an Indian wanted for murder. *Name's Boone Terrell. Half Osage. Mean as hell. Murdered Sammy Buffalo Killer, a full-blood boy. Beat 'im to death. Approach with caution. He's dangerous. You bet'cher boots he is.*

By this hour Tan Labeau knew and likely he and the county sheriff were there also. Labeau, Boone reasoned, would not believe that he had killed poor Sammy; as a matter of fact, Boone could not recall ever hearing or reading where an Osage had killed another tribesman. He saw irony in that the Osages, who had never gone to war against the whites, were now the most exploited of all Indian tribes because of their wealth.

As the afternoon lengthened, the heat became breathless, banking up in the close-growing timber, and the cars of the posse thinned out one by one until the yard was empty and there was no coming or going on the dusty road.

He stayed put. Once he observed movement around the barn and sheds; that was all — he couldn't see much through the trees around the house. He conjectured whether some of the possemen were concealed there, on the logical theory that he would show up at the house sooner or later.

Thirst tormented him incessantly. In desperation he placed a pebble in his mouth and waited for the darkness that seemed never to come.

When it arrived at last, finally, crawling over the hills, he eased down to the road and watched from the woods, still suspicious of what the silent house might hold. Close to an hour had passed when he slipped along the road and crossed and, circling, approached the house by way of the outer sheds and now the rear of the garage. Here he could see the kitchen door. There was no light, no sound. Where was Nate?

Boone waited. A car whined past on the road for Paradise. The night serenade of insects whirred higher and higher. He was becoming edgy, wary of the dark house, wondering whether Nate had been hauled into town on some trumped-up charge, when an under-sized figure left the murk around the front of the garage and stopped midway to the kitchen, apparently watching the road.

Boone took the pebble from his mouth and tossed, and heard it strike the ground. "Nate," Boone whispered, and saw the figure step toward him at once.

"Wondered how soon you'd show up after the herd of drugstore cowboys headed back to town with their big shiny pistols an' rifles an' silk shirts," Nate Robb said scornfully, not muffling his voice.

"I was afraid they'd left somebody in the house."

"Too much trouble. They can't show off out here. They'd rather Cadillac up and down Main in Paradise where they can look important." He spat with moist disgust.

"Teresa told me about Sammy. I was at the schoolhouse, waking up from a drunk." Again, in self-reproach, he had no wish to shield himself.

"She came by here."

"Nate, there's one thing I want to make clear: I didn't kill Sammy."

"Hell, I know that. I told Sid Criner and Dane Horn so. They was all here. Claimed you's the last person seen with Sammy. Well —" he said, making a get-ready motion, "you hungry?" Basic needs always came first with Nate Robb.

"I could eat one cow raw, but first I'm gonna drink a bucket of well water."

"Stay here. Somebody might drive up." Nate fetched a bucket of water and dipper and a sack, which he dropped with a thump at Boone's feet. "Here's some grub. Some clean clothes. Old Jake's tied in the timber south of the barn. There's a carbine on the saddle, box of shells in the sack."

Boone was gulping greedily, downing dipper after dipper of sweet water. And stopping for breath, gasping, swallowing, he sluiced his face and head to soak up more water, and threw down another dipperful.

Nate said, "I figured you might lay low for a while till this blows over."

"Medicine Hill. I'll go there. I sure can't do any good in the county jail. I can always turn myself in."

"Better hit the grit," Nate said. "I hear a car."

Boone heard it at the same time, blasting across the still night. He did not go yet, troubled for something to say to this trustworthy old one, whom he remembered from earliest childhood, this white man who could be as cantankerous as a grizzly at times, but more times generous and loyal to a fault, who gruffly dodged any show of sentiment and was, in his bluff way, as much a father as steadfast friend.

Of a sudden Boone slapped Nate on the shoulder, jerked up the sack and struck out south, trotting. Soon he passed the sheds, the barn and the corrals. Behind him he heard the car rattling the cattle guard; pausing, then, he caught the lift of voices, and found that he was holding up because he was afraid for Nate. A while, and the car clattered the cattle-guard pipes again, and Boone saw its headlights bobbing on the Paradise road.

He quickened stride. In the timber his horse stamped nervously. Boone untied and swung up and rode out. The night was clear and cool. Moonlight was a white ash upon the tall-grass pasture. About him hummed the night insect chorus. In that moment he was wholly at peace, untroubled, unafraid. He shook off the unreality and rode on.

When the dark hump of Medicine Hill stood out before him, Boone dismounted and led the gelding, remembering the dense blackjacks and thickets and the clutter of rocks seemingly on guard here. Branches ripped at his face and arms. He stumbled over slabs of rock. Deep into the dense tangle he came to a little opening which appeared awash in the moonlight. A pool of silver marked the little spring. The uncropped grass was so tall that it lapped at his knees. Not far away was the dark hole of the cave.

As he looked, there settled over him the strangeness of time retreating, of bits and flashes of vivid scenes relived, of young words spoken, for most of all this was the hallowed place of his youth. Here, on their Olympus, Acey and he had acted out their impossible dreams.

Hunger intruded, launching him into a frenzy of preparations for camp. He unsaddled the gelding and dug into the gunny sack of supplies, gorging on canned beans and cold biscuits and a hunk of roast beef. In addition the sack yielded coffee and pot, tin cup and plate, fork and spoon to go with the knife he had commandeered for the beans, a battered frying pan, and a slab of bacon.

Afterward, he took rope and halter off the saddle and tied the gelding for night grazing. Behind the saddle he found two rolled blankets. With these he made a bed on the ledge in front of the cave and lay down. For one lingering moment the droning insects and the gelding's unbroken cropping of the rich grass reached him and seemed to collect in his spinning head; then, expelling a groan, he slept.

CHAPTER 11

He opened his eyes to sunlight parading upon his face and mourning doves calling, and lazily he thought, If the Osage has a song, it's the plaintive call of doves, which you hear almost everywhere. He was not yet fully awake, as if some instinct would not let him escape his dreamlike state. He seemed to be half out of an old dream and half into a new one, the dream of this unchanged place, and which was shattered as he remembered what had happened and why he was here. Alarmed that he didn't hear his horse, he jackknifed up and saw the bay named Jake standing at the edge of the timber, eying him with the patient, now curious, eyes of an old roping horse.

It was a rule at the Terrell ranch that you tended the saddle stock before you ate. Boone got up and led the gelding to the spring, then tied him in a fresh grazing spot, idled back and washed and temptingly considered the coffee pot. Not till tonight, however, would he make a fire.

After breakfast, he mounted the conical hill.

Here were the flat sandstone rocks of the vision quests where Acey and he had lain and dreamed, each wrapped in a blanket at night, down to breechclouts during the hot days, starving their slim bodies to illuminate their perceptions, waking just as the sun was beginning to light the day. For three days and three nights they had fasted here, rising only for water and nature's needs.

Standing on the highest flat rock, flame-colored under ascending Grandfather Sun, Boone looked out upon his surroundings. To the north appeared the miniature of the Little Chief School. A frantic bug of a car was scurrying along the road there. Elsewhere the pastures rolled away to gentle hills, the grass flowing like waves before the wind, which carried the scolding voice of a crow.

He sat on the warm rock, not moving, not yet prepared to come to grips with the present. In his boyish dreaming that long-ago time he had assumed several heroic forms, partly self-induced through hunger's hallucinations and partly because of his own vivid imagination and longing for significant signs. He could see that now.

Once his spirit had entered the body of an

eagle and he soared high above the shaggy hills and rich prairies. From his sky perch he saw all things, including a great village of the Osages beside a stream; and just as the Cherokees were creeping up to attack, he flew down among the lodges and screamed warnings at the unsuspecting people. In gratitude for his noble deed, the Osages set up a lodge for him and filled it with food; however, he was content to glide in long circles throughout his sky home and never lived in the village.

And once his dreaming spirit became a gray prairie wolf and he learned the wise ways of a wolf. When he was hungry, he caught rabbits or, with other wolves, surrounded and dragged down a buffalo. His senses were indeed keen and although he had not the eagle's advantage of the sky, he could hear all sounds and run faster than the strongest wind, even faster than the black-tailed destroyers of spring striking out of the sky. Therefore, when white men on horseback came hunting him with lean hounds, he merely ran faster and led them over rocky slopes and through timbered stretches, until the spent horses and hounds fell exhausted. He was very wise in that way.

In another dream he was a warrior and he rode a spotted war horse, and Pawnee and

Kiowa and Cherokee scalps hung from a pole outside his lodge for the villagers to see. He even rivaled *Shonkah-Sabe,* the great giant Black Dog. Alone, he crept into a Kiowa lodge and touched a chief with his coup stick; alone, he took a herd of fine Comanche horses and sang a brave and contemptuous song as he drove them away, and the Osages gave him the name of He-Brings-Many-Horses. (As close as Boone, in his limited knowledge, could arrive at that meaning in the Osage language was *Ka-Wa-Hiu-Bi-A,* which meant many horses, and which evoked the suggestion of a smile later when he confided in Acey.)

And the beautiful, mythical Evening Star, the embodiment of his aspirations for a wife when he reached manhood — he had dreamed of her as well, discovering her as he rode over the hill on the spotted war horse.

His eyes followed her graceful body as she took the path to the stream, the fringes of her buckskin dress swaying with every movement, as she tarried like a child to pick wild flowers, as she strolled on to the bank and, after a look around, removed her dress.

He slid from his horse and followed, seeing her outlined in the evening haze before she stepped into the pool. The perfect small breasts, as round as bells, the slim body the color of soft copper, the long, tapering legs, the flat, smooth belly, and the dark tufted mystery of her womanhood. She was smiling as she entered the water, pleasure mantling her high-boned face.

He reached the grassy bank and looked down at her. Swimming in the clear water, her movements rhythmic and languid, she seemed to perform some ritualistic dance. He tensed for her to shout him away, but the dark eyes only smiled. Stripping quickly, he dived in and surfaced beside her. Her limpid eyes were teasing as she swam away.

He struck out after her. To his confusion he found his arms around her. Her skin felt as smooth as satin. She turned toward him. Tenderly he cupped her breasts in his hands. They kissed, her parted lips warm and full and sweet. Then his hand moved down and he touched the softness that hid the wonder of her.

He woke to find his thigh drenched in himself.

And so, sometimes he was an eagle, sometimes a wolf or warrior or lover in these dreams, but always he was brave. That was the most important goal of life. And since his medicine power came from both the eagle and the wolf, he was extremely strong.

Contemplating the past, he perceived what he had not before. While Acey and he were seeking to discover who they were, they had, instead, found out who they were not. He still did not know his identity or where he belonged. What forms had Acey's dreams taken? What brave deeds had he performed for his people? What animals had transferred their power to him? The wise coyote, the strong bull, the silent panther, the powerful bear, the fleet wild stallion? Boone wondered. Whatever, their powers had not been strong enough. Perhaps nothing had really happened because, being very young and very foolish, they had not sought their visions apart? He could only wonder.

Still, by returning to this high, secret place this bright morning, where the eye could travel with the beginning of an eagle's, and experiencing the solitude, drinking at the sweet spring and feeling the wind out of the southwest and smelling the perfumed grass, he felt cleansed and rejuvenated. And he no longer wept. His pain was released and he felt no particular apprehension. Had the sought-after primitive powers come to him at last, just when he needed them? He permitted himself a faint smile at his youthful superstitions.

How long he sat there musing he did not

know, nor was he concerned about time. He had the unreal sensation that his mind was at rest far away, floating free of his sore body, an omniscient force capable of flight far beyond the hill. He suppressed his hunger, declining to go to his sack of supplies in the cave, and presently he realized that unconsciously he was fasting and preparing himself for tomorrow, when he must do something. Rising, he strayed to the other side of the hill and back, his mind reaching out. Sammy's death was somehow connected with Acey's, and blaming Sammy's murder on him was the quickest way to silence him. And what else was Sammy struggling to tell him during those last fearful moments? He lay down, letting his mind roam again.

He woke with a start. Warmed by the sun, he had slept and slept, for it was on its downward path and the wind felt cooler. He stood and scanned his surroundings, feeling refreshed, his mind rested and clear. Tomorrow he would ride to Salt Creek and look around.

Bobbing movement between the hill and the schoolhouse caught his eye. A single figure afoot, keeping to the brushy cover of a little summer-dry branch which came down out of the hills. Gradually the figure closed into focus. A woman. It was Teresa.

Feeling swept him as he went down the hillside and through the timber and thickets to meet her outside the tangle.

Her face was flushed. "I brought you some goodies," she said breathlessly, handing him a laden brown sack.

He murmured his thanks and led her inside, making a way for her through the dense growth, parting and holding back the branches. As she ducked down to enter, she brushed against him and he got the delightful warm scent of her. She had changed to riding breeches, and although he had never liked them on girls because he thought breeches made them look thick behind and awkward, he saw that Teresa, long-legged and slim-hipped, wore them as admirably as a boy.

"You shouldn't come here," he said as they went toward the ledge by the cave. "You could be implicated."

"I wanted to make certain you made it. Did you know that if you follow that little branch, you can't be seen from the road? I looked from the road before I started, just in case." Deliberately, she seated herself away from him, and he did not miss the propriety. Being betrothed, she ought to keep distance between them. And the reflection filled his mind that while going away and saving himself, he had lost something irrecoverable.

"Any news?" he asked.

"They think you left the Osage. They're looking for you in Texas." She sounded tense. She kept brushing at her hair, at that one wisp that seemed forever to fall across her forehead.

"That's good."

An earnestness suffused her face. "Boone, what are you going to do?"

"I know about tomorrow. Tomorrow I'll know about the next day."

"What, tomorrow?"

"Salt Creek. I want to look around there." His voice implied a confidence he didn't feel, and he could see that he hadn't convinced her.

"I keep asking myself what you can prove this way?" she said, crossing her long legs and leaning on the palm of her left hand, movements which traced her breasts against her blouse.

"What can I prove if I run or turn myself in?"

"The latter," she said, giving him an intent look, "would be better than getting yourself shot. You could hire a good lawyer."

"We're back on that again."

"There are some honest ones despite what you think. You could prove your innocence. You could testify that you saw two men in the car following Sammy after you let Sammy out." Her voice betrayed a rehearsed quality, making him think that she had carefully lined up her battery of arguments in advance and now was firing them one by one.

"Who would believe me?"

"I do — for one," she said.

Her tone caught him off guard and the tenderness he saw in the wide-set eyes, escaping through the bounds of her determined restraint, made him uncomfortable.

"If I turn myself in," he said, speaking carefully, "I'll never find out what happened to Acey. There'll be no more questions asked. Maybe that's what somebody wants to happen . . . to steer this thing away from Acey's case." He paused. "There's something else that bothers me. Something I had to go away from and come back to see. At first I thought I was seeing a change that had taken place at home. But it wasn't. I just didn't see it before. Guess I was too close to it, or too busy helling around."

"What do you mean, Boone?" In her puzzlement and also her desire to understand, her large eyes looked enormous and more luminous, and for a delayed instant, no more, the past was now and the closeness that had been between them existed still.

He shunted the feeling aside, saying, "It's the fear I see in peoples' faces, especially old men like Judge Pyle. The fear I hear in their guarded voices; the way they beat around the bush. The same fear I found in Sammy; something he sensed but maybe couldn't see. He wasn't like that in the old days. Sammy said Acey was afraid too. Afraid of what? Being murdered? What's the reason for this? Who's responsible?"

"Part of it is the times," she said thoughtfully, her brows forming a tiny frown. "The oil boom. The wild towns like Whizzbang. The violence. All this Osage money and everybody after it in all the county towns. It's not only Paradise, Boone. The whole county's on the make. It's not just one man, it's just about everybody. From Smiley Kemp and his overpriced tombstones, and Dane Horn lending money at atrocious interest rates to Indians and making slick livestock deals, to my own father at the big store. I ought not say this, but I know 20 per cent is added to Indian purchases."

All at once her expression lightened and she feigned a benign attitude and her voice became mockingly paternalistic: "Now about that little extra charge there on the store's books, Mr. Shunkahoppy, sir. We have to do that in order to carry your account till payment. Otherwise, sir, we couldn't afford to extend your credit that long, Mr. Shunkahoppy, sir. We know you understand." She smiled with a saccharine sweetness, furiously blinking her lovely eyes.

"Thank yuh, Mr. Frien'-of-Eendin," drawled Boone, not to be outdone; it was a game they used to play, mimicking the town's many colorful characters. "I'se just a-wonderin' is all. Ain't much, is it?"

"Hardly anything at all, Mr. Shunka-hoppy. You'll never miss it."

"Yuh ma' frien', ain't it?"

"Of course, I'm your friend, Mr. Shunka-hoppy, sir. Now, would you like to look at the shipment of brand-new Indian blankets we just got in from Pendleton?"

"Say, that's a good notion."

"And" — smiling sweetly — "we also have some very nice new diamonds over in the jewelry department that Mr. Clutch can show you."

"Reckon I could use a few more. 'Cause I'm gonna go Washin'ton 'fore long see Great White Father, purty soon I am."

"May I ask what you are going to tell the

Great White Father, Mr. Shunkahoppy, sir?"

"I'll jus' tell yuh what I'm gonna tell 'im. Gonna tell 'im: Paradise on map — that's what I'm gonna tell 'im. Yuh bet'cha, ma' frien'."

"Good for you, Mr. Shunkahoppy, sir! Paradise is a great little town!"

She delighted him and they laughed together in the old way they had laughed and, as suddenly, their laughter stilled. The intimate past vanished. He saw that recede in her eyes, in her guilty flushing and drawing back, and felt it within himself as his mind went back. "Somebody has to make a stand. If they get away with killing Acey and Sammy, what next?"

"You think Acey was murdered?"

"I do now. I feel it."

"Who?"

"I have no idea. But I intend to find out."

"You always were an idealist," she said softly, looking down at her hands. "A laudable trait, Boone, but it can lead into dangerous places."

An awkward silence set in. Teresa continued to look at her hands now and then. Boone could find no words. His thoughts kept veering off into the past they were both avoiding. He said, "Did Andy tell you that he knocked Staley off me twice at the garage

270

when Staley's crew was holding me?"

She looked surprised. "No, he didn't."

"Well, he did. About that time Dane broke up the fight. How's Andy doing at the bank?" Boone was finding the conversation much easier when he discussed Andy.

"Fine. Did I tell you he's building me a house? It's high on the hill, overlooking the town. You can see for miles. I guess all that money which Dane spent so begrudgingly on Andy's education is paying off. Dane thinks anyone who gets past the eighth grade is an educated fool . . . Andy's very capable and people like him."

"Andy's a good man. I don't think he would take the hide Dane does on a loan. I trust him. He'll be a big man someday. You won't have to worry. Andy's the best-educated man in Paradise."

"Andy's honest," she said. "I know that. And I know that he doesn't always agree with his father. They've had their arguments over interest rates charged Osages. Andy's conscientious. He wants to improve the Paradise schools. He's a builder. He wants to bring some kind of payroll, maybe an industry, to the town besides the quarterly Osage payments . . . It's repugnant to him to see the merchants hovering like vultures on payment day, waiting for the Indians to blow their money, to pay up their old bills and start new ones. He's . . ."

She ceased suddenly and gazed down, a self-arresting gesture. And seeing that naked inward expression, he was surprised and the insight went through him that by enumerating Andy's many fine qualities she was, although unaware of it, seeking to reassure herself of her choice of him.

Boone looked away; he didn't want her to read his face. A moment later he heard her speak in a voice that was drastically changed and softened. "There was so little time to talk the first day I saw you at the school. I remember why you said you went away. Why you didn't say good-by. Why you didn't write — not even once. And yet . . . I don't know . . . nothing's quite clear to me today. Everything's so confused."

When he turned and looked at her, she had drawn nearer. The deep hurt stood pooled again in her eyes, and instantly he wanted to change that. But he made no move to take her in his arms, and he was going to be honest if it hurt her more.

"In a way," he said, "it's pretty simple what happened then. I knew I was going downhill, as the old Indians say. I was about to become a drunkard, like many of my Osage friends. So I left. I didn't ask you to run off with me — even though I wanted to — because . . . because I was afraid I couldn't make it and I didn't want to drag you down with me. I don't want that to sound noble. It's not. But it's the truth."

There was a long silence, and then she said, "I could have helped you, Boone . . . if you'd only let me."

"I know that now."

As if reaching backward in thought, she murmured, "You said there was no one else. I guess that's important for a girl to know."

"There wasn't."

"Three years and just that — that's all?"

"There isn't much to tell." Why tell her now of his torment when he thought of her, of his constant longing for her, of when he knew he had whipped the bottle. A recalling entered his voice. "I never blamed your father for forbidding me to see you."

"He didn't know the times I slipped off to meet you, and we would drive and drive."

Silence.

"It's getting late and school starts in the morning," she said suddenly, rising. "I'd better go." She was clasping and unclasping her hands, and looking down.

"Thanks for everything." He was, he knew, being so damned stiff and proper with her. He hadn't touched her yet, but now he took her by the hand and drew her after him into the tangled, shadowed woods.

Just before they emerged on the other side, he let go her hand. When he glanced back, she was still close behind him. He stopped, waiting for her to pass into the open. Instead, she went straight into his arms and laid her cheek against his shirt.

Her voice rose, small and troubled, "Oh, Boone, if you hadn't gone away."

"If I hadn't I'd be dead."

"I mean . . . if you'd just said something. Just kept in touch. Just *once*."

He could feel her tense unhappiness, her confusion. He held her close. She stirred and looked up at him. Her eyes were wet and he could never stand weeping. "Hey," he said softly, and as he started to wipe away a tear at the corner of her eye, something flowed swiftly into her face that was irreversible and true, and as he bent his head and kissed her he knew that deep down nothing had changed, and that which had been there was still there.

She drew slowly away from him, turning his lips aside with the tip of one forefinger, and he saw the forced return of her inhibitions. "You were right," she said. "I ought not to have come here, although for a different reason than you said."

He felt a plunging affection for her. He wanted to protect her and make up for the pain he had caused her, and in the next moment realized he could not.

By then she was walking rapidly along the wooded branch toward the schoolhouse. When he could no longer see her, he made his way back through the woods and climbed the hill. Dusk laid a thick veil over the hills. It wasn't long until he saw headlights come on and heard her car as she drove away from the school and turned east on the road to Paradise. In the woods below a whippoorwill voiced its first nocturnal call. A pang of loneliness stole over him.

He was suddenly angry with himself. Well, by God, he had better quit daydreaming and get a hold of himself again. She had just come here to help him, and what if they had kissed? It meant nothing now, not any more.

Old regrets punished him as he went down the hill and made a small fire in the mouth of the cave and cooked his supper.

Late in the night the wind came crying on the wings of a fast-moving thunderstorm, shouting and screaming and wailing through the timber. Lightning danced across the boisterous sky. In the midst of the uproar, Boone wrapped a blanket around his shoulders and climbed the hill and stood on the flame-colored rocks and turned his face to the tempest, reveling in its clean fury as buckshot rain peppered his face. More wind than rain, fleeing within minutes, growling and complaining off to the northeast.

After the storm passed, the stars appeared again and there was a stretch of silence when he heard only the raindrops dripping off the trees; afterward, the foxlike bark of coyotes set in and, deep in the woods behind his Medicine Hill, he heard the sequential hooting of a great horned owl.

Boone felt uplifted, at peace. There was a rhythm to these hills. And there was beauty in the wild night, beauty and harmony with nature, more beauty even than in his boyhood dream world.

CHAPTER 12

The morning was still fresh when he saddled the red horse and set out for Salt Creek, his objective that section west of the Standing Elk ranch. Two hours later, keeping the hills between him and the road and riding the draws when he could not, he reached the creek.

As he dismounted and tied up in the brush, a somber reflection crossed his mind:

It happened somewhere along here. Along here Acey died.

He began a slow and methodical walk. A few whitefaces grazed in the pasture. Acey could have come here to look about his cattle. He liked to do that. If so, why cross the creek? Boone could see no cattle over there. There was a stillness under the shadowed elms and sycamores and cottonwoods. A strange melancholy. His throat tightened and went dry. He noted that the creek was down, though still wide and deep; the banks looked steep everywhere. As yet he saw no ford. He shivered as he walked on, trying to re-create the order of those ultimate moments: Acey riding up the creek. His balking horse nervously entering the swift waters . . . suddenly stepping off the bank and going under and Acey struggling . . .

Boone rested his chin in his hand and peered up and down the creek and pictured that final scene over again, step by step — and shook his head in rejection. He couldn't see it that way. Somehow he couldn't; not even a drunk being so foolhardy.

He moved on, searching for a ford, where passage had worn away the high bank and a rocky shelf might rise out of the creek; hoping there was a ford, for then he might be wrong. But the high shoulder of the wooded bank continued unbroken. He came to a barbed-wire fence and saw a gate not far away. He stopped. He could see no reason to go farther because if Acey had attempted to cross, he had done so south of this fence in his own pasture.

Discouraged, Boone looked across the creek; for the first time, he noticed habitation in the distance. The usual rich Osage-type house: two-story, red brick, about half a mile from the creek. That would be Buck and Rose DeVore's place. Donna Standing Elk had said the DeVores were her nearest neighbors and lived across the creek.

Boone was ready to turn back when the racket of a car reached him. The noise grew louder. Soon after he heard the rumble of bridge planking and sighted the car approaching from the west, the DeVore side of the creek. He watched it make dust on to the east, traveling like a bat out of hell, Nate would say.

Boone had forgotten about the old county road and the wooden bridge that the winding creek hid from sight here. That bridge . . . he gazed hard in that direction, and hard at the gate, not fifty yards from the creek, and stiffened with comprehension. If Acey had wished to cross the creek, all he had to do was open the gate and ride the short distance to the bridge.

The cold logic startled him, and now baffled him. Why hadn't Acey taken the obvious way, one he undoubtedly knew about?

Motor noise swelling again from the De-Vore side of the creek disturbed his thoughts. Not one but many cars, the volume of sound indicating that possibly they traveled in a pack. Alarm rushed through him. He drew deeper into the timber and waited.

He heard the lead car take the bridge, and before its rumbling passage died another rumble began and another. He quit counting to fix his attention on the crowded road as car after car appeared. He heard voices. The cars were slowing, and as the dust settled he saw the front car stop. It was a purple Cadillac. Now all the cars were stopping. That was when he noticed the horse trailers, when their meaning struck him. Each car pulled a loaded trailer.

A chunky, big-hatted man strutted back from the lead car, shouting and gesturing importantly. He wore a bright yellow shirt. Others started getting out of cars and letting down trailer gates and leading out saddle horses.

Boone stood motionless, feeling cornered, yet spellbound. He saw the men mount up and form beside the road, rifle butts slanting up from long scabbards alongside the saddles, and he saw some of the riders already flourishing long weapons. Everybody wore a broad-brimmed cowboy hat and gaudy shirt, such as you'd see at the Fourth of July 101-Ranch Rodeo, and everybody seemed to be jabbering and laughing nervously and reining horses this way and that. It all reminded Boone of a Saturday afternoon Western movie, a bad one at that. They were too far away for him to recognize faces, but the loud-mouthed, heavy-bellied man in the bright yellow shirt, still giving orders and strutting around like a turkey cock, and now mounting a beautiful Palamino, looked like Buck DeVore. He was leading the posse.

A blue roadster was drawing past the parked vehicles. The driver stopped just beyond DeVore's Cadillac and a slender man got out. Boone stared hard. That was Andy Horn, and he was walking back and speaking to DeVore and shaking his head. The preparations continued. After a bit, Andy walked back to his car and drove off. Boone felt an unlooked for warmth. Andy had tried to stop them.

He watched in fascination. The rowdy riders, the nervous horses, the flash of weapons — everything seemed imagined. He could be watching through the film of a dream. Then the milling of the horses slackened and DeVore took the lead and rode through the pasture gate.

That sudden motion sent Boone retreating farther into the brushy woods, thinking of his mount downstream. He sprinted into a run. Not far ahead, checking up to look back, he saw the last of the riders crowding through the gate. He ran on. When he looked backward again, they were stringing out across the pasture, close enough that he caught the drift of larking voices and hoof clatter. One rider dropped his rifle in the grass and dismounted to retrieve it to the accompaniment of bantering laughter.

Boone could see his horse now. But once there he discovered what he had not remembered at the fence, that along here the creek made a dogleg turn to the east. At the angle the posse was taking, they'd spot him if he tried to outrun them down the creek. He'd have to sweat it out.

The old gelding began to twitch its fox ears forward and lifted its head to nicker a greeting to the posse horses. Boone grabbed the bit and pulled the bay head down and clamped his hand over the quivering nose. Rigid, he watched the noisy pack straggle past.

Darkness was about an hour away when Boone reached Medicine Hill. He watered and unsaddled and slipped on the gelding's halter for grazing and climbed the rough hill for one more look around. Seeing the blur of the Little Chief School, he wondered whether Teresa had come here earlier and decided she had not; in one way he wanted to see her very much, in another he did not, because he had sensed within her the headlong feeling that he had, and he was afraid for them both.

He was down below gathering wood for an after-dark fire at the cave when Old Jake threw up his head and flicked the sentinel ears, every sense alert. Boone stood still but a few moments, hearing no sound beyond the timber and brush, before he dashed to the cave and back with the carbine. Jake continued to twitch his ears, but nothing happened. Boone was about to climb the hill to look when he heard brush crackling and someone stumbling over rocks, obviously coming through without regard for stealth.

In moments Teresa Chapman came to the edge of the woods and waved and paused to regain her breath. She carried a light sweater.

"Didn't expect you back," Boone said, coming out to her.

"A cowboy found your car and reported it." In her plain blue dress, belted at the waist, and her reddish brown hair drawn back with a blue ribbon, she looked as fresh and appealing as if she were starting the day's schooling rather than having ended it.

"That's sooner than I thought anybody would find it," Boone said, guiding her toward the cave. When she was seated on the ledge, he laid the carbine aside and said, "I'm glad you're here, but I still don't want you involved in this. Won't your folks wonder where you are this late?"

"I room with a girl in town who teaches at the high school."

"What if the posse saw you coming here?"

"The posse's in town, boozing up for tomorrow. They're calling in officers from all over the county to comb the country east and northeast of Paradise; even officers from adjoining counties. They asked Andrew to join them, but he refused. He said it was barbaric."

There it was again. Her formality. Her saying Andrew, instead of Andy. "Good for him," Boone said.

She shrank from relaying the next bit of news. He saw her eyes reflect that reluctance as she said, "Sammy's funeral was this afternoon."

He compressed his lips, before him the frozen tableau of the Gray Horse cemetery. The chanting of the old priest. The wind of many voices in the trees. The cars parked on the hill. The grieving faces of the older Osages come to pay respects to the senseless passing of another young one. The primitive wailing of the blanketed older women.

"No doubt there was a big crowd," he said, with bitterness. "The attraction of murder. I know Lester Oliver took care of everything in his usual inimitable style, with integrity, dignity, beauty." He shook his head. "It doesn't help to talk like that, only I've seen so much of it."

A burdensome silence began to build between them, something unrelated to the events swirling about them. Boone, feeling it acutely, could find nothing more to say at the moment. She looked so earnest and appealing in the soft light of early evening. Her eyes were constantly on his face, a suggestion of sadness in them, he thought. He felt uncomfortable under that intentness. A sudden importance struck him.

"Was Mary Elizabeth at school?"

"Yes."

"Did she have flour on her face?"

Teresa nodded worriedly. "And the kids teased her until I made them stop. However, she kept it on. I thought I ought to talk to Donna about Mary. I didn't make her clean her face. In fact, I didn't even talk to her about it. I was afraid I'd upset her, poor child. She's been through so much."

That bothered Boone. He said, "When I went by the house after the funeral, I saw her like that. It kinda threw me at first. Donna says Mary Elizabeth is ashamed of her Indian blood after all that's happened. Acey's drinking, I mean. These past few years I guess she never saw him when he wasn't."

By mutual assent they dropped the subject there. The silence took hold again. They were, he realized, just sitting there looking at each other. Finally, she said, "People in town think you ran because you're guilty. Boone, you've got to give yourself up and fight this out in court."

"Not yet. I need a little more time."

"You're so stubborn," she said, shaking her head in dismay, her expressive eyes full of the sadness again.

"Well, I'm finding out some things. Acey

didn't try to cross Salt Creek."

She cast him a startled look. "How do you know that?"

"All he had to do — if he'd wanted to cross — was open a pasture gate and ride a little way to the bridge on the county road. That's all. The bridge has been there for years. I remember it when I was a kid. I rode over there today. It hit me when I saw the bridge."

"Would he have been near the gate?"

"He's got cattle in the pasture, which runs along the creek there for a quarter mile or more. Sammy, who was with the searching party, told me they found Acey where the creek turns east. That's in his pasture."

Her eyes became deeply questioning. "And if he didn't try to cross?"

"Something else happened to him in the pasture before he drowned."

"But you don't know that anyone was with him, Boone. Could have been an accident. Maybe his horse threw him, or slipped suddenly and Acey fell from the saddle. Maybe he just passed out."

"I've thought of that too. Any number of things could have happened. But," he said firmly, "I can't believe he tried to cross at high water, even drunk, when he could have taken a bridge that's been used for years.

Another thing: There's no ford across the creek in the pasture. No place I found where you might even *think* you could cross in high water."

"Now what?" she inquired after a pause, not quite sharing his conviction.

"I think I'd better talk to Tan Labeau or Nate."

"You can't hide here much longer. They're going to run a fine-toothed comb through these hills."

"They'll have to beat that noisy bunch I saw today in the creek pasture. Looked like Andy tried to head them off. When does the big manhunt start?" He was being sarcastic.

"You mean when do they start playing Cowboy and Indian in deadly earnest? I'd say tomorrow or next day. Very soon."

Their talk fell off again, and Boone didn't mind. He was content with the warm veil of twilight around them, meanwhile mindful of her deliberate propriety, of her determined observance of the gap between them. He respected Teresa, he'd always respected her, and the truth bored into him that was another reason why, long ago, seemingly longer than it was, he hadn't asked her to run off with him. Now he could ask himself what would have happened had she gone with him? Would they, married, have made it together? Now he had no doubts: they would have. He continued to look at her, seeing her eyes turning on him, at times looking away, her frank concern for him contradicting her seemly manner.

When she drew the sweater around her shoulders, he thought of time passing and made a hasty decision. "Let's go to the top of the hill for a look before you start back. I want you to see this place. Acey and I used to come here when we were boys. Here we could feel like Indians."

"Are you sending me home, Boone?" she asked, pretending hurt.

He held out his hand to her without replying. She stood but did not take his hand. Still, when they started up the rough slant and he lightly took her arm, she did not pull away. At the top they stepped upon the vision quest rocks, the dimness turning their flame color a muddy hue, and gazed off. No cars raced along the darkening line of the schoolhouse road. The hills, the prairie seemed to slumber in timelessness.

"It's so peaceful," she said, watching beside him. "How I wish that were actually true. You wouldn't know our quiet little Indian trading post on the banks of Salt Creek . . . It's like a boom town. Loaded cars coming and going at all hours. The

Blue Bird's open twenty-four hours now. Seems everybody's packing a pistol or has one in his car. Everybody's wearing a big white hat and boots and new gunbelt. Snipe Murray's enjoying a rush trade. Headquarters is Judge Pyle's office . . . When the judge is closed, it's the Goodtime Billiards. Haney's Hardware has sold out of pistols and rifles. The Oklahoma City and Tulsa papers have had reporters in town interviewing local officials." She moved away from him and sat down. "Boone — you just can't go on like this. Living in the hills like a" — she hesitated and plunged on, flinging the words at him — "like a wild Indian. The buffalo are gone, Boone. You've got to face up to reality."

"I told you my hands would be tied in jail," he said, and sat beside her on a great rock, upon him the unruliness that refused to obey. "I know there isn't much time left. A day or two." However, he wasn't going to talk about tomorrow because he couldn't see beyond to tomorrow. There was nothing to talk about. So he sat still and felt the silence swelling between them once more. He didn't understand her. Not at all. Although it was getting late, she showed no restlessness, no wish to leave.

After a little, he said, "I think you'd better

go," and came to his feet. She sat a moment longer before she stood up, reaching no higher than his shoulder, but as she did she seemed to lose her balance on the rocky footing.

He caught her arm, lightly, then roughly, stepping around, to prevent her falling, and that momentum swung their bodies together. Feeling raked him instantly; his breathing became rough. She was there, completely against him. He expected her to pull free at once. She did not. As his arms slid around her, he felt hers around him. She turned her face to his and he laid his mouth across hers, conscious of a blinding sweet haze. A storm struck his mind: Why, in God's name, had he ever allowed himself to lose her?

When he lifted his head, she looked up at him and he heard her voice trailing a sweet sadness, "Why did it have to happen that way?" speaking as much to herself of her obsession of the past, saying there was no answer, there could be none, that she expected none.

His throat was full. He said nothing, set for her to push away. But she stayed there against him, and over him then fell the swift certainty that this time there would be no sudden breaking away, no avowal of wrongness, no self-ordering display of restraint. This he sensed at the same instant that he wished to protect her, as he had been responsible for her in the past, yet knowing that he was powerless to do so. They were both being swept away and he didn't care. He knew now that she really wasn't about to fall a moment ago. His hands became almost rough and she turned her face to him again and he bent his head and kissed her, her lips giving in a way he had never experienced before when kissing her. He felt her go lax.

They seemed to slip deeper into the depthless and wonderful, mysterious sweet haze. Now they lay pressed together on the great rock, her head cradled in his arm. He rained kisses on her mouth, on her cheeks, her eyes, her throat. He felt her clean-scented hair loosely brushing his face like a caress. He could hear his own pulse racing; her uneven breathing was warm against his ear. He found himself bringing his body over hers. For a space her body was resistant, then passive, then, in a crash of knowing, he felt its gradual acquiescence, its parting. Her face below him, twisted away, looked so young, so lovely as it swam through a green mist.

He moved suddenly, powerfully. She

voiced a small cry and flung her arms about him as if to join them together forever and ever.

"Boone . . . dear Boone . . . oh, why?"

"Teresa . . . sweet Teresa . . ."

He lost all sense of time and place. His mind fled. They lay still, drained of emotion, arms around each other, eyes half shuttered. He cuddled her as though she were a frightened child needing protection from the unknown night. She kept touching his face. He stroked her hair. Now and then, tenderly, he kissed her lips or cheek, and was moved when he found her face wet with tears. Together they watched the star-lit sky like two lost souls adrift in eternity. What now? Tomorrow — what then?

But he was beginning to feel a terrible lash of guilt. He had stained her new life with Andy. He had spoiled everything for her. Andy's honest image accused him from the darkness. But wasn't Teresa his girl first? Hadn't he loved her and lost her? Didn't he still love her? Yes, if that helped.

She pressed closer against him, and he held her for a wordless interval, incapable of thinking beyond now.

She turned a little to look at the stars again. She said, "For a long time you didn't seem to know that I existed. I remember the first afternoon we went riding, down to the river and back. I don't think you said more than half a dozen words, and I sat as far away from you as I could . . . I didn't think you were ever going to kiss me. Yet I was afraid you would. You thrilled me when you finally did. You're a shy person, Boone . . . I remember at the games how fearful I was you'd get hurt, but you never were, seriously . . . I used to lie awake at night thinking about you . . . I could always talk to you about anything — the world, my girlish dreams, my hopes. And you always listened to me, just as you're listening now."

He could only hold her closer.

When she spoke again, a languid sadness lay traced in her voice. "I wanted this to happen long ago. You were always so watchful over me. So protective. Boone, the idealist, the young god. Dear Boone, who read the English poets . . . That was another reason why I loved you. Then you went away."

"I told you why," he said, reminded that nothing was explained or could be.

A night breeze rose and an early-fall coolness clutched the hill, impressing upon Boone the inexorable constancy of change. He remained still, wanting these moments to continue yet a while longer before they vanished like smoke on the wind.

In dread, he felt her stir and heard her voice, small and resigned, "Guess I really do have to go now."

They sat up and held each other briefly, without kissing, then stood. There were faint rustlings as she made ready to go. To him the silence surrounding them was oppressive and heavy. He turned at her touch. He held her as he guided her down the rocky hill, for she could fall in the darkness. Entering the woods and thickets, vigilantly warding off branches and helping her over and around rocks, he led her through to the open prairie washing away on a mirage sea of silver.

When she paused, expecting him to go no farther, he put his arm around her waist and, in silence, they went along the branch to the ghostly white of the schoolhouse.

He opened the door of the Hudson for her and she got in and he closed the door after her. She sat a moment, then she said thoughtfully, "You know, Boone, I don't feel ashamed at all. I ought to, but I don't, even though it was wrong."

He couldn't speak past the fullness of his throat, past his stifling doubts.

She found the ignition key and turned on the switch. "I can't bear to think of you alone on that hill. I can't. What will you do?"

"I won't wait for them to come after me."

"You won't give yourself up?" Her voice had the bittersweet trailing tone that made him ache.

"Not to them. If I do, it will be to Tan Labeau."

She started the engine and looked straight ahead. He thought her eyes were closed. A moment. A longer moment. She stirred. As she shifted the gears, he bent and kissed her and she kissed him, and as he stood back from her, the premonition shocked him that they were saying good-by.

He watched as she backed around and rattled across the cattle guard. The headlights of the Hudson flicked on as she turned out on the road to Paradise.

When the drone of her car faded out, he left the schoolyard. It was the worst moment of his life.

CHAPTER 13

He slept little that night, flashes of half dreams, half awakenings tormenting him. Sometimes he was back on the flame-colored rock with her. Sometimes he imagined that he caught the sweet scent of her hair, so real that he felt the ache of the emptiness around him. Had that been her way of telling him good-by?

By daylight he was up and ascending the hill, there to stand appalled at its barren coldness where last night there was the tenderness of complete love. His spirits sank when he looked off. He decided that he was getting nowhere. Maybe the sensible course was to ride to Nate's and call Tan Labeau on the phone to take him into custody. It was that, else wait for them to flush him out. His dearth of options depressed him, and he shrank from giving up. Hadn't his ride to the creek convinced him that Acey hadn't tried to cross? And there was poor Sammy, left murdered in the pasture like a castaway dead animal, also unavenged.

He left the hill and boldly cooked breakfast and made coffee and forced himself to eat and drink, while he struggled to clear his thinking. Even with his mind concentrating on the posse and the little time allotted him, he retained a picture of Teresa that would not lessen or go away. She floated there still, in the unreal green mist. He went to saddle up.

Around ten o'clock he was posted in the blackjacks south of the home ranch, watching the house and the road. Cars passed now and then, heading east, drawing horse vans. As yet he couldn't bring himself to go to the house and call Labeau. That was too much like quitting, like betraying your friends.

Afternoon had come when he saw Nate Robb amble to the main corral and bridle a horse and throw on blanket and saddle. At the same time Boone heard a car turning off the road and clanking across the cattle guard. Nate went back. Boone lost sight of him when he passed behind the barn.

Not long afterward the car pulled away from the house and Boone saw the streak of its dust going east. Nate did not return to the corral. When the saddled horse had stood for a long while, Boone began to puzzle why. That wasn't like Nate. You didn't saddle a horse and let it stand a long time.

Possibly an hour had elapsed after Nate had saddled the horse when Boone decided to venture to the house. An occasional car still hurried by. Evidently something big was building up east of the ranch, just as Teresa had said.

When within a few rods of the house, Boone called Nate's name. There was no answer, no audible movement within the house. He called again. Still no answer. But Nate Robb would not have gone off in the car and left his horse saddled.

Boone was worried now. He advanced to the back yard, intending to enter the house through the kitchen, and called again. No answer. He was passing the corner of the garage, when he heard an indistinct moan of pain. Whipping about, he saw Nate lying in the yard.

Boone ran to him.

Nate Robb lay face down, arms flung forward. Apparently he had tried to crawl to the house and lost consciousness. Boone turned him over, flinching at the dried blood on Nate's face. The old eyes had difficulty focusing on Boone; in fact, Nate didn't know him.

"Nate — it's Boone."

Nate couldn't talk.

Boone got his arms underneath and carried him into the kitchen, and on to Nate's room at the rear and laid him on the bed. Taking towels and a pan of water from the kitchen, he set about cleaning the battered face, his hands gentle, his anger flaming higher and higher. Whoever had done this was thoroughly brutal. Nate was hardly recognizable. Remembering the pint of corn whiskey in his room, Boone ran upstairs for it; holding Nate's head up, he poured a trickle between the swollen lips.

Nate's response was a strangling spluttering and blinking and gasping. He was coming around. He moved his arms and legs. Recognition poured into his eyes. "When'd you ride up?"

"Just did."

"Where am I?"

"In your bed and you're gonna stay here for a while."

Nate protested and strained upward, only to fall back. His head rolled. "Maybe you're right," he muttered, collecting himself again. Boone offered the bottle. Nate turned his head away and growled as of old, not without a trace of humor, "Back in the early day we'd shot the bartender for servin' that bug juice."

"Don't be so choosy," Boone said, relieved. "This is what brought you to. The one time Snipe Murray's rotgut ever revived anybody." He corked the pint and set it on the table by Nate's bed, and the brief jesting was over. "Now tell me who did it."

"Fellow in town."

"What fellow?"

"Look here," Nate snapped in his early day voice of independence, "I can handle this. You got enough troubles."

"You're not handling anything right now," Boone squelched him. "You're gonna stay in bed. You probably have a concussion. I want to know who did it."

"Herb Staley," Nate said, gruff about it. He lay back for needed breath, murmuring, "Believe I will have another touch of that poison."

Boone held him up so he could drink, and then Boone asked, "Why'd he do it?"

"Claimed I knew where you hid out. When I said I didn't, he started in on me. What really set him off was when I said I wouldn't tell if I did know. That's when he hit me first."

"Where'd he go?"

Nate reared back in protest. "I said I could handle it."

"Where did he go?" Boone insisted.

"Hell, if you have to know . . . to the posse camp in the Diamond D pasture by the big spring. Bunch of 'em stopped by here this morning. Had to show off their new pistols an' nose around." Nate's scorn bit through the swollen mask of his face. "Wonder who'll fix milk toast for them drugstore dudes . . . tuck 'em in at night when the dew falls?"

"Sure he went there?"

"Where else? That's where they're all headed. Tomorrow they start their big manhunt for Boone Terrell." When Boone showed no surprise, Nate appeared to take that for lack of concern. "They mean business, Boone. Nothin' more dangerous than a dude with firearms — if they don't shoot off their own foot first." And when Boone started to the door: "Just what're you up to?"

"You need a doctor. I'll call in town, get a taxi driver out here. He can bring you back — if Doc Mears doesn't put you in the hospital."

"Hell, I wouldn't go to him."

"He's the only doctor in town."

"You'll play hell," Nate swore. He strained to rise and fell back weakly. "Just fix me a big pot of coffee."

Boone eyed him critically, knowing him. Nate would not see a doctor unless completely incapacitated. "All right," he concluded, although not liking his decision, and went to the kitchen. He was thinking ahead as he built a fire in the iron stove and put the coffee pot on. This thing had to be done tonight. Staley had run roughshod too long. Nate was family.

"I'll be back sometime tonight," he told Nate when he came into the room.

"Listen to me. I'll take care of Mister Staley later."

As if he had not heard, Boone went to his

room and donned a broad-brimmed white hat he had seldom worn. Downstairs he sacked a helping of bread and meat, left a lamp burning in the kitchen, looked in on Nate, who seemed to be resting comfortably, and hurried to the corral. After unsaddling Nate's horse, he hastened to the blackjacks and rode off to the east.

To Boone the broken land around the spring in the Diamond D pasture resembled a camp ground for a summer revival meeting. Only the big tent was missing. He could see cars and vans parked without order, horses haltered close, others on long ropes. Someone had rigged up a chuckwagon on the rear of a truck. He saw one A tent, which he took for the headquarters, where possemen strolled in and out. Mostly, however, the manhunters stood around in small groups and smoked and gestured, or idled over to their horses and back, or took rifles and carbines out of long scabbards for umpteen checks and put them back, or loitered over to the chuckwagon for more coffee.

Failing to locate Staley's black Packard on the west side of the spring, Boone worked around through the timber to the east side. By then the light was dimming and he couldn't distinguish all the cars. He'd have to wait for full darkness before moving in.

Never had he been so determined about a thing, this stalking, this biding his time. A duty he must carry out before he surrendered tomorrow to Tan Labeau. Waiting, he munched his cold rations. He was in the unusual position, he reflected, of acting out the role of a tribesman on a revenge raid and it was not an illusion born of the vision quest rocks on Medicine Hill. Those cars could be hide lodges, and when darkness fell he would go among them and touch the enemy he sought and bring him out. To be true to himself and his people he must perform this deed, which was as binding as blood, because from his earliest memory Nate Robb had belonged among his own.

So now he waited with solid patience.

He saw fires springing up, and presently he smelled food on the wind. When darkness cloaked the camp, he pulled the broad hat low on his forehead, took the saddle gun and made for the east side. If challenged, he hoped to pass for a posseman while he searched for Staley. The hum of voices deepened as he neared the cars and vans. He heard a man ask, "What time we pullin' out in the morning?" and the careless reply, "This bunch won't be up till after daylight. Le's have another drink."

Boone was checking each car. He had gone about thirty yards when a man stumbled around a horse van, gave him a brief look and reeled on. Boone stiffened as the man halted and turned and mumbled, "That you, Ross, ol' hoss?" Boone, moving on, said, "He's back there."

A long hulk loomed ahead, as shiny as a black hearse. Staley's Packard. But no one was around it. Looking toward the nearest fire, Boone saw four men filling tin plates from a black pot. Past the fire stood the headquarters tent. The chatter of voices was steady. One man prominently wore a big star on his calf-hide vest. A revolver wobbled at his gunbelt.

And slowly, like an ugly dream, Herb Staley's unmistakable broken face slid into focus as he crouched on the other side of the fire. Staley was talking between wolfish bites. Blowing, Boone could tell, saying: "That red ass won't fight. Ever see one that would? . . . He'll quit like a whipped dog if you corner him. . . . You'll see."

"I wouldn't be so sure about that," the man with the star said. "Get an Indian mad, well —"

"Wait'll tomorrow," Staley said.

The son of a bitch, Boone thought. Listen to him brag.

Boone lounged against the left front fender of the Packard, mindful of a current of men around him, strolling back and forth, smoking, talking; there was always the chance, of course, that someone from Paradise might recognize him. He breathed the raw fumes of whiskey. He didn't see Buck DeVore, and inasmuch as DeVore had led the posse that first day, Boone looked for him here tonight on the eve of the big manhunt.

Boone saw Staley get up and fill his plate again and crouch down and resume talking. The light accented the deep-socketed eyes, the heavy brows, the rock jaw, the crooked ridge of the nose, a brawl-marked but rugged face.

Behind Boone came the husking of feet through prairie grass, and a man stepped out of the darkness. He was reeling a little, and Boone could smell the corn whiskey as the posseman asked, "Got a drink?"

"I'm out," Boone said, not turning his head till late. He'd seen that flat face in the Goodtime.

"Where you from?" the drinker inquired.

"Tulsa," Boone said.

"Come over for the fun, huh?"

"Yeah."

The drinker angled across to the fire

where Staley was and spoke around, and receiving no encouragement went on. Two men idled by Boone. One asked, "Wonder where Buck DeVore is? He was all hot for the hunt. Offered some of the boys extra horses."

"Damn'f I know. If you ask me, we can get along without him. Enough givin' orders already."

When Boone shifted his attention back, he failed to see Staley and for a moment he feared he'd lost his man. Then he saw Staley near the tent, stacking his plate and swiping a hand across his mouth, left out of the powwow now as more men came to the fire to group around the man with the star.

Casually, Staley strolled around the fire toward his car.

Boone, back-peddling into the muddy light behind the Packard, thought: He's leaving, he's not pulling a horse van; the son of a bitch is leaving.

Staley came to the car and reached into a pocket for keys and opened the front door.

Now! With Staley's body and the car door between Boone and the firelight.

Boone moved quickly. Just before he got there he saw Staley jerk, sensing something; by then Boone was jamming the carbine's barrel into Staley's back and he was saying,

"Keep quiet. One word out of you this goes off. Back up."

Staley, although betraying surprise, didn't obey.

"Move," Boone snarled, giving the barrel a brutal shove. "Be quiet."

Staley backed up then, and when they reached the darkness behind the car, Boone ordered, "Turn around — keep walking."

Within moments they were beyond the camp. Staley, slowing step, turned his head to look at Boone, and Boone jabbed him and Staley went ahead. Coming to the gelding tied in the woods, Boone led the horse away, then mounted.

Camp sounds fell behind. A car, lights bobbing, roared up toward the camp from the west side. Boone made his prisoner walk faster. Sometimes he made him trot. That wasn't enough. He wanted to punish Staley, to make him hurt as he had hurt Nate. So he unstrapped the rope on the saddle and fashioned a loop and tossed it around Staley's neck and drove him like a horse, lashing Staley with the slack.

Staley stopped stubbornly, balking. Boone jerked him down like a steer, and when Staley refused to get up, Boone heeled his horse onward and dragged him. A little of that and Staley jumped up, gasping, "You tryin' to kill me? Who are you?" He had lost his hat.

Boone said no word. Let Staley wonder, let him worry. He forced Staley into a trot. A saucer moon was coming up.

The prairie gave way to a rounded hill rising eerily out of the gloom of the early darkness, as mysterious as a prehistoric Indian burial mound. Boone drove his captive around the hill and onto a stretch of prairie.

"What're you gonna do?" Staley called back, panting. "Who are you?"

"Keep moving. Don't look back."

Staley balked. Boone walked the gelding into him and knocked him to the ground. Staley got up and walked on.

"Trot," Boone ordered, slashing the rope.

When Boone figured they were a mile or more from camp, he reined up and said, "You can take off the rope now and turn around."

"Who th' hell are you?" Staley demanded, tearing at the loop and whirling around. His voice was shaking. He was gulping hard for wind.

Boone slipped the carbine into the boot alongside the saddle, coiled up the rope, and tied it to the saddle and dropped to the ground and went over to Staley. Very slowly Boone removed his hat and pitched it back and turned his face to the light.

"You —" Staley exploded, and immediately let out a long yell.

"Yell all you want," Boone taunted him. "They can't hear you."

Staley quieted down. Boone could hear his choppy breathing.

"What're you gonna do?" Fear leaked through Staley's voice as he struggled to regain his usual bluster.

For reply Boone smashed him. The blow to the belly carried all his strength.

Staley bent double, whereupon Boone smashed him in the face, and kept smashing him. Staley hit the grass, but he was heavy and tough and not hurt much. Boone taunted him, wanting him to know why:

"Did you go into your little act — crack your knuckles — before you beat up that old man at the ranch?"

Staley lumbered up heavily, in silence. Boone waited for the familiar rushing charge, the way the man had fought at the garage, shuffling and feinting as he bored in. This time, however, Staley delayed and stood back and appeared to await Boone's charge.

Boone hesitated, sensing something out of place about the hesitation — because that wasn't Staley's style — and suddenly Boone grasped his mistake: He hadn't searched for a handgun.

Late, he saw Staley digging inside his coat, and late Boone left his feet, diving low, and felt his shoulder smash Staley's thick thighs. A roar filled Boone's ears, a roar without pain. Slashing upward, he saw the brief blur of Staley's arm whipping down like a club with the little handgun. Boone closed and grabbed, felt his hands on Staley's arm. Staley gave a mighty lurch, tearing free of Boone's hold.

There was an overhead roar, but no pain. Boone drove his right knee into Staley's groin, feeling the squashiness there, aching to destroy him. Staley cried out and went limp, doubling up, and the handgun fell to the grass.

Into Boone surged the emotion to finish him with his hands. He began to throttle the thick neck column, hearing the gasping "Ahhhh — ahhh — ahh." Moments, and something tugging at his mind, a kind of late-coming urgency that transcended violence, caused him to break off, to growl, "What about Sammy — Sammy Buffalo Killer? That was you and Criner in that car — wasn't it? You followed us — didn't you? Both you bastards?"

Staley groaned, not answering. He had

quit gasping.

"Answer me! Goddamn you!"

At that moment a shot sounded at the camp. Boone paused. Another shot and another and another. Each spaced, he realized, in answer to Staley's. Before long people would be hurrying this way.

Boone could see Staley's open eyes. Boone kicked him in the ribs, shouting, "Answer me! You followed us from the pasture, didn't you? You saw me let Sammy out by the tracks?" Boone booted him again.

Staley said not a word.

Boone hurried. "Or would you rather talk about what happened to Acey at Salt Creek? It all ties together, doesn't it?"

There was no reply. When Staley tried to sit up, Boone kicked him back. Did he hear horses running? Yes. But there was yet time. "I want some quick answers," he said, kneeling over Staley. "Was it you or Criner that killed Sammy? It's more your style. Or did you both beat him?"

"Go to hell," Staley said and suddenly raised a high, strung-out yell.

Boone grabbed him by the throat and dragged him to his feet, and as he wobbled there Boone battered him to the grass again, short, savage blows. He raised Staley to his feet and beat him to earth again. The man was helpless. By this time Boone was weary of punching him and aware there would be no revelations.

Something happened to him then, strange and dreadful and impelling, blazing up from his depths, from his roots, as he found his pocketknife in his right hand. For one swift and terrible moment he considered taking Staley's scalp, and telling him that was for Sammy and Nate, marking him for what he had done. Less swiftly, aghast at himself, turning away in revulsion, he let go the knife and rushed to his horse. And not too soon. Because he could hear horses coming hard and Staley's guiding shouts. Staley had played possum.

As the sounds back there grew less and died altogether, Boone faced himself. Had there been time would he have taken Staley's scalp? That the impulse had occurred astonished him and frightened him a little. Would he? He was certain and not certain.

The lamp still burned in the kitchen when Boone approached the house afoot more than two hours later after a roundabout ride. He watched. The road was dark and still. Wary, he circled the house and found the yard empty and entered the kitchen.

Turning up the lamp, he took it to Nate's room.

Nate lay on his back in his bed, one leg strangely drawn up.

"Nate," Boone called softly.

The old man did not stir. In dread Boone stepped closer, feeling cold misgivings. He looked down.

Nate's eyes were open, staring sightlessly. Nate was dead.

An awful horror crept over Boone, then head-shaking disbelief. He could not accept this — no. . . . He stood motionless, numbed, while he fought to refute what he knew was all too true. Nate was gone.

At once an intolerable guilt burst upon Boone. If only he'd made Nate see the doctor in town! Worst of all, if only he hadn't left Nate alone!

With deliberate care, he placed the lamp on the table by the bed. It was then that he noticed the whiskey bottle still there.

Furiously, then, he broke out of his inertia. He swept his eyes hawking to the bed. He read the fresh marks on Nate's face, the fresh dried blood, Nate's torn shirt, the rumpled bedding: the signs of an old man's brief struggle. And suddenly, in further fury, he rushed about the room for other signs. There was nothing. He took the lamp and rushed to the kitchen. There was nothing there.

Slowing, he paced back to the bedroom and set the lamp on the table, sank into Nate's cane-bottom chair, bowed his head in his hands and sobbed.

Afterward (he had no idea how long), he called the Paradise telephone operator and left word for her to have Lester Oliver come for Nate in the morning. And from the tall, old-fashioned wooden wardrobe, the lone piece of furniture that Nate had fancied for as long as Boone could recall, he took Nate's blue suit and dark tie, and from a drawer his one white shirt and laid them out.

That, and he blew out the lamp and put the dark house behind him. The night seemed unusually still.

Chapter 14

Late in the night Boone dismounted and led his horse through the tangle to Medicine Hill, after very nearly reconsidering and returning to the house to wait for Lester Oliver, and going with him to surrender in Paradise. So heavy was his depression that he turned back and rode some distance, until reminded of Sid Criner's city jail, dark and foul, where he would be held until county officers arrived to take him in custody to Pawhuska. Anything might happen in Criner's jail, he knew. And like a shouted warning out of the legendary past, Nate's stories rang through his mind of violence on the cattle trails to the northern pastures, "in the early day," when the surest way for a town marshal to kill a man without consequences was to arrest and jail him and next day, with regret, of course, report having shot the prisoner for attempting to escape.

Boone shuddered, thinking how close he had come to making a likely fatal mistake while overcome by grief, when a person's judgment was often faulty and too giving in. Nate also had taught him that. No, when Boone surrendered, it had to be to Tan Labeau, and not now, not quite. There was yet today and perhaps tomorrow. He needed a little more time. He wanted to think.

He moved mechanically, from channeled habit, tying Old Jake the gelding for grazing, gathering wood, making a small fire by the cave, only to fall deeper into despair. He couldn't eat, he had not the faintest need for food. His body cried for rest, but his shocked mind wouldn't let him sleep. He wept.

And then, after a while, a kind of comfort

seemed to envelop him and he became conscious of an unforeseen peace of mind, of a vague but consoling release. How glad he was that he had known a man like Nate Robb, who had lived on the frontier, who loved horses, who understood water and grass, wind and sun. How glad he was that he had loved Nate, though unsaid, and respected him and listened to him, though not enough.

He thought of Nate's life, of his simple pleasures and needs. "By God, a man's gotta have his coffee." Coffee and brown-paper Bull Durham tobacco cigarettes. "Them tailor-mades you get in town just don't satisfy a man." For years Boone had mailed Nate a monthly check for wages. A letter came, though rarely did Nate write. Inside Boone found a packet of uncashed checks. "Tear these up," read the terse note in the all but illegible scrawl. "I don't need much." Boone had sent them back, with the suggestion that Nate go out and buy himself a pair of new boots.

He thought of Nate's old-fashioned court-liness toward all women, including city girls, "who can't boil water without burnin' it an' make a fuss about servin' salads that 'ud starve a hummingbird." Of Nate's unbending contempt for "drugstore cowboys —

why, they'd have to pull leather to hang on a stick horse." And Nate's disdain for "old fartheads," a category of man which, though unspecified, somehow failed to meet lofty cowboy standards, a rather sweeping loss of status which Boone suspected could be traced to the subject's lack of generosity. Nate's concept of security was modest: "I always keep a hundred dollars back in case a horse falls with me an' I get laid up."

Nate's past, that interval before he became part of the Egan Terrell family, was largely mysterious except when he talked about trail-driving. Boone gathered there had been a deadly gunfight over a girl in Elgin, the rail terminus across the border in Kansas, where herds were driven out of the Osage Reservation. And that Robb really wasn't Nate's last name. Other than colorful references to "in the early day," Nate had not revealed his younger experiences, and the Terrells had respected his silence.

Boone became sensitive to sounds beyond him. Coyotes were singing nearby. A nighthawk swooped down, so close he caught the brush of beating wings. Life was going on despite his depression, his remembrance of things past. He grew drowsy. The fire burned down to a bank of cherry-red coals. All at once he dropped into a bottomless pit of exhaustion.

He woke to a chorus of twittering sweet
birdsong and a squirrel barking reproach-
fully from the hilltop. Farther off a crow
scolded in flapping flight. The sun was well
up.

But the harmonious voices of this natural
world had not roused him so late. Distant
voices had — men's voices, he realized suddenly, springing up. He could hear them
still.

Boone ran up the hill and looked and felt
a jolt. Horsemen were approaching the hill.
A crowd. Noisy and blundering. Momentarily he could feel some of Nate's old
disdain. In that time the actuality escaped
him that he was the hunted, that these larking riders, though out for a frolic, would kill
him if he resisted or ran.

Jerking to rush downhill, he saw them fanning out and pointing, and by that he knew
they intended to search the timber around
the hill. Last night's happenings had triggered the search hereabouts. His call from
the house for Lester Oliver to come out this
morning had been enough. And now he
understood the distant noises that had
reached him during his exhausted sleep.
Those roars and rumblings were the posse's

cars and horse vans passing on the road in the early hours.

He saddled Jake swiftly and slung on his gear and led off toward the other side of the hill. Hallooing voices became audible. He held the gelding's head. Before long he distinguished voices calling back and forth. The calling changed to a disordered mingling of voices; apparently a parley was going on. There was disagreement. Boone made out that some thought the thickets surrounding the hill were too dense and troublesome, that no man would hid in there. A distinct and differing voice seemed to take over. Boone wondered if that was the man with the star.

A spell of silence followed, as if the possemen were yet undecided. A hush soon broken when shod hoofs began sliding on rocks, when brush began snapping. So they were coming through. He had badly underestimated their determination.

He mounted and swung away at a trot, ducking branches, reining from side to side through the shaggy blackjacks. A short way ahead the woods thinned. And just before he fled the timber, shouts and the clatter of horses rose behind him. The posse had found his camp.

He kicked flanks and the old roping horse

responded bravely, stretching out. Wind tore at Boone's face. He plunged downslope, across a grassy draw, up another slope; and when he jerked to look, he saw horses clearing the Medicine Hill woods. Somebody whooped. They saw him now.

He raced on a couple of hundred yards, which was playing the other side's game, became there were quarterhorses in the posse, chunky, short-backed speedsters he had noticed at the camp last night. A patch of stubby blackjacks jutted ahead. He beelined for them. The first shot cracked as he cut in behind that dark shield and kept running hard.

A quick dismay went through him when he looked ahead. He was entering much rougher country, yet country he knew and the men pursuing him did not. For sometimes Acey and he, while acting out their boyhood dreaming, were as Osage runners coursing these hills for signs of tribal enemies, the Pawnees, the Kiowas, the Cherokees, the Comanches; and sometimes they had hunted through here for quail, and sometimes on horseback they had chased coyotes with lean greyhounds and often the sly coyotes had fooled them and the eager dogs. Sometimes the hard-pressed coyote appeared to falter and become weak, when all the while he was merely making certain that he was seen; and then he would disappear into the roughest place, a rock-cluttered hill, a jungle of blackjacks and post oaks and brush, and Acey and Boone, quirting their sweaty ponies, would ride madly after. And drawn in, only to encounter incredibly broken footing, slowed to a walk, fending off low branches, and finally forced to lead their mounts.

Meanwhile, the coyote had doubled back on his headlong pursuers and vanished. ("That coyote is smart, that coyote. But next time we catch him, I bet.")

The rough hills and ridges evoked these rapid-fire images, erased as Boone felt the old gelding tiring. They kept on, running raggedly now. The thought seemed to spring naturally to Boone's mind, and he steadied on it. But doubling back worked only when all the pursuers followed the pretense blindly and entangled and lost themselves for a while, and these were not impulsive boys behind him. Yet he had no other choice.

The slanting shoulder of a timbered ridge bulked forbiddingly closer, its rugged face rushing into detail as though Boone looked through a swiftly adjusting lens, seeing reddish rock slabs and scrubby black trees and clumps of squatty brush. At the ridge's sloping base, he pulled up and looked back and made a show of indecision, of being forced to let the old horse blow while he lingered to be seen as the coyote had lingered.

Riders stood out suddenly, scudding into view around the blackjacks where Boone had heard the shot. They drew up and milled about, joined by more riders. Everything struck him as so unreal. For one breath he saw them as quixotic figures, defined against the dark green cloak of the trees, or as puppetlike figures jerking here and there; fleeting impressions, instantly gone, when they sighted him and fired without effect and whooped and rushed pell-mell after him.

He tore into the timber and rocks, finding the ascent far rougher than he remembered, and when out of sight, he dismounted and led his horse, knowing that he could move faster on foot. The grade steepened sharply. With the old gelding following nimbly, for Jake had lived all his useful life carrying Terrells and Nate over such up-and-down places, Boone came to the spine of the long-running ridge.

His doubts hit hard as he paused, straining for sounds of the chase down below. By this time they should be clattering up; he should be hearing voices. The waiting dragged on and he began to doubt his hasty judgment of running to this shut-in wilderness, which could trap him as well. While he waited for pursuit that never rushed up the ridge, they could be flanking the sides, cutting him off, content to wait him out.

He shut down on his panicky waverings. By God, did he expect a way out at once?

In not many moments he picked up the rumble of running horses. The volume swelled to a roll of sound, heavier and more ominous than he had anticipated. His insides shrank with coldness. Tensed, he heard the rumble change suddenly in tone, breaking off to piece-meal shouts and leather squeaks and spur jingles and bit rattles. They were pulling up, bringing a closer wave of querying, excited voices.

"Hell, he's up there," a loud voice sang out. "Didn't we see 'im go in? What're we waitin' on?" Now a confusion of more voices.

The voices tailed off.

Now what? Boone couldn't tell.

Gradually, he received the impression of riders in motion, of an undertone of indistinct voices. Now of shod hoofs over rocks and of brush crashing.

So they were coming after the coyote, all of them, he hoped.

These sounds turned him onward along the ridge top, ears cocked to the crashing and rock clambering lifting higher. Now and then he got the shrill of a sporting voice. He moved deeper into the web of timber, faster as the rocks thinned. His mind was constantly judging the location of the noises. And when he decided the posse had time to mount the ridge, he made his cut to double back, leading Jake downslope.

He had covered some thirty yards at a stiff-legged trot, when, directly below, he saw a swish of motion through the trees. His heart seemed to miss as he pulled up sharply and froze.

A horse and rider materialized, parallel to the base of the ridge. More riders followed single file. They passed.

Boone whirled away uphill, aware suddenly that he was stripped of time. He could only hope that the other ridge flank was open. He climbed as fast as he could, dodging trees, trotting, running, now forced to break through a clutch of brush, the old gelding kicking up a racket at his heels.

He was sawing for breath when he reached the top. It was clear for the moment, though he could hear the posse toward the end of the ridge. He plunged on, down the other side. There was an opening in the timber.

He aimed for that. There he looked down and stopped dead-still, seeing another single file of prowling horsemen.

He whipped around and started back up, once more hanging on the noisy approach of the riders he couldn't yet see. He dug a hand to his forehead. If he rode to the open end of the ridge, what then? He'd run into the flanking parties. Jake couldn't outrun them.

He dashed that from his mind and tied the reins to the saddlehorn, took the short rifle, slapped Jake across the rump and sent him startled and flying onward. Boone held up, watching, fearful the old horse might stop after a short distance. Jake didn't.

Slipping downslope, Boone saw the brushy crevice. Into it he crawled and lay still, his head canted upward, listening.

A single horse was coming along the spine of the ridge, coming slowly, hoofs clacking on loose rock. The horse stopped, then started forward, and there was a jangle of hoofs as the racket of the first horse was lost amid the others, and a chorus of vexatious voices complaining of the rugged footing. Evidently the clamor carried down to the flanking party below Boone, for a hallooing floated up from there. At once a rider on the crest clattered out and started down

Boone's side.

He crawled deeper into his shelter. The hoof sounds above conveyed that the rider's route was taking him near Boone, though around the waist-high hunk of rock behind which Boone lay.

Immediately afterward, not ten feet away, Boone saw broadside the head and fore-quarters of a quarterhorse sorrel, and the rider's pinkish, unshaven face, and silver-mounted saddle and hand-tooled gunbelt on which a pearl-handled revolver joggled. And white steer heads decorating shiny black boots, and a cream-colored Tom Mix hat. The rider's attention was on ducking tree limbs. He clattered by.

Boone thought, He wants to get off this damned ridge. He thinks maybe they've found something below. When he finds out they haven't, he won't come back up the slope.

The rackety passage of the posse hung over the ridge several minutes. Boone grew cramped and restless. When he could hear no more horses or voices, he raised up to look and ducked down at two stragglers halted on top, just resting slouched in their saddles. One said:

"Let's hold up here or go down. My ass is tard."

"We're right on his tail."

Far down the ridge a shout was raised. It sounded again.

"What'd I tell you? Come on!" They took off in a rush.

Boone crawled out and stood, knowing the shout could have but one meaning: Jake had stopped and the lead posse riders had caught up with him.

Boone scrambled to the summit. It was clear both ways. He cut away running, doubling back. Panting up to the open end of the ridge, he saw no one in sight. So far they were all behind him. In lengthening strides, he took the downgrade.

A naked vulnerability clawed at him as he left his cover and struck across the open prairie, but he also had a buoyancy of body and mind. Like the coyote, he thought, he was running for his life.

CHAPTER 15

At the first motte of blackjacks, Boone looked back at the massive ridge. Nothing ruffled its serenity, no movement. It still slept, ageless and eternal, a stern guardian overlooking the prairie sea lapping its feet.

He moved on carefully, from cover to cover.

The sun was high when he entered the woods surrounding Medicine Hill and discovered the wreckage of his camp. Every-thing — his few supplies dumped and scat-tered, his tin utensils trampled, his blankets gone. It didn't matter. He had to leave here. He had to reach Tan Labeau. He would never return to this mythic place made real. He had come to the end of something, a passing. An absolute severance from the dreaming past into brutal reality. Nate — and the remembering pained him — was really his last tie.

A crackling disturbance sheared across his musing. Someone was tearing through the thickets on the side facing the schoolhouse. He stepped past the cave and stationed himself against the wall of rock, holding the saddle gun ready.

A man ran out of the woods. Andy Horn. He didn't see Boone until Boone lowered the carbine and walked out and waved.

Andy kept running, his face strained. "Hey, Boone. You all right? Teresa sent me to look for you. She said the posse came this way."

"They did. I ran and hid. I've decided to surrender to Tan Labeau."

"Something's happening, Boone." Andy's voice was baffled and angry. "Mary Elizabeth's in danger."

The strangest coldness fastened upon Boone. Once more he felt himself flailing out blindly against unknown forces, elusive yet near, unseen yet openly striking the innocent. He dreaded to ask, "She's been hurt?" and felt the instant flash of a furious outrage.

"She's safe — for now," Andy said gravely. "Yesterday evening somebody tried to run her and Donna off the Salt Creek bridge north of town. It was deliberate. That big Packard just wouldn't go over." His words came faster: "Last night an attempt was made to blow up the house . . . Donna was still scared when they got home. She locked the house. She couldn't sleep. She got a gun . . . Around midnight she heard a noise outside. She went down. There was a man trying to open the basement window under the bedroom where Mary Elizabeth sleeps. When Donna screamed, he ran. She shot at him, but doesn't think she hit him. She found enough dynamite sticks to blow the house sky high . . . Boone, I don't know what this is all about, but I think it's time we found out. We can talk as we go. Teresa's waiting at the school. She wants you to drive her car."

They trotted across, ducking into the

brushy woods.

"Where's Mary Elizabeth now?" Boone asked.

"Before daylight this morning Donna took her to Louis Climbing Bear's house at Gray Horse. Donna thinks it's safer there."

"Where's Donna?"

"At home."

"Did she call officers?"

"No. Just Teresa, early this morning. Donna didn't say over the phone what happened. Just asked Teresa to come at once to the ranch. Donna's afraid to call Sid Criner in town — or anybody — afraid to say where Mary Elizabeth is. Teresa called me from Donna's. I went out. I talked to Donna. Teresa came back to the schoolhouse. When I got there a little bit ago, she said the posse had been here."

They struggled through the dense thickets and out. In Boone's mind a door kept opening and closing on Donna Standing Elk. He didn't trust her. Was her story a coverup for later when something happened to the child? With her out of the way, a victim of "unknown persons," Donna might yet grab a piece of the estate through some slick lawyer. He said, "I think we'd better take Mary Elizabeth to Pawhuska as fast as we can."

"That's what Teresa said. Donna agreed. We need you to drive Teresa's car. I'll follow in mine."

Boone, who was slightly ahead, turned to Andy as they went on. Doubt tore at his mind. "Why didn't Donna go to Pawhuska, to the sheriff's office, instead of Climbing Bear's place?"

"After what happened on the bridge, she was afraid to drive that far alone. I can't blame her."

"Unless the whole thing was arranged."

Andy stopped in stride. "Boone, you're wrong. Donna's scared to death."

"She's a good actress."

"Not that good. I saw her. Teresa saw the dynamite sticks. The fuse wires and the long lead wires. The window he tried to pry open. So did I. It's all true, Boone. If Donna hadn't gone down to look she and Mary Elizabeth would both be dead."

Boone wavered in the face of Andy's conviction, but not completely. Now wasn't the time to argue what couldn't be proved. He said, "I haven't told you about Nate — Nate Robb." And so, telling, he saw the blank shock widen Andy's temperate eyes, and next Boone said what he had done to Staley, not omitting blaming himself for leaving Nate.

"You had to do what you thought was best at the time. Let the law handle it. You can testify in court that Nate said Staley attacked him."

Boone's bitterness ripped out. "That won't bring Nate back. Now, I wonder whether I'd be believed." They hurried on a way before Boone spoke again: "In case you wondered, Andy, I didn't kill Sammy."

He saw Andy's head come up, his eyes searching Boone's face, a candid appraisal that was without hesitation or doubt. Andy believed him!

Neither spoke after that as they pressed along the wooded branch. Teresa was waiting in the schoolyard, impatiently walking back and forth. Her eyes rested on Boone for the briefest of moments, and then she said to them both, "What do you think? Should we take her to Pawhuska?" She was taut with worry and uncertainty. She looked pale and lovely.

"That's the only thing to do," Boone agreed. "We can call Tan Labeau from Gray Horse . . . tell him to meet us on the old Pawhuska road. I just hope he's there."

"He will be," Andy said. "Tribal council meets today. Let's go."

"Wait," Teresa cautioned. "A man in a car was watching from the road when school took up. He left, then came back. He was there a little while ago when I dismissed the children for the day." She regarded them both in tragic appeal. "I know he's looking for Mary Elizabeth."

"Show us," Boone said.

Walking fast, they went around to the front of the schoolhouse. Teresa stopped, looking west. She shook her head. "He's gone. He was down the road there not ten minutes ago."

"All the better," Andy said, moving to his roadster. "Nobody to follow us. Boone, you drive Teresa. I'll be right behind you." He looked at the saddle gun. "I'm glad you brought that thing. We may need it."

Boone laid the short rifle on the back seat of Teresa's old Hudson Super-Six touring and took the driver's seat. Teresa got in. He started the motor and backed around and drove across the rattly cattle guard and turned east.

Gray Horse was some four or five miles southeast. He held the Six in second gear for about a hundred yards before shifting into high, missing at once the breakaway power of his Stutz. If they had to make a run for it with Mary Elizabeth, the touring was short on horses.

The way was clear, and in Boone's eyes

the narrow dirt road winding beyond was as a strip of ribbon tossed carelessly between patches of black timber and humps of grass-covered hills turning brown. The scene was so peaceful, so incongruous.

Teresa watched anxiously ahead. Sometimes she twisted about to look behind where Andy ate dust. The wind played in her hair, whipping it capriciously across her forehead and down her cheeks. Brushing it back kept her busy. At the moment she was staring straight ahead, her normally smooth face troubled.

He looked away to concentrate on the rambling road. This way they would come in on the east side of Gray Horse from the north, past the Indian cemetery on the wooded hill, turning west over the creek bridge and up the hill past the village grocery store. Climbing Bear's place, where Acey's funeral feast was held, lay west of the store several hundred yards, then south off the road leading to Paradise.

Driving, which seldom failed to clear his thinking, helped now. He guessed that he was too emotionally concerned to see a possible link in the killings and the attempt on Mary Elizabeth's life, but there had to be a connection. For motivation: headrights, land, the twenty-five-thousand-dollar life insurance policy. Was Donna involved? In his biased judgment, he kept thinking so, contrary to what others said. A new point of view occurred to him. Donna would have died with Mary Elizabeth had the house blown up, if Donna had told the truth. . . . He sensed that the solution lay quite close and unsuspected, just beyond his grasp, yet hidden and obscure, possibly behind a façade of friendliness; for both Acey and Sammy had to an extreme the vulnerable Osage trait of naïveness, such as Boone himself did, but which he had learned to recognize and guard against.

Boone tore past a stand of blackjacks crowding up to the road on his right, and he glimpsed a wire gate which opened on a dim wagon road worming into the timber. He remembered: Once a house had stood there in the blackjacks.

Teresa was looking back. She leaned farther out. She stayed there, intent. Suddenly she jerked around and shouted, "We're being followed. A car came out of the timber back there. It pulled in behind Andy."

Boone glanced in the rear mirror. The Hudson was kicking up clouds of dust which blotted out all but the dim shape of Andy's roadster. Approaching the cemetery road, Boone eased off the gas and braked gradually, swinging out. As he came into the square turn and straightened, he hit second gear and the Hudson, voicing a deeper roar, went tearing south.

Boone looked then; so did Teresa. A black sedan rode Andy's dusty tail on the east-west road. But, by God, Andy was doing some driving himself, weaving back and forth in the center of the road so the sedan couldn't pass. Boone whooped encouragement.

When Boone looked again, Andy had made the south turn and was coming hard. Onward, Boone remembered, the land pitched and rolled away in undulating swells, the road bearing straight. He drove fast, but not all out; need for that would come soon enough, and he was afraid, damned afraid, the Six wasn't bred for long-distance running.

Boone took them over a hill. Teresa leaned out to look. "That car's falling back now," she shouted above the wind, and Boone thought darkly: *They'll follow us right up to Climbing Bear's. Well, we'll see about that.*

That threat still dogged him when he saw the conical shape of the hallowed cemetery hill and its shaggy crown of blackjacks rising on his right. He let up and took the easy turn downhill to the bridge over the creek. "How's Andy?" he yelled at her.

She looked. "He's coming. Don't see the other car."

Good. Boone shifted into second gear for more power as they charged upgrade. It looked better now. By God, if they could increase their lead a little more, they might yet turn off at Climbing Bear's without being spotted. He punished the Six all the way up the hill, past the grocery store and onto the flat stretch beyond. By then he was doing sixty-five. Teresa jerked him a look of white-faced alarm. Houses and fence posts flashed past.

There it was, the lane leading to Climbing Bear's house, as square a turn as could be.

Boone heard and felt the touring shiver and buck on loose gravel, swerving violently. He cut speed, braking lightly, off and on, not too much, on the verge of skewing into a slide, out of control. He spun the wheel savagely, felt Teresa thrown against him, felt the car right itself, almost stopping. Blooms of trailing dust caught up, powdering a grayish film on their faces. Teresa coughed.

He whipped onto the lane and bulled ahead, past one house, another. He saw the yellow house of Louis Climbing Bear. He wanted to pull in on the other side, out of sight from the road. But a stout wire fence closed off the house. Boone stopped and cut the motor and stepped out to the gurgling of the overheated radiator.

"That was some ride," Teresa remarked, showing him a wan smile. She got out and leaned on the front fender, the wind shaping her blue dress tightly about her, tracing her slim hips and long legs.

"May have to do some tall talking," he said, scowling, "if Louis doesn't believe us." He turned at the roar of a car turning off behind them. It was Andy. And before Andy reached them, the black sedan roared by on the Paradise road.

Now they know where, Boone thought. He waited for Andy.

The three of them hurried across the yard and climbed the steps. Boone knocked. He waited what seemed a long time. Nobody appeared. Next time Boone pounded on the door. Nobody came. Inside, however, he detected heavy movement, and Louis Climbing Bear was a heavy man.

"Louis!" Boone called sharply, pounding again. "It's Boone Terrell!"

The door opened and Climbing Bear barred the way, a shotgun slanting across his broad body. A formidable great brown bear of a man defending his lair. His thick

338

lips moved. "What you want?" His flesh-heavy face was drawn tight, his dark eyes suspicious. "Ever'body's lookin' for you, Boone."

"I didn't kill Sammy, but I think I know who did," Boone replied, aware that they were wasting time. "Louis, we've got to take Mary Elizabeth to Pawhuska for her protection. You know what happened last night. What they tried to do." Boone turned his head. "You know Teresa Chapman, here — Mary Elizabeth's teacher. You know Andy."

"Where's Donna?" Climbing Bear was still suspicious.

"She's home," Boone said. "Teresa has her permission. It's all right, Louis."

Climbing Bear did not speak, but he stirred uncomfortably.

"Donna's place is being watched," Teresa explained. "I was there this morning, after she brought Mary Elizabeth here. I saw a car on the road, a man watching. So was the school being watched." She fixed imploring eyes on Climbing Bear. "You can call Donna."

"No phone here."

"Then call her from the store. But hurry."

Although Climbing Bear continued to stand his ground, some of his guardedness seemed to leave him. No one spoke for a moment.

Andy broke the deadlock, his voice both urgent and reasonable. "No place near Paradise is safe, Louis. If they'll try to blow up Donna's house, they'll come here. At night, anytime. They knew we stopped here. A car followed us. It just went by."

Without changing expression, the Osage said, "Come in," and led them to a rear room where the door was closed. "We have no children at home any more," he said softly. "We hoped we could keep her for a while, this little one."

A large Osage woman came to the kitchen door, watching. Her troubled eyes said whatever decision her man made was right.

Now Climbing Bear, carefully, set the shotgun in a corner and opened the door.

Mary Elizabeth Standing Elk sat rocking by the window. She held a brown-faced Indian doll, the one Boone had purchased at the Salt Creek Trading Company; it peeked from the folds of a bright shawl.

Boone was moved at seeing the child again. His eyes sought her face. It was no longer flour-white. While he looked at her, a distant roar reached him. A car was tearing east on the road.

"You woke up my baby," Mary Elizabeth pouted, scolding them all. "I just rocked her to sleep."

"Gosh, I'm sorry," Climbing Bear said at once, feigning abject apology and hanging his head. "Better be careful or I'll get a good spankin', huh? That doll will be big girl someday, I bet, that purty doll." He was, Boone saw, seeking not to alarm her. Climbing Bear, smiling and nodding, said, "Some frien's are here to take you and your doll to Pawhuska. Be good, won't it? That doll will like that, I bet."

Mary Elizabeth had been smiling until mention of leaving. Her smile vanished entirely now. "Where's Donna?"

That was Teresa's cue. She went in and patted her and put her arm around her, saying, "Donna's all right, darling. She's home. She told us to take you to Pawhuska."

"Why? I like it here, with Louis and Esther. I'm not afraid now."

"I know, darling. You can visit them later."

"You bet you can," Climbing Bear promised. "Long as you like. We'll have big time."

Mary Elizabeth's face fell, acquiring the somber mask that distressed Boone. She turned her eyes upward to look at Teresa. "Is something bad going to happen?"

"No, dear," Teresa assured her. "It will be all right. And Boone and Andy are here. We're all going together. Oh, we'll drive fast.

But won't that be fun?"

There was a jot of time, broken only by the slowing rhythm of Mary Elizabeth's rocker. Boone saw her gradual acceptance, saw her sit a moment longer, then rise with her doll. But the print of fear was back on her face, turning it solemn. He saw that also.

Chapter 16

The men went outside to the cars.

Boone could see yet the small face turning in questioning appeal to Teresa.

"They'll expect us to rush into Paradise with her," Andy said, looking grim, and Boone nodded. "And they'll be looking for you driving Teresa's car. Maybe you'd better take mine. It's faster."

"Take mine." Climbing Bear pointed to a frame shed under which a red Pierce-Arrow sedan was parked. "Runs good. They sure won't be lookin' for you in a Pierce." He pressed the keys into Boone's hand.

"All right," Boone said. "We'll go ahead on the old Pawhuska road. Sooner we get out of here the better."

Andy was already getting in the roadster. "I'll call Tan Labeau from the store. Tell him to meet us."

Boone ran to the Hudson for the saddle

gun and was on his way to the shed when Teresa and the little girl came out on the porch with Esther Climbing Bear. He waved them toward the shed. "We're taking Louis's car."

He started the Pierce-Arrow and backed out. "Up front, you two." They hastened in, Mary Elizabeth's smoky eyes intent on the saddle gun on the back seat before she sat between Boone and Teresa.

Boone backed out into the lane. He saw Andy, who had gone ahead, come to the road. There he stopped and looked westward, a long look, then pointed for Boone to see and drove on.

When Boone came to the road and looked, he wasn't surprised to see a car parked boldly, less than two hundred yards away, facing east, posted in the center of the road, in position to block a car going west toward Paradise.

With slow deliberation, Boone turned east and held that designful pace to the store, in time to see Andy running inside to call La-beau. Coming to the downgrade leading to the creek, Boone began to let the sedan out. There was a resounding roar as they crossed the bridge and rushed up the cemetery hill. He liked the power he felt.

The road split a short distance on, the left

fork slanting north past the cemetery, the other continuing east. Eventually, Boone knew, it meandered southeast to join the main road between Paradise and Hominy. Slowing up for the turn, he looked down the east fork and went rigid.

Sunlight glinted on the windshield of a parked car. A red Buick, likewise blocking the road.

Boone caught the dismay on Teresa's face as he made the northward turn in a cloud of dust. He downshifted to regain speed. Ahead rose the knob of a little hill. The road there was empty. Relief surged over him. They swooped up the hill and down it, running free. Yet a question gnawed: They'd blocked the west and east roads. Why not the north?

Ahead reared the hump of another low hill. At the same instant Boone saw the car. For a wishful briefness he thought it was moving. But it wasn't. It, too, was parked in the middle of the road. However, one side of the hood was up and a man was waving for Boone to stop.

Boone almost smiled at the ruse. He needed no urging to ignore the flagdown. Only there wasn't room to pass on the narrow road. He rolled on, headlong, unchecked. Briefly, as he roared upgrade, he saw the indistinct face of a hatted man inside the black sedan, while the bulky figure beside the car frantically waved him to stop.

Boone yelled, "Hold on!" and was aware of Teresa throwing her arms around Mary Elizabeth as he took to the ditch and the Pierce-Arrow dipped sideways. Instantly there came the slapping crunch of his machine knocking down weeds and bumping over washed-out places and the unsettling impact of the right wheel and fender shearing dirt off the high bank of the ditch. The car and the man blurred past on his left.

He fought the wheel left and was clear of the bank, and then right, as the sedan keeled, about to go over, then left, savagely, and right again, straightening on four wheels, and suddenly they were back on track and he had the big red car going like a bat out of hell, disdainfully flinging dirt and gravel, drumming staccatos against its underbelly. He could tell the right front fender was knocked down, its headlight smashed. But, by God, they'd made it and nothing could catch them now.

He remembered his passengers then. Teresa still held Mary Elizabeth. The child seemed a frozen image, as immobile as the brown-faced doll she clutched.

Ahead the road was open and the mirror showed no pursuit yet. His mind whipped backward to the sedan. A black Packard sedan, he was pretty sure. And the man in the road was Staley; he was sure of that, too, and of seeing a revolver in Staley's hand. Boone's last glimpse was of Staley running to the car. By this time he would be turned around and coming.

Boone was approaching the intersection with the schoolhouse road. Some miles on to the northeast it came in on the main road west of Pawhuska. Somewhere along the upper stretches of this old road Boone hoped to meet Tan Labeau, if Andy's call had gone through. There was one sure way through these sharp-angle turns. You curbed your passion for speed, you eased off, braking just enough to avoid skidding, then swinging out and in. Coming out of the turn, he downshifted for more speed. His elation rose as he pushed the sedan faster.

That feeling deserted him abruptly, crushed out, as he smelled something hot and burning. Like rubber. At the same time Teresa yelled and pointed and he saw smoke. He should have known. The knocked-down right front fender was rubbing the tire.

A glance in the mirror showed the road clear behind them. He brought the heavy sedan to a lurching halt and jumped out, and with dust fogging in he dug into the tool box on the running board and found the jack handle. Dashing around, he pried under the smashed fender. It refused to budge. Forcing the handle farther underneath, he pried with all his might. Metal shrieked as the fender rose protestingly, only to settle back. He pried again, higher this time, and the fender stayed. He peered underneath. The tire was about free. He wrested once more, higher, higher. He peered again. The tire was clear. It was also badly gouged.

Running back, he dropped the jack handle on the floorboard and took off, running hard in second gear. The delay had cost a minute or more.

The road, ever lengthening out to the northeast, seemed to narrow more. Once a wagon trace to the agency, now graded and ditched, it dipped and gamboled over the rolling bounty of sweet grass like a free spirit, except for the sharp turns.

There was the stir of movement up ahead, partially hidden by the curving road. Tan Labeau? He clamped his lips together when he saw a wagon and team headed this way, and a Model-T Ford headed the other direction, both stopped. Obviously the two drivers had paused to visit.

Boone rode the horn. He saw the wagon driver look up and turn his head, unconcerned, and say something more. Boone cut speed, giving the horn a series of peremptory toots. The driver took up the reins, yet continued talking.

Boone, for a moment, was tempted to try the ditch, but it looked too deep. He had to stop. Honking with his right hand, he leaned out and motioned hard for the man on the wagon to hurry past. An old man, Boone saw, and not a little stubborn judging by the thrust of his whiskered jaws. Displaying the obstinacy of the mules he drove, he slapped the reins and waved to his friend and the wagon began to crawl. The flivver's driver was no more hurried. He waved and called out some last word, after which the flivver, much like a mother hen shaking free of dust, jiggled off.

Inch by inch, it seemed, a narrow gap appeared between wagon and car. When Boone shot forward, the mules danced sideways and the old man on the wagon muttered and shook his fist. Boone shot around the flivver in second gear, slewing gravel and dust.

He was doing sixty-five on a level stretch when, through the pall of trailing dust, he took a sighting in the mirror and saw the shape of a car. It was traveling fast, and not far behind. Boone moved up to seventy-five. A cold knot rode the pit of his stomach.

A sharp curve snaked ahead. He eased off on the gas at once and played the brakes off and on. Even so, he roared into it too fast, feeling the sedan beginning to wing a little, pulling away from him, tires squealing, skimming the road. He touched the brakes again, lightly, and then the Pierce-Arrow was grabbing track and they were through.

Glancing back, he saw the car go into the curve, and in moments saw it emerge, coming on rapidly. If that was Staley, he could drive.

Wooded hills rushed past. Boone had no sense of time and little of his whereabouts in relation to the Pawhuska road. The race was settling down, see-sawing back and forth. He would gain on the turns, then Staley would gain on the straight runs, for the Packard was a shade faster.

A landmark shot by. A certain conical hill. Boone remembered. It told him that he was nearing the upper end of the old road. And now, for the first time, he made out two cars behind Staley. One, he hoped, was Andy's.

It had to be.

Shattered glass tinkled all at once as the rear window went out.

"They're shooting at us," Boone yelled. "Stay down."

He didn't know when he first noticed his car pulling to the right. Maybe when he took the turn just before he spotted Staley back there. Now, suddenly, he had to oversteer. He worried. Was Tan Labeau somewhere ahead? Was Andy behind Staley?

A second later he heard a violent bumping up front, felt it quaking the whole car. That gouged front tire. Hell, yes. It was going out. Down, down. From the rim of his eye he saw Teresa pin him a look of alarm. But he didn't look at her. He was looking up the road, far up the road. At a car. And, by God, it was stopped. And there was another car coming up. Both blocking the road. This time he couldn't bull through.

Wild Boone Terrell had run his race. Lost it.

An explosion blasted through his thinking as the tire blew, flapping and banging like crazy. His car was swerving and sun-fishing. At seventy-five on a graveled Osage county road when a tire blows, you fight the wheel and not the brakes and pray you don't go over and start rolling through a barbed-wire fence.

Boone fought. He muscled the sedan back on even keel. In the split second that it straightened, he hit the brakes. But he was still much too fast, and he could feel it skewing again, nose down low on the right side, bucking and whipping, that wheel thumping the busted fender.

As if he watched a spinning cyclorama, he saw the deep ditch hard before him and blackjacks close beyond. Saw that whirling away as he fought the wheel left, saw the road tilting into view, and now the careening other ditch, which righted itself as he braked the sedan screeching still, slanted across the road, dust fuming up like smoke.

He stayed there, thrown against the wheel, struggling to collect his scattered senses. His passengers stirred before he did, their eyes upon him unbelieving that they were safe.

The oncoming roar of the car behind them filled Boone's ears. That roused him. He reached for the saddle gun, hurrying them. "Come on! Run!" With the road ahead blocked, he could see but one choice.

Somehow he had his charges across the ditch and was hastening them into the blackjacks before he heard Staley's car sliding to a stop. Boone jerked around.

Two men jumped out running. Staley and Buck DeVore, who had a rifle.

Boone snapped a shot at them. DeVore hesitated, surprised, then came on with Staley, who hadn't stopped. Another car rushed up. A red Buick touring. Dane Horn got out. He started running with the others toward Boone.

And then, unaccountably, Boone, who had taken a stand at the edge of the timber, saw DeVore lower his rifle and saw Staley halt and Horn hold up as they passed the Pierce-Arrow and at that moment discovered the two cars blocking the onward road.

And the armed men running this way from those cars were not whom Boone had assumed. For Tan Labeau led them, his short, roundish body seemingly bouncing with each unaccustomed stride in high-heeled cowboy boots.

Horn went to the middle of the road. His head was high, but his voice sounded forced. "Glad you fellows got here. Saved us a lot of trouble. Just getting ready to take Boone Terrell into custody for you. We jumped him up at Gray Horse. Gave us quite a race." He eyed the blackjacks. "There he is, armed. You heard him fire at us."

Labeau did not so much as glance toward

Boone. "Don't believe it's exactly like that," he said distinctly, and had to pause for wind. "It's that little girl you're really after — she's the one you want dead. You could always claim she was killed accidentally when you shot it out with Boone."

Another car had roared up. Boone saw Andrew Horn running along the road and stopping just as Dane Horn said, "That's about the craziest talk I ever heard, Tan. Boone Terrell's wanted for Sammy Buffalo Killer's murder. You're all balled up."

"You're all under arrest," Labeau said. He made a motion that sent his men fanning out and around. One relieved DeVore of his rifle. Another took Staley's revolver. Another shook down Horn and emptied a shoulder holster.

"Now just a minute, Tan," Horn said amiably, once more forcible Dane Horn on the streets of Paradise, the generous town leader who understood the caprices of men as well as their strengths and was wiser for so knowing. "I hope you understand the seriousness of what you're doing."

"I do," Labeau replied. He reminded Boone of an old bird dog whose age-weary eyes had been made lively again by today's hunt.

As the talking continued, Teresa and Mary

Elizabeth had left the woods to stand hushed beside Boone. The child was watching intently. Boone moved to the edge of the ditch. He was startled when Mary Elizabeth, in the most plaintive of voices, pointed and said, "That man rode off with my Daddy that morning."

"What man?" Labeau pounced on the words.

"Him." Her pointing hand was aimed unwaveringly at Buck DeVore. "He did. Daddy never came back."

Boots scuffed suddenly on gravel as DeVore, his face like putty, wheeled on Horn. "They can't put this on me, Dane. I rode off with him, but I sure didn't kill him."

"You stupid fool," Horn exploded. "He's lying, I tell you he's lying."

"Like hell," DeVore gushed. "I didn't know the kid was at the house when I told Acey I had some whiskey hid out at the creek. I thought she drove off with Donna." His voice shrilled. "But I didn't kill him. You were there — by the pasture gate near the bridge — when we rode up. Acey was drunk. I gave him the doped whiskey, but I didn't kill him. After he passed out, I held back . . . It was you, Dane — you — who dragged him to the creek and threw him in. It was you — Dane — not me."

Dane Horn's moon face had acquired a frozen quality. "I have nothing more to say at this time." He folded his arms and stood away, as if to remove himself from all this.

"You can say it in court," Labeau said, his voice as bleak as wind out of a wolf-gray winter sky. "You'll all stand trial, and not just for Acey. For Sammy Buffalo Killer. For the attempted murder of Mary Elizabeth and Donna Standing Elk. Somebody has to answer for Nate Robb too. . . . Dane, you had to hatch this plot. Rest of 'em don't have the brains. Idea was for Acey's six headrights to go to Rose DeVore, a first cousin of Acey's — though Rose wasn't in on it. But Sammy was also a first cousin. You had to get rid of him. You made it look like Boone killed Sammy, also to stop Boone's prying about Acey's murder. De-Vore promoted the fool posse. . . . That just left the little girl. You had another motive there: to eliminate a witness. Buck was beginning to sweat. It was general knowledge in Paradise that Mary Elizabeth was in the house when Acey rode off that morning. Except by that time she was too scared and shocked to identify till now the man he rode off with."

Tan Labeau gave a little jerk of his head. His voice was like a file: "Buck, you slipped

355

off from the posse last night to dynamite the house. You're still wanted in South Texas for killing a rancher ten years ago. Dane held that over you and was to share in the headrights. Your real name is James J. Fowler. You and Dane are behind this night terror campaign around Paradise to scare unrestricted Osages into selling their ranches cheap. . . . Now spill what you know about Sammy and Nate. Might help you a little. You're gonna need all you can get, believe me."

DeVore began, "About Sammy — well, Staley and Criner —" Then his mouth became a trap, shut tight, as a kind of wordless exchange seemed to take place between him and Dane Horn.

"I can fill in the rest," Boone said. "A car trailed Sammy and me from the pasture that night. When I let him out at the tracks the car passed me. I saw two men. They followed Sammy. Nate told me Staley beat him up to find out where I was. Few hours later, when I came back to the ranch, Nate was dead. And Herb Staley was the *only* person who knew Nate had survived the first beating — because I accused him of it. He went back to seal Nate's lips."

Staley, standing behind Dane Horn and DeVore, whirled running.

Boone moved as Staley moved, leaping the ditch. He saw Andy make a grab for Staley, and delay him momentarily; saw Staley knock Andy aside and sprint for the Packard.

Boone caught up as Staley was yanking on the car door. When Boone pointed the saddle gun at him, Staley drew around and spread his hands in a gesture of surrender.

His eyes gave him away.

Boone saw it coming as before, Staley's right hand slipping inside his coat. Boone drove the butt of the rifle against Staley's jaw. Something cracked. Staley flopped against the car door, he sagged to the running board, then to the ground, hands to his broken face. Blood streamed from his mouth, from his ear.

Boone took the little hideout revolver from under Staley's coat and stood over him. He said, "You never change your style, do you? I'd like to kill you, but you've caused too much sorrow, too much pain, to get off that easy. I want you to suffer for Sammy and Nate."

Labeau and his men, crowding around, took over.

"There was a third car," Boone told Labeau, handing him the hideout weapon.

"Criner, likely. We'll pick him up."

"I was wrong about Donna," Boone said. "How wrong I was."

"Yeah," Labeau said. He was beginning to look weary again. "You know you damned near ended up in that ditch. You kept crowding things. But I guess that's what it took."

It's finished, Boone thought, taking slow steps back. He was suddenly quite tired. In time he could return to his oil-slick tracks and screaming engines, for there, clearly, lay the fulfillment of his vision quest. It was there, now, in the present, not in the dreaming past. . . . What was it Acey had said? *Make 'em eat dust.* That was it. Yes. Acey's last words to him.

He paused as voices rose.

Dane Horn stood apart, arms folded, his composure like stone. A change passed over his face as Andy came up to him.

"You've got to try and understand," Dane Horn said. "I can explain everything." His uncommonly strong voice broke, trailed off.

"Even the twenty-five-thousand-dollar life insurance policy Acey took out . . . with you as beneficiary . . . which I found at the bank?"

"Andy . . . *son* . . ."

"That could have been said a long time ago."

Andrew Horn turned his back and walked

away, the wreckage on his downcast face terrible to see, as if someone had just died before his eyes. His mouth twisted convulsively.

Teresa went straight to him. Young Andrew looked up at her. Their eyes met and clung and something sprang alive through the shock on their faces, something spontaneous and true, surfacing for the first time, unknown to each other until these ruinous moments.

Boone kept his glance on them a moment longer, then turned thoughtfully away, conscious that what had happened had irrevocably changed all their lives, and would change them further in the days ahead, drawn them all to the lean of their beings, closer to the absolute, to the truth about themselves. Just as poor Sammy, ill, fearful, doomed, had tried to reach Boone that last night as the final tragedy of his life neared.

Boone heard a faint voice, plaintive and tired-sounding, and it was addressing him:

"I want to see Donna. Take me home. Please."

Why, he had forgotten her. She still had her Indian doll. Through the wild ride and afterward, fleeing across the ditch and into the timber, she had held on to it.

The sight wrenched him. He scooped her

into his arms, holding her so close and for so long that she squirmed a little. Now he looked at her. At the softly molded face the color of dusk. At the great smoky eyes. Solemn, yes, yet different. Like a small flower just beginning to open.

His throat caught. Different because her haunted look was gone. That struck through him. She wasn't afraid any more. Mary Elizabeth Standing Elk, this fullblood child.

ABOUT THE AUTHOR

Fred Grove was born in Hominy, Oklahoma, and he graduated from the University of Oklahoma with a Bachelor's degree in Journalism. While working on newspapers in Oklahoma and Texas in the early 1950s, Grove began publishing short stories in some of the leading Western pulp magazines. His first four Western novels were published by Ballantine Books and include some of his finest work, especially *Comanche Captives* (1961) which earned him the first of five Golden Spur Awards from the Western Writers of America. *Comanche Captives* also won the Oklahoma Writing Award from the University of Oklahoma and the Levi Strauss Golden Saddleman Award. *The Buffalo Runners* (1968) won the Western Heritage Award from the National Cowboy Hall of Fame.

Grove's Western fiction is characterized by a broad spectrum of different settings and time periods. *The Great Horse Race* (1977) and *Match Race* (1982), both of which won Golden Spur Awards, are concerned with modern quarter horse racing. *Phantom Warrior* (1981) and *A Far Trumpet* (1985) are set during the time of the Apache wars. Two of Grove's most memorable novels, *Warrior Road* (1974) and *Drums Without Warriors* (1976), focus on the brutal Osage murders during the Roaring Twenties, a national scandal that involved the Federal Bureau of Investigation. *No Bugles, No Glory* (1959) and *Bitter Trumpet* (1989) are notable for their graphic settings during the Civil War. Grove himself once observed that "thanks to my father, who was a trail driver and rancher, and to my mother, who was of Osage and Sioux Indian blood, I feel fortunate that I can write about the American Indian and white man from a middle viewpoint, each in his own fair perspective . . ." Grove now resides in Tucson, Arizona, with his wife, Lucile, and has just completed *Man on a Red Horse.*

We hope you have enjoyed this Large Print book. Other Thorndike, Wheeler, and Chivers Press Large Print books are available at your library or directly from the publishers.

For information about current and upcoming titles, please call or write, without obligation, to:

Publisher
Thorndike Press
295 Kennedy Memorial Drive
Waterville, ME 04901
Tel. (800) 223-1244

or visit our Web site at:

http://gale.cengage.com/thorndike

OR

Chivers Large Print
published by BBC Audiobooks Ltd
St James House, The Square
Lower Bristol Road
Bath BA2 3SB
England
Tel. +44(0) 800 136919
email: bbcaudiobooks@bbc.co.uk
www.bbcaudiobooks.co.uk

All our Large Print titles are designed for easy reading, and all our books are made to last.